The Finder's Tales: Britt

Tiffany Jo Howell

Books written by Tiffany Jo Howell

The Finder's Tales: Marco

The Finder's Tales: Britt

Contents

Chapter 1

My name is Jordie, and I am a Finder.

I'm sure you have never heard of me. You may have seen me around but quickly forgotten me. I do my best to blend in and go unnoticed. I look like an average male human of medium height, medium build, brown hair, and brown eyes. Keeping a low profile is important in my line of work. For you see, we have found that humans make exceptional pets on other planets - and I am the one who chooses the best possible human pet for my clients.

~~

Jordie

My alarm buzzes me awake at precisely 6:30 a.m. I never hit snooze; I simply wake up and begin my day. I step into the shower and am out in eleven minutes. Exactly. Every day. I often travel to different countries and cities, so I understand the importance of keeping a schedule.

I dress in a suit and tie that I laid out the night before. I have five similar suits for my current project - black pants and jackets with a different shirt and tie. I shine my shoes weekly, keeping them looking nice.

My work as a Finder has me traveling to all countries on Earth. I adhere to the customs of each location so that I blend in with the local humans. I often go unnoticed. You may have seen me, but you wouldn't remember.

I'm in Australia for my current project, and my breakfast (or brekky as they say here) consists of a boiled egg, some cold-cut meats, a plain pastry, and a glass of orange juice.

And coffee.

I always have coffee. I bring my grinder and freshly roasted coffee with me. No matter what country or planet, I enjoy a cup of freshly ground coffee in the morning. My favorite comes from the Central American country of Costa Rica.

I am highly sought after for my ability to match a pet almost perfectly to its owner. This is because I make it a point to learn the customs and mannerisms of each culture. Humans are fascinating little creatures. No matter the differences in skin color, hair color, or even brekky food – they are more alike than different.

Humans are becoming popular pets, but I am the Finder that clients hire when they want the very best. I understand that pets and clients are both happiest when matched with similar lifestyles.

When matching a pet with my client, I consider climate, attitude, activity levels, and hobbies.

I would never put a quiet human with a loud owner on a bustling planet; that would terrify the pet. And I would never put a high-strung pet with a retired client. I take the extra time to match an owner and pet properly. It's my knowledge of humans that raises me above other Finders.

Some human children mature quicker than others, but I make sure they can care for themselves before I take them to live on another planet. Few clients want a baby human since they are too much work. Baby humans need constant care, feeding, and diaper changes.

I devised my own pet program and put it in my Finder's Brain Book. It looks like a computer tablet from Earth, but it's so much more. It is set to track all the optimal pets that I have picked out. My tablet is programmed for me; it automatically turns on when I want to use it, registers my fingerprints anywhere I touch, and recognizes my movements such as how high I normally lift it to work. It tracks my heartbeat, perspiration, and other vitals. This tablet understands my job and notifies me of any situation that needs my attention. Of course, it works in any galaxy, allowing me to check on current and possible future pets no matter where I am.

First, I enter all of the traits I'm looking for, and my pet program tablet shows me several possibilities. I then narrow down my search based on details about my client. From here, I can see a picture of the possible pet.

Most recently, I have been assessing a human that I believe will be a good fit for my current client.

Zussta is a female from the planet Janti. She enjoys traveling and adventures, so I must find a human who can keep up with her active lifestyle.

I came to Australia about two weeks ago to check on a possible match for her. The human saw me but quickly forgot about me. Now I'm back to visit the pet again.

Britt is a ten-year-old human female. She lost her parents when she was two years old and has been living in the foster care system since then. Britt is bright, energetic, and independent. She is old enough to dress herself and do other self-care with little supervision. She is a bit more talkative than I usually prefer, but I don't think this will be a problem with my client.

She is currently boarding out with another foster family but should be back at the group home later today. It is common for a foster family to take her in temporarily. These families believe they are giving her a sense of home life.

Whenever possible, Britt wakes up early in the morning and visits with the older male humans in the park before she continues her journey exploring the neighborhood. It's quite interesting, really. The men gather to play games and talk about the weather, their ailments, their grandchildren, and everything else. This gathering of older human men is something I have noticed in several countries. They gather to play chess, dominoes, checkers, or other various board games in this part of the globe.

Britt's route stays the same, but she constantly finds something new to inspect, climb on, or crawl through. This is why I believe her activity level will match that of her future owner.

It's almost 10 am, so I wait for her to make her way past my park bench. Sometimes I have to wait for several minutes, depending on what she finds to do along the way.

After seven minutes, I see her coming. She is twirling a piece of string with something tied to the end. I don't know what she found, and I don't need to know. She is about to walk past me. I hear her humming a song to herself when she stops to look at me.

I stay quiet and let Britt speak first.

"Hi there. I don't know you," she says, tilting her head and studying me. "And I know just about everyone here, or at least I've seen them. I come this way almost every day." She pauses and tilts her head the other way. "You're not from here, but you seem to like sitting on this bench. Where are you from?" With that, she smiles and steps closer to me. Before I can answer, she keeps talking. "My name is Britt, and I've lived here all my life. I live in a foster home on the other side of the park. So, are you visiting someone here in town? Or are you staying at the hotel over on Sydney Street? That's pretty close, and you could walk here each day. You're dressed all spiffy. Are you from the Secret Intelligent Services?"

I pause before I speak in case she keeps talking. Since she stopped, I finally answer. "I'm here on business, and yes, I'm staying at the hotel. I'm not sure what the word 'spiffy' means, but I'll take it to mean well dressed, so thank you."

"The old guys in the park use the word spiffy when one of them is dressed nicely. Ms. Williams says I have picked up too many words from the old guys, but I like them." She then holds up the string. "Look what I found, it's this metal piece with a hole in the center, so I tied string through it. It makes a cool noise when I spin it. Listen." She steps back and begins to spin the metal and string. Sure enough, it begins to make a whistling noise.

"Yes, it does make a noise. That metal piece is called a washer." I tell her.

Her untamed blonde hair seems as if it's trying to break free from her headband. This girl is not afraid of strangers. Her confidence and intelligence are traits that will make her a good pet.

She sits down on the bench and keeps talking. It's an odd conversation that goes in several directions, but I don't mind.

Talking with her confirms my choice. She will be perfect for my client.

Britt

"Brittany, come here, please." Mrs. Morgan calls me Brittany, even though I have told her many times that I would rather be called Britt. I sigh and get up from the guest bed to see what she wants. I walk into the kitchen and stand in the doorway.

"So, Brittany," she continues, and I try not to roll my eyes. "Mr. Morgan and I need to run to the hardware store. Since you got into everything and knocked over several boxes of screws and bolts last time, perhaps you should wait here."

I don't argue and tell her that I tripped on one of the brooms the store had leaning into the aisle, and that's how the screws and bolts got spilled. She doesn't want to hear my side anyways. But being here alone… now that I like! I can't let her know that, so I keep my face neutral. "Okay, I'll stay here."

"We will only be gone a short time. Perhaps it would be best if you stay in your room." She means the guest room, but she likes to feel generous by calling it my room. "You can color one of the books we gave you."

"Sure, I'll color."

I'm so not going to color.

She bought me a coloring book for little kids. It's childish, but I'm polite enough not to tell her.

"Please don't get into trouble." She looks right at me when she says this. Again, I just agree with her instead of trying to explain myself.

Mr. Morgan meets us at the front door. He isn't big on conversation and usually leaves all the talking and decision-making to her. She turns back one more time. "We will be right back. Be good." And with that, they are out the door.

Yes! I got the whole house to myself! I run, making a large circle through the kitchen, into the dining room, through the living room, and back into the kitchen. Then I turn and run the course the opposite way. I think I was faster the second time.

After a couple more laps, positive that it's faster to go through the living room first, I make my way upstairs. The guest room is on the first floor, so I've rarely been upstairs the entire week I've been here.

The house is one of those older homes. The first day I was here, Mrs. Morgan explained that this is a Victorian-style house that she remodeled. She went on and on about how they took down walls and opened the interior. I must have looked interested because she talked about the house a lot. I was actually bored and tuned her out most of the time.

I stop in the hallway when I see the trapdoor in the ceiling.

Bonza, an attic. I bet it has heaps of boxes and trunks and is full of old, interesting stuff.

I find a chair in the main bedroom and drag it under the trap door. I climb up and can just barely reach the string that's hanging down. I pull gently in case something falls on me. As the door opens, I peek up into the attic. No raccoons are coming to attack me, and nothing is falling. I scoot the chair out of the way, and the steps easily pull down to the floor.

Perfect.

I climb up and stop at the top of the ladder to check out this new space. It's great. I step all the way in. It's dark and stuffy but wide open. There are boxes against the three walls, old plastic totes covered in dust, and folding chairs against the back wall. I walk to one side and open one of the boxes next to me; it's full of clothes. Boring.

The next tote I open has Christmas ornaments and decorations. It's not bad, but it's still boring. I keep looking, hoping to find a diary or something interesting, but there is just not anything worthwhile. The Morgans aren't very exciting, so I guess their junk isn't either.

It's hot up here; I check the window at the far end. It's not locked, but it sure sticks. I bet this window hasn't been opened in years. It takes some work, but I finally get it to slide up. I stick my head outside, gulping air and wiping the sweat off my forehead.

Wow, this is defo a good view. I bet I can see all the way to the park. I stand on my tip toes but can only make out the tree tops. If I were higher, I could see better. I lean out further and check out the roof. It slopes upwards. Yep, I need to get higher.

I carefully climb out the window and crawl to the top of the roof. I sit down with my feet above the window peak. This way, if I start to slide. I can catch myself.

See, I'm not reckless.

The breeze cools my back. I lift my hair off my neck and let the wind do its job there too.

I was right; I can almost make out the old guys in the park. I bet I could see better if I had some binoculars.

I wonder why more people don't sit on their roofs; it's awesome up here.

I feel the sun on my face, listen to the squirrels' chatter below me…

And then I hear the scream.

Shoot, shoot, shoot. I didn't see the Morgans return home, and Mrs. Morgan is in the driveway screaming and pointing at me. I can't hear exactly what she's saying, but I'm sure it's not good.

I slide down the roof and scramble into the window. I bolt down the attic steps and haul the chair back so I can push the attic door closed. I'm dragging the chair back into their room when I hear the front door open, and Mrs. Morgan is all in a tizzy.

"Brittany Christine Marie Lee, get down here right now!" Shoot, she used my full name. You know you're in trouble when adults call you by all of your names. I fly down the steps and stop short in front of her. I push the hair out of my face and stand up tall. I wasn't doing anything bad, but I know I'll be in trouble again. "What were you doing on the roof? You could have been killed!"

Okay, well, now she is being a little extreme.

"You are due back at the home tonight, but I don't think my heart can handle any more of you. Pack your bags, young lady; we are taking you back now."

Fine, I want to go to the group home anyway. I silently turn and stomp down the hall to the guest room. I already had my bag packed – I was ready to leave.

Me and my bag are at the front door lickety-split, surprising both of them.

As soon as we pull up to the front doors of the group home, I jump out and run ahead of the Morgans. I need the headmistress, Ms. Williams, to hear my side of the story first. I bolt down the hallway and burst through her office door.

Ms. Williams jumps but doesn't yell at me. I slam the door and lock it behind me. "Ms. Williams, I promise I wasn't being bad. I just wanted to get a better view of the park and the town. And I did. I could see the entire world up there. I wasn't misbehaving at all, just looking around. You know I would never do anything bad on purpose. You gotta believe me; I wasn't trying to get in trouble. You know, back in my day kids were allowed…"

By this time, the Morgans are banging on the door.

"Britt, you're ten years old; you haven't been around long enough to say 'back in my day'. You really do need to stop hanging around the old guys in the park." With that, she gets up and gently touches me on the shoulder. "Why don't you go to your room and put your things away." She opens the door and greets the Morgans.

Good, she isn't going to make me stand there while Mrs. Morgan says all kinds of nasty things about me. Mr. Morgan gives me a slight smile and hands me my bag. So maybe he's on my side.

I quickly scoot past them and make my way upstairs.

I toss my bag on my bed and begin to pace. I can't stay still. I have to get out of here before they come to scold me some more.

Mrs. Morgan's shrill voice is still going strong in the office as I quietly slip out the front door.

I'm kicking a rock along the sidewalk when I see a round, flat piece of metal. It's smooth and has a hole in the center. I take it with me and continue kicking the rock. With one final kick, I send it sailing off the sidewalk and into the grass.

I wonder what I can do with this metal thing. I toss it up and down in my left ha. Then I pull some string from my pocket (you never know when you're going to need string) and tie it around the metal. It's not quite long enough to bang on the ground like a yo-yo. I'm always on the lookout for some life-saving device such as this metal piece. I like to think I'm a secret agent or a ninja. I'm always prepared to fight off any bad guys; this string and metal circle might save my life one day.

I keep playing and walking, hoping the guys are in the park. I know they're old, but I like talking with them. They don't talk down to me or treat me like a child. They let me hang out with them as long as I want and aren't offended when I leave. Sometimes, being friends with old guys is easier than with kids my age.

I swing the metal piece in a big circle next to me, and it makes a whistling noise. Whoa! This is too cool! So, I do it again and again. Spinning and whistling.

I see a guy in a suit sitting on a bench. Not looking at his phone, not feeding the birds, just sitting there.

Weird.

Who is he?

I stop in front of him. "Hi there. I don't know you." I introduce myself. "I'm Britt. And I know just about everyone here, or at least I've seen them. I come this way almost every day." He doesn't say anything, so I keep talking. "You're not from here, but you seem to like sitting on this bench. Where are you from? I live in the group home that way." I point to show him the direction. "Are you staying with family or at the hotel over on Sydney Street? That's pretty close so you could walk here. You're dressed all spiffy. Are you from the Secret Intelligent Services?"

He's not one to talk a lot, and that's okay. He says he is staying at the hotel, I bet it's because he works with the Secret Intelligence Services. So, I show him the metal piece I found. He tells me it's called a washer. Whatever. I think he's pretty impressed that it makes noise when I spin it around.

I flop on the bench next to him. "Did you see the guys playing chess right over there this morning? They're my friends. I visit them when I'm close enough to walk to the park. I like to hang out with them. They don't yell at me for doing anything wrong. We can talk for hours. I tell them all about my days, and they never tell me I talk too much like other adults do."

"Maybe they never say that because they can't hear you. You know, they are old." He simply states.

I stare at him

He stares at me.

I stare at him.

I burst out laughing! "They may be old, but they can hear just fine. I not sure if you were being serious or funny. But I think you might be funny without trying." I push his leg and keep laughing.

"It was simply an observation."

He may not talk much, but he's funny. Kind of like those people that are funny because they don't understand the proper way to behave. I like those people.

I can't stop laughing. It's like he just said the most hilarious thing I've ever heard. I clutch my gut laughing. I fall off the bench, still laughing.

I laugh until tears stream down my face.

And that's my last memory of being on Earth.

Chapter 2

I'm not sure where I am when I wake up, but that's not new to me. I often wake up in a temporary home. I stay still before moving around, trying to remember who took me in this time.

Wait, I don't remember who I'm living with right now. I think back to the Morgans, but I shouldn't be there. I should be at the group home. I peek open an eye and check out the room. Nope, I'm not in the guest room of the Morgan's house, and I'm defo not at the group home. I fully open my eyes and sit up.

I don't recognize this place at all.

And I'm still wearing the clothes I had on yesterday. Or at least, I assume it was yesterday. Maybe it's still today.

I get out of bed and check my surroundings. It's sparse but not scary. It's kind of homey here. A bed and a small couch are along one wall, and a table with two chairs towards the end. There are two doors past the table… time to explore.

I get up and step in front of the door on the left. It automatically opens to a nice bathroom. The walls are light green with an area in the back looks like a shower, except there are no handles or showerhead.

A shelf is next to that, with towels on the top rack and a change of clothes on the bottom. Yep, that must be a shower.

I go out and stand in front of the door on the right. It doesn't open. There aren't any handles or knobs, so I tap the wall around the door in case there is a button that opens it. Nope. Maybe there's a button located higher on the wall. I'm kind of short, you know. I'm only ten, after all. I drag a chair over and climb up, tapping around the door. It still doesn't open.

I'm locked in a strange room.

Now I begin to panic.

I rush back to the bed and find my bag zipped closed. I open it and see some of my clothes, shoes, a comb, bathroom supplies, and four headbands. I dig deeper and find the flat metal piece with string.

I sit and think.

The last thing I remember is talking with the funny guy in the park. We were laughing and… that's it, my memory is blank.

I hear a whooshing sound, and the locked door slides open.

The funny guy walks in.

I'm not sure if I'm more scared or confused – but I'm definitely both.

"Hello Brittany, I'm glad you are awake."

"Britt. I'd rather be called Britt." I automatically correct him. "Where am I? Why are you here? I thought you lived on the bench. I want to go back to the home. So, if you could just show me how to get out of here, I know, I can find my way. I tried to open the door, but it wouldn't open. But then you came in, does it only open from the outside? If so, that is really weird. Why is my bag here with my stuff in it? Did Ms. Williams pack it for me? Okay, I'm going to go now, so please show me how to open the door."

I stand in front of the door, hoping it will open this time. It doesn't.

The guy sits at the table and answers me. "My name is Jordie. You are in an orientation facility and not in Australia anymore. I am a Finder, and it is my job to pair pets with a more advanced species. I have matched you with a client from the planet Janti. I believe you two will get along quite well."

Wait, what?

I understand the words, but they don't make sense. This guy is certifiably crazy.

Jordie pushes out the other chair. "Please, come and sit down with me."

I stay standing.

He keeps talking. "I will not hurt you. I have studied you and believe you will make a wonderful pet for Zussta. Now please, sit, and I will tell you more."

Well, that's a whopper of a story. I don't believe him, but I sit down anyways, glaring at him. Wouldn't that be cool if you could actually hurt someone with a look? Like, a really mean look would cause them to turn to ice or something?

"As humans, you feel that you are smarter and above all the animals on your planet. And you think your planet is the only one with life on it. But Earth, and all the species on it, is quite young compared to other planets. There are many galaxies and thousands of species that have been around much longer than you. Most are much more evolved than humans. Out there," he points towards the wall and not the ceiling. "Out there, you are not at the top of the food chain. You can barely take care of yourselves and your planet. It is kind for other species to take humans as pets."

Huh?

"Okay, weirdo, whatever you say. Now if you'll show me the way out, I'm going home." I stand up and give him a quick salute goodbye. I stand in front of the door with my arms crossed and my foot tapping. I try to give the vibe that I'm angry instead of totally and completely freaking out.

"Would it help if I let you see some species from other planets?" He asks. "Or, aliens as you call them?"

I slowly turn around. "Mister, if you can introduce me to an alien, then I'll believe you," I call his bluff.

He gets up, and as soon as he is next to me, the locked door opens.

Traitor door.

He calmly walks out and turns left.

I turn right and take off running.

I don't know where I'm going, but I'm sure not staying here. I run around corners and come to an empty hallway. I stop and look around. It's just a long hallway with doors on each side. I bet Jordie will look for me at the end of it or in one of the rooms. I see a vent close to my right ankle. I try to pry it open.

Success!

I quickly slip into the vent system and gently pull the cover back in place. I always wonder why people don't close the door or pull the vent cover back in place in television shows. Leaving it open means you might as well have a neon sign pointing to where you are.

I quietly crawl through the vents until I see the light for another entry point. I slowly creep there and peek out.

Jordie's face is looking in at me.

"Waaah!" I scream and jump back, hitting my head in the process.

"Britt, please come out of there. I thought you wanted to see the other species?" He opens the cover. I sigh and climb out. But I don't apologize.

I dust myself off. "Fine, let's go see the aliens."

This time he walks next to me instead of letting me out of his sight. Smart, I wouldn't trust me, either.

We walk for a bit, occasionally turning left and right. I run my right hand along the wall, stopping in front of each doorway in case it opens. Then I scoot to the other side of him and run my left hand along that wall. I tap the doors as we go by them. Nothing happens. I stop to tie my shoe, even though there aren't any laces. Jordie pauses and waits for me.

See, I made him stop.

I don't plan on making things easy for him.

We walk some more, me looking for anything along the way to distract him. But no, it's just empty hallways with locked doors. I wonder why I don't see any people around. This is freaky.

He stops in front of a large door. It slides open to a small empty room. I look sideways at him. "We will enter through the next door. Please step inside." He holds his arm out to usher me in.

We walk in, and the door behind us closes. "The next room is the maintenance area. Here many different species work together. Please don't touch anyone, and please stay behind the yellow line on the floor."

So, keep your hands and feet inside the ride the entire time. Sure, okay.

The next door opens.

What the bloody heck?

Chapter 3

Actual aliens are walking around. Like, real-life aliens. Just all going back and forth, looking busy. I do a quick head count and guess about fifty of them. Well, forty-nine if we don't count both heads on that one guy.

One alien looks like a fuzzy ball with short, stocky legs walks by, talking with another that has the longest spaghetti arms and legs I've ever seen.

Another tall creature is blue with blue waves on his body. He has four arms and hands and flippers for feet. How does he walk without tripping? Does he live in the water but can walk on land too?

I don't realize that I've stepped too far forward.

Jordie touches my arm. "Please stay behind the yellow line." He says as he points to the floor. Sure enough, there's a yellow line around the perimeter of the room.

I look around the room; it's huge. Like, big-enough-to-fit-several-airplanes-in-it huge. Once my mind starts to understand what I'm looking at, I realize it's similar to an airplane hangar, but, like, really big.

Is that a humungous door at the other end?

Are those spaceships? I didn't notice them at first with all the aliens walking around.

I've heard people talk about being so overwhelmed that their brains can't register it all. That must be what's happening to me.

There are twelve ships parked inside this area. Most of them are plain grey in color, but one has a yellow strip down the side. What makes that one so special? Maybe it's a police car – a space cop car. Most of the ships are in the center of the hangar, but some are along the edges. Freaky-looking beings are talking with each other and climbing into and out of the ships.

One guy has orange fur like a cat and walks all sleek and smooth like a cat. Are Earth cats actually aliens and descended from this species? Another weird creature walks by and looks at me - with all four of its eyes that are in a line and go halfway around its head. There's another alien about the same height as me, but it has the biggest hands I've ever seen. Ha, imagine the card game Slap Jack with that one. Except it probably takes it a long time to get its hand to the cards. I bet I'm faster.

There is no end to the weirdness around here. There's one guy with polka dots and one that's completely purple. Some are tall, and some are short.

And they all get along and are talking. Do they all speak the same language?

There is so much color walking around that it hurts my eyes.

This can't be real.

I look at Jordie, and he gently smiles at me as if reading my mind. "Yes, this is real."

I don't believe him. I totally break the rule and step past the yellow line. I walk up to a tall female space creature with jewels on her head and around her eyes. She seems like a girl by the way the gems look like makeup, but I could be wrong. I tap on her leg. "Excuse me, are you an alien? My name is Britt, and I'm from Earth. Have you ever been there? Probably not, since people would have certainly noticed you. Where are you from?"

The tall lady alien looks down at me but doesn't answer.

Jordie is next to me, pulling my arm and talking to her. "Please excuse the human; this is her first time off her planet." He pulls me back to the edge of the room.

"Why didn't she answer me?" I ask as soon as he lets go of me.

"Because she doesn't speak your language, and please don't disturb anyone else. They are working." He steps forward just a little, turning to face me.

"But you spoke to her in plain English. That's fishy that you think she understands you and not me. I still think you're lying to me." I huff and put my hands on my hips. Are they people in costumes? I bet that's it!

I don't think Jordie ever gets mad because he calmly tells me. "All species hear me in their language. You hear me speaking in English, and she understood me in her language. My species is gifted with this ability."

Wait, what?

"What do you mean '*my species*'? What are you? Aren't you human? You're a little odd, but heaps of people are a bit off. I once met this kid who only walked backward. I think he did it for attention, so I ignored him. But everyone else stared and pointed. So, you're not the strangest person I've met."

Jordie puts his hand up to stop me talking. "I look human, but I'm not." He turns and waves over a square alien.

It walks towards us and stops just outside of the yellow line. Maybe it's not allowed on this side of it. Jordie introduces it to me, "Britt, I'd like you to meet Stan. Stan, this is Britt, and she just arrived from Earth."

An arm shoots out from the body and gives me a small wave. I give it a confused wave back. Then I reach out and touch it. I lay my entire hand on its arm to see if it's real. Stan holds his arm still and doesn't pull away.

"Stan has met other humans before and understands you've probably never seen his species. You're lucky he was walking by and you got to meet him; not everyone talks with other species on their first day here." Jordie is nodding at me.

Am I special?

I let go of the alien, and he walks away.

So, aliens are real. They are really real.

No. This can't be real… I must be dreaming. Maybe I have a fever, and I'll wake up back in the home with Ms. Williams putting a cold, wet washcloth on my forehead.

Jordie steps in front of me so I have to look at him. "Let's go back to your room and talk about what you have seen." He takes my arm and guides me back to the door. I let him gently pull me as I look back over my shoulder. The colors… the shapes… there is so much to look at.

I keep staring until the door closes and I can blink again.

I look wordlessly at Jordie.

The other door opens into the hallway, and I follow him this time instead of running the other way. I'm in too much shock to think of anything. Thankfully he doesn't say anything. We keep walking until he stops in front of a door. It slides open to the room where I woke up. Was that only about an hour ago? Or was it a day? A week?

I don't know.

I'm all confused.

I sit down at the table, and Jordie takes the seat across from me.

"Do you want to talk about it?" He asks.

I try to put everything in order in my mind. "So much has happened so fast. It seems like just yesterday that I was walking in the park near my group home."

"It was just yesterday," he calmly states.

"Oh. Well. There you go," as if that explains it all.

It must not explain it at all because Jordie is sitting there looking at me. My thoughts are confusing and all over the place. "This is all in my head. right? The aliens can't be real."

"I understand it can be a lot to understand at first. But yes, this is real." Jordie answers.

"So… it's true, what I saw? Because I think I saw heaps of aliens walking around. How are they here on Earth without anyone knowing about them? Are we in the Outback? Because there are heaps of open space there and I bet you could have a big building and no one would know. Why are they here? What are they doing? And why am I here? It would be amazing if I really met aliens, but I can't figure out why. Do any of them speak English or Spanish or German? I guess they don't have to if they aren't interacting with humans. Why did Stan let me touch him? The lady alien didn't hurt me, and Stan seems nice…"

Jordie interrupts me. "Let's slow down. I admit that I normally let the humans settle in more before I take them to the hangar, but I thought you could handle it."

"Oh yeah, I can handle it."

Maybe.

"Where are we?" I start with one question

Jordie is ready. "We are on a large ship outside of your galaxy. I rent space here for orientation before I take pets to their new homes. I share this ship with other workers. This is a maintenance and repair station for various types of transportation."

"How many kids have you kidnapped before? Wait, did you say we're on a spaceship?" I'm not sure which I should think about first. One scares the bejeezus out of me, and the other is way too cool.

"Yes, we have left your galaxy. And no, I don't kidnap children. I carefully choose them. As I told you, it is my job to find the best possible pet for my clients. I am one of the best Finders in this part of the universe."

"And you think you found an alien to own?" I turn things around on this Jordie guy. I pretend they are going to be my pet, not the other way around.

Jordie mutters something incoherent but then speaks up. "I think you will get along quite well with your owner. She is active like you, always traveling or hiking. I think you will like her."

I'm not so sure about that.

"I will let you shower, and then I'll come back soon with some food. Are you hungry?"

Whoa, talk about a quick change in topic. But now that he mentions it, yes, I am hungry.

"I'm starving. Do you have pizza? I really could go for a slice of pizza or maybe some ice cream."

Jordie taps something on his tablet. "The food I have for you is not what you are used to. But it is full of all the nutrients you need."

Eww. It probably doesn't taste good.

"While we wait for the food, let me show you how the shower works." He stands and walks into the other room.

I get up and follow, still not sure what's happening. I'm not sure if my head is spinning from the whole idea of aliens or how quickly Jordie changed the subject.

"Wave your hand in front of the panel here." He waves his hand in front of a black square on the wall. Water starts to rain down from above. He waves his hand again, and it stops. "And this is your shampoo, conditioner, and soap all in one." He places his hand under an indent in the wall and liquid drips into his hand. He takes a towel, cleans his hand, and drops the towel on the floor when done.

"There are clean clothes on the bottom shelf. Please shower and dress. I will be back soon with food." He walks towards the door but pauses, looking back at me. "Are you okay, Britt?"

I don't know. Am I okay?

I have no idea.

"I guess, but I still don't understand why I'm here. And I really want to go home." I whisper.

Jordie stops and really looks at me. "My apologies. I have shown you other species without properly explaining it. Please shower, and when I come back, we can talk more."

With that, he leaves, and I'm still standing here; dazed in this new place.

Chapter 4

I have to admit; this is a bonza shower! The water comes out of the entire ceiling, not sputtering out of a little showerhead like back at the group home. It's like standing in warm rain.

I use the all-in-one shampoo-conditioner-soap to wash all of me. There, I'm now clean from head to toe. I step out of the shower and take one of the towels. I wonder why he thinks I need two; I'm not that big.

Anyways, I'm clean and dry and find new clothes on the shelf below the towels.

I totally don't mind sleeping in my clothes and wearing them again the next day. It makes getting ready in the mornings easier. But since there are new ones here, I'll try them on.

The pants fit perfectly. They are comfortable, like leggings, but not as tight. The shirt has sleeves just past my elbows, and it seems like it was made for me.

Well, it's a bit creepy that he knows my size.

I try not to dwell on it too much. I want to know where I really am and what funny-looking people are really doing here. If they are alien, which I doubt, why are they here? I mean, I don't believe I'm on a spaceship and out of our solar system in one day.

Mostly, I want to know when I'm going home.

Ms. Williams probably thinks I ran away. I admit I did consider just that a couple of times, especially while living with the Morgans.

I don't bother trying to comb my hair. Instead, when it's about halfway dry, I grab a headband and pull it back like I normally do. One of my foster moms tried to brush all the tangles out of my hair once. After what felt like hours of pain, she finally gave up and bought me four heavy-duty headbands. I absolutely love them.

Alright, so let's figure a couple of things out.

The secret agent guy kidnapped me; I can't get out of this room; he shows me aliens (or people dressed as aliens), and I'm hungry.

Yep, that about sums it up.

There's no clock in the room, so I'm not sure how long I wait for Jordie. I hear the door swoosh open, and he walks in all calm, cool, and collected.

But he is carrying a dinner tray… so that's a good thing.

"Hello, Britt." He says as he sets the tray on the table. "I brought some food for you."

I'm beyond hungry. I rush to the table, but he stops me. "Before you eat, I should tell you that this does not look like food you are used to eating. It's full of needed nutrients to keep you healthy and active."

It worries me that he said this twice. That means it's code for nasty-tasting food.

He removes the cover and I see a bowl of watered-down porridge.

Well, that's disappointing. I often eat porridge at the group home, so I was hoping to see something better. I mean, if he's going to keep me here, the least he can do is give me good food. I wouldn't object to a bacon and egg sammie.

"Do you have anything else? Can I have some Milo to drink? Ms. Williams doesn't let us have chocolate milk, but maybe you will. I'm starving to death. I don't know when I last ate. I don't know what day today is, so that's why I don't know when I ate. I had brekky at the Morgan's house, and then got in trouble and brought back to the group home early. I snuck out, and that's when I met you. Remember? You were on the park bench, and I was walking through the park. You said that funny thing about the old guys not hearing me, and that's it. Poof, here I am. And, by the way, where am I for real? Wait; let me at least eat while we talk. Do you have any sugar to put in it? I like my porridge with milk and lots of sugar. Is there somewhere I can place my order?"

I'm still trying to figure all this out when Jordie interrupts me. "You will like the food; it tastes like anything you want. Just think about what food you want to eat, and it will be the best-tasting food you've ever eaten."

Really? Anything I want? "What if I want ice cream? It could be snack-time. And if it has all the nutrients anyways… can I imagine it as ice cream?" I poke it with my spoon doubtfully.

Jordie stares blankly at me. "Yes, go ahead and imagine ice cream."

I definitely could use some ice cream at a time like this.

I close my eyes and think of a sundae. One with chocolate ice cream that has chocolate and caramel sauce on top. I love caramel. And sprinkles; every sundae needs sprinkles.

I dip my spoon in and take a small bite.

Ice cream sundae!

I bob my head and hum and keep eating.

"What did you think of the species you saw earlier?" Jordie asks. I finish my bite before answering him. I'm not an animal; I do have manners after all.

"You mean the aliens? I'm not sure they were real. Can you prove that aliens, in general, are real? I know I saw them, but does that make them real or are you lying to me?"

"They are most certainly real. I promise that I will never lie to you."

I pause and study him. I'm pretty good at reading people and knowing when they lie. I have to be good at this since I'm perfecting my ninja street skills and all. People usually have a tell; like they can't look me in the eyes, or they fiddle with their fingers – something always gives it away. But this guy openly looks at me when he says this.

I believe him.

Which means…

"I knew it! I always knew aliens were real!" I exclaim as I jump up from the table.

Jordie sits there, all cool-like and barely moving. "How could you know there are species on other planets before you came here?" He asks.

I study him for a moment and realize he isn't talking down to me like some adults do when they ask you to clarify yourself; he's simply asking.

So, I answer. "The way I figure it is that there is more out there than my foster home; there's a city. And there's more than my city; there's a country. And there's more than my country; there's the world. So why can't there be more out there than my world?" I shrug and look around. "It just makes sense. I mean, just because I haven't seen it doesn't mean it doesn't exist."

I sit back down and eat my ice cream.

Jordie stares at me for a moment and then taps on something that looks like a computer tablet.

"So," I say in between bites, "when can I go home? I assume you want me to spread the word about aliens being real and they're not here to attack us." I pause. "Are they here to attack us? They didn't hurt me when they saw me, so it's not like they hate humans. How do you want me to tell the world about them? Will I be on TV? That would be so cool!"

"Britt." Jordie interrupts my dreams of stardom. "You're not going to be on television. You're not going back to Earth. You are to be a pet. I have already explained this several times." He's looking at me like I'm some little kid and can't remember things.

But I did forget that; at least for a few moments.

"You seriously think I'm going to be a pet? For an alien? A pet?" He's still stuck on this? "Nope, not happening." I push the ice cream porridge stuff away. I'm not going to be a pet to anything, and I'm not going to eat this pretend mush food. "Besides, I don't know how to be a pet. I've never had one. We weren't allowed pets at the group home. Maybe you should choose someone else."

I think that's a good argument. Maybe he will agree with me, and I can go home.

"I know this is hard for you to understand. But you will have a good life with your owner on the planet Janti. I never place a pet with a bad owner. She will take care of you and treat you wonderfully." Jordie tries to convince me. He's not doing that pleading voice that grown-ups do when they try to get you to do something you don't want to do. He says this like it's a fact - and that's what scares me.

"But I don't follow commands very well. Watch, tell me to 'sit,' I bet I won't do it." Again, I think this is another valid point.

"Britt, you are not on Earth anymore. You are in pet orientation now. Over the next couple of days, I will teach you about your owner and her language and show you what she looks like. That way you won't be quite so nervous when you meet her. You need to get used to the idea of being her pet. But first, we have to do a full checkup on you. We will clean your teeth, check your eyesight, and try to tame your hair."

That's the last straw.

"No! Nobody touches my hair. I know I have lots of hair, but I like it! Why does everyone try to make my hair all straight and pretty? I'm not all straight and pretty!"

I double dog dare him to try to cut my hair.

Jordie sighs. "Fine, we won't straighten it and make it pretty. But we will give it a trim. All pets should be tidy. We need to check your eyesight, clean your teeth, and do a basic physical on you. You will also begin to learn the language so you understand some basic commands. You are lucky I am your Finder. Some of the others simply hand over the humans to the owner with no preparation at all. Now, we have a lot to do during the two weeks in this orientation facility before you move to Janti. I'll let you relax for now, and I'll be back later to take you to your first appointment."

"Wait." I stop him right there. "I didn't agree to any of this, and I bet Ms. Williams at the group home didn't agree to this either."

"I repeat, we are not on Earth anymore, Britt. This is your future. In two weeks, you will become a pet on another planet. You must prepare yourself for this." Jordie tells me. No fanfare, no pleading, just tells me.

OMG, he's serious. How am I supposed to prepare myself for this?

"Now please, relax, and I'll be back in a couple of hours. You can sleep if you want. I left some water on the table. Here, I brought you a pen and paper if you want to draw. Humans seem to like to do that." And just like that, he leaves.

Why does he assume I want to draw?

I tear a piece of paper from the notepad and make a paper airplane. I make it short and stubby, so it will curve and fly all over the place. Sometimes I make them straight to see how far they will go. But today, I want to see it go in circles. Like my mind - flying in circles.

I lay on my back on the floor and aim the airplane straight up. It curves and lands away from me.

I don't bother to get it.

Maybe I won't cooperate, and instead, I'll go limp. I'll show Jordie that I don't follow commands very well, and then he will take me back to Earth. Okay, that's my plan. Whenever he comes back, I won't move. I'll show him that I won't make a good pet.

Now I just have to wait.

And wait.

I'm bored.

Chapter 5

"Hello, Britt." Jordie waltzes in like nothing is wrong.

I must have fallen asleep at some point because I'm still on the floor when he walks in and scares the bejeezus out of me.

But I remember my plan.

I don't answer. I'm pretending I can't hear him. Maybe I've passed out. I keep my eyes closed and don't take any deep breaths. I'm not moving.

"I know you're awake. Please stop pretending; we have a lot to go over. Here, I brought you some more food."

I stay still.

"This will not be bad." Jordie doesn't even check my pulse. He goes on talking. "We will go to the spa to have your hair trimmed. Then we will do a physical on you. I have already run some basic tests. You are healthy with no major problems. I'm not sure when you last had your eyes checked or your teeth cleaned, but we will do that today."

My eyes fly open. "A dentist? You want me to go to the dentist? Nope." I jump up and run to my bed, throwing the covers over me.

Jordie stays sitting at the table. "Dentists are not bad here. On Earth, you humans sometimes do harmful things to your bodies in order to do good; we don't do that here. There won't be any pain when they clean your teeth. You may feel some tingling, but definitely no pain."

Yeah right. That's like the doctor telling you the shot will only hurt for a moment.

"It won't take long. The entire cleaning will be done before you even realize it. Besides, your owner will need to bring you back here every six months for a complete check-up, teeth cleaning, and hair grooming. It's best to get used to it now."

I have to come back here? Why does he keep saying things that scare and confuse me?

Now I really stay under the covers.

"Please come out from your bed. We have an appointment and need to stay on schedule. I told you I would not lie to you. Having your teeth cleaned is nothing to be afraid of. It won't hurt."

I peek out.

"What if I don't come out?" I ask.

Jordie pauses. "I know this can be scary. But if you do not come willingly on your own, I will have to put you to sleep and take you there. It is an option, but I don't think it is a good one. Having you awake and aware of your surroundings will help you accept your situation as being here in orientation and a pet on another planet. The sooner you accept the things I ask of you, the easier the transition will be."

I peek out. "Do you mean 'put me to sleep' like when you have to put a dog down? Or 'put me to sleep' like actually make me sleep?"

Jordie looks confused by this question. "I'm not sure I understand what you are asking. But I mean that I will gently have you fall asleep, and you will wake up later. It's similar to what happened when I brought you here."

I sit up now. "That's what I thought. I figured you wouldn't want to kill me. That would kind of defeat the entire 'being a pet' thing."

Jordie tries not to smile. "You're right. No one wants a dead pet human."

I try not to giggle, but that's silly. "Yeah, playing fetch would really be a bummer."

I get out of bed. "Fine, but if this hurts, I'm going to be really mad at you." I think it's best to forewarn him. I'm a happy person… until I get mad. One time Billy tripped me. I fell hard and hurt my knee and elbow. I jumped up and punched him square in the stomach. He couldn't breathe for several seconds. I told him if he ever tripped me again, I'd punch him two times. He never messed with me after that.

I spot more food on the table and decide to eat slowly and take up more of his time. I sit down and close my eyes, thinking about what I want to eat. I'm hungry for brekky food, and a lot of it. I picture fried eggs, bacon, a slice of fried tomato, and hash browns. I want the eggs first and imagine the yolk just a little bit runny. I dip my spoon into the mush and take a bite. I can almost feel the yolk running on my tongue.

"You know, you could be a millionaire if you make this stuff available on Earth," I mumble through my mouthful. I take sips of water in between and slowly savor the meal. Bacon, hashbrowns, tomato… yum.

When done, I push the bowl away and sit back in the chair, patting my belly. I'm really glad Jordie didn't speak the entire meal. I wanted to concentrate on the food.

"I'm ready, but I'm still not looking forward to the dentist."

Jordie looks up from his tablet. "I promise it won't hurt."

I get up and stretch. Jordie leads me out the door. I sort of feel like I'm walking into a torture chamber.

I didn't pay attention when we went to the hangar area, but this time I watch where we are going.

Crud, I forget to pay attention to our route.

"Is there anything to do here besides sit in my room?" I ask. "At home, I normally go for a walk through the park. I hang with the old guys playing checkers, and I climb trees. I climbed onto the roof of the Morgan's house, and they didn't like that. But what I'm saying is that I'm like really bored. Are there any other kids to play with? Are there any other humans on this ship? Wait. Who's going to clean my teeth? Will it be human adults or aliens? I don't think I can sit still if I have some scary alien all in my face." I stop walking when I think of this.

Jordie looks at me as if waiting for me to keep talking. I stare at him until he speaks. "There are not any other humans on this ship, which means no kids. You don't have to worry about 'scary aliens' touching you. Just because a species is not human and is different from you doesn't mean they are scary. You must get used to seeing all kinds of different beings. And we don't call other species aliens; each has their own name – such as your species is a human."

My mouth is hanging open as I stare at Jordie. I honestly didn't mean to make him mad. But what else do you call someone from outer space? I thought aliens covered anything not from Earth. I guess I learned something new today.

Maybe it's best not to talk for a while.

We make two more turns before Jordie stops in front of a door. It looks exactly like every other door. How does he know which room is which? There aren't any signs on the doors. I wonder if he can see through them.

The door slides open, and he walks inside. I pause a bit. I've never had to deal with a bad dentist, but I've never met an alien dentist either.

I step inside and look around. The room is much smaller than my room. It's a nice maroon color but with bright lights. There is a future-like curvy chair in the center of the room and a more normal-looking chair along the wall near the door. I scoot into the normal chair. I'll be fine here. Jordie thinks otherwise. "You will need to sit in the other chair." He sweeps his arm out as if guiding me to a beautiful place instead of a weird chair.

I get up but don't sit in the chair yet.

A door opposite where we came in opens, and a female alien walks in with five other alien people following her. They all look odd. Not totally alien, but not totally human either.

The one in charge speaks first. "Hello, Britt. Please have a seat in the chair, and we can get started."

I don't want to sit in a chair and let aliens drill on my teeth.

I dart towards the door – and it opens!

I bolt into the hallway, turn left, and stop.

Chapter 6

I run in the other direction as soon as the door closes. Since Jordie saw me turn left out of the room, he'll think I'm running in that direction. I use my ninja street smarts to know how to do this. I used to spend afternoons pretending I was running and hiding from people, so I've practiced ditching the bad guys.

All that self-training is starting to pay off. Okay, so I was goofing around back in the good old days, but hey, I can pretend it was training. I always thought I'd need these skills someday, and I'm glad I have them now.

I take the first corner at a full run, barely slowing down. Glancing right and left, I only see doors that probably won't open. I keep running.

Every now and then, I stop in front of a door, hoping it will open. I have to be smart about this. If we really are on a spaceship, I don't want to run in a circle and accidentally wind up back at the dentist's office. Wouldn't that be my luck?

I slow down and try to figure out what to do next, the old guys taught me that. They would say, "Britt, stop for a moment and think about your situation. Then find a solution. Don't make too many snap decisions."

My options are to hide on the spaceship or hitch a ride with it. But who knows where I would end up? How do I know which ships are headed for Earth?

And am I really on a spaceship?

Just because *I think* I've seen space creatures doesn't really mean I'm in space on a ship. Jordie said we are in a different galaxy, but what if he lied?

Okay. I'm going to go with the assumption that we are still on Earth because my other option is to give up, and I'm not ready to do that yet.

So, I have to look for an exit door.

I doubt it will actually have the word 'exit' on it, so I either have to try all of the doors or look for one that's different. I start to jog slowly, looking closely at each door and stopping in front of each one, hoping it will open.

Jog, stop in front of a door; jog, stop in front of a door; jog, stop in front of a door… It opens!

OMG, a door opened!

I step forward and peer inside. It's loud. Metal pots and strange machines are clanging and buzzing, and aliens yelling back and forth. But they all stop when they see me.

Everything goes quiet.

Is this where my porridge comes from?

I think I'm in the kitchen.

Never show fear.

I decide to speak first. "G'day, everyone. My name is Britt. Can someone please show me the ship's exit door? Point me in the right direction, and I'll be out of your way."

None of them answer me.

I try again, this time a little louder and a little slower. "I'm not here to bother you; I'm simply looking for the exit. You know, a way out of here."

The noise resumes as they all go back to work without answering me. I quickly step around one alien who is using all four hands to shake the pans in front of him. I tap a different one on its shoulder, "Excuse me, do you speak English?" Maybe they don't answer because they didn't understand me.

"Out? Leave? Door?" I try using simple words that may be something they might know. Nothing.

I hear the swoosh of the door open, and I quickly duck behind the counter.

Even though Jordie isn't yelling, I hear him perfectly over all the kitchen noises. "Britt, please come out. They are working in here."

I don't move.

"Hi." Jordie is standing next to me. It didn't take him long to find me.

I stand up. "Hi," I mumble from my hiding place.

"Come," He says, "let's let them work, and we can talk in the hallway."

Fine, whatever. I follow him out the door.

"Bye," I call out to everyone or everything. Some glance up at me, and one blue guy with wavy, underwater stripes on his body opens his mouth really wide.

Once we are in the hall, Jordie starts talking first. "Were you afraid to get your teeth cleaned? Is that why you ran away? I told you it wouldn't hurt."

I take a deep breath. "This mess I'm in is all too much. First, you kidnap me, then aliens want to put their hands in my mouth. You say I'm in a different galaxy, but I don't know for sure. You feed me mush that tastes like real food. It's all too much."

I plop down on the floor. I'm exhausted, and my head hurts.

Jordie sits on the floor next to me. "You are safe here, and nothing will hurt you, but we have a lot of work to do before you go to Janti."

"But I don't want to be a pet on another planet. I don't want to be a pet at all. I stayed with a family once who had a dog that kept running away. Maybe the dog wants to be a pet on a different planet. I'll show you where he lives so you can take him instead of me." I'm hopeful that we can make a swap.

Jordie smiles. "It doesn't work like that. Let's reschedule your teeth cleaning and go back to your room. Come on." He stands and brushes his pants off.

I stand up, but I don't brush off my pants. I stay dirty.

So there.

I wonder if pets know they are pets. I bet dogs think they are members of a pack, and cats know they are in charge. Maybe that's why they accept their role so easily; they don't fully understand their situation. I know some humans think of their pets as family, but at the same time, they don't allow dogs to go outside unless they are on a leash or in a fenced yard, and many cats are never allowed outside.

I'm starting to scare myself, so I change my line of thinking. I wonder if the sky is blue on every planet. Are trees green? See… change of thinking.

I'm so lost in thought that I forget Jordie is next to me. I totally jump when he resumes his lecture. "After your checkups, you will get to see a hologram of your owner and begin to learn her language."

That could be interesting. "Is a hologram similar to virtual reality? I've never seen either one, but I know what they are."

"Yes. The hologram is three-dimensional, and you will get to see what your owner looks like. And as I said, you will also begin to learn her language."

I'm going to learn a new language?

I decide to try something.

"Bee boop boing bok ewk boop."

Yep, that got his attention. Jordie pauses and tilts his head, looking at me. "What was that?"

"I was speaking alien," I tell him.

"No, you weren't."

"Really? Huh, I was hoping that maybe I just automatically knew how to speak alien."

Jordie sighs, "There is no language called 'alien.' Each species has its own language."

I can tell Jordie is trying to keep calm, so I decide to keep my act up.

"So, I have to learn a lot of languages?"

Jordie sighs again.

I make some clicking and whooping noises. "How about that? Was I speaking alien then?"

Jordie sternly looks at me. "Britt."

I try not to smile. Messing with Jordie is my new favorite pastime.

I can see he is trying to stay calm as he continues. "How about this? Let's go back to your room, where you can relax or nap for a while. Then, we will have your teeth cleaned and your eyes checked. Once your checkups are done, I'll show you outer space."

Well, now I'm curious. "Okay. I'll let the aliens clean my teeth and check my eyes, and you'll show me the real outer space." I hold my hand out for Jordie to shake it.

We shake. We have a deal.

Chapter 7

After some sleep and another shower, I see that I now have several outfits to choose from. Before, I only had white pants and a white shirt; now, I have three different colors of pants and shirts to choose from: white, yellow, and orange. I pick out some yellow pants and a white shirt. I know the yellow pants were matched with the yellow shirt, but it's not my style to be so matchy-matchy. I really don't have a style, so I choose the orange pants and white shirt. On Earth, I only had a couple of pairs of jeans and seven shirts, so that made getting dressed in the morning easy.

I don't bother trying to tame my hair. Instead, I grab my black headband to wear.

Jordie enters and informs me that it's time for my eye and dentist appointment… again. He stresses the word *again*.

Yeah, yeah, I get it.

I'm ready this time when we walk into the dreaded room. I go straight to the curvy chair in the center. It takes me a bit to get brave, but I eventually go ahead and climb into it.

As I settle in, the lady from last time walks in followed by her alien helpers. "Hello, Britt. It is good to see you again. My name is Sha." I wonder if all doctors are formal. Maybe all aliens are formal. Are they proper in general or just with pets, kinda like being nice to guests? At least she doesn't pat me on the head and do that whole baby talk thing that some humans do to animals. Why do people talk weird to their pets? "We will first clean your teeth." As she says this, the other aliens roll trays next to the chair. At least I don't see any knives. "This patch will wrap around your teeth. You will feel a tingling but nothing else. We will do your top teeth first. Please open your mouth."

I look at the blue wrap in her hand, then at Jordie. He gives me an encouraging nod.

Be brave.

I open wide.

The blue paper stuff forms itself around all my teeth. Thankfully, I don't gag. I barely know it's there. Then the vibration starts. This isn't bad, but weird. I rub my upper lip. I wonder how long I have to sit here. Should I keep my mouth open? Will it turn my teeth blue?

The vibration stops.

"Very good. Let me remove the patch, and we will continue on to your bottom teeth."

That's it? Are we done already?

I run my tongue over my top teeth, and sure enough, they feel clean and smooth. I normally don't like getting my teeth cleaned, but I like the clean feeling afterward.

She removes the blue thing, and the aliens around her pretend to be busy without really doing anything. "I will now place a patch on your bottom teeth," she informs me.

I keep my mouth open and wait for the vibrations. They are not bad. Wow, if this was how dentists were on Earth, I wouldn't mind going at all. Before I can even get lost in thought, we're done again. The lady removes the patch, and the alien helps whisk everything away.

I start to get up.

Sha touches me on the shoulder. "If you could stay still, please, we will test your eyes and hearing next."

Jordie didn't say anything about my hearing. Maybe he did, and I didn't hear him. I look at Jordie for an explanation, but he's too busy with his tablet to notice me.

I guess it'll be fine since it didn't hurt to clean my teeth.

Before I nod and sit back in the chair, the helpers have a new tray next to Sha. I take this moment to look closely at the helpers. There is one with too long of arms. And I think another one has an extra eye, but he's wearing dark glasses, so it's hard to tell. And one more whose head is too small and he tries to hide it by wearing a hat. It's like looking at a picture and trying to figure out what is not quite right.

I smile. This is kind of cool.

One of the aliens smiles back at me but then quickly returns to work.

See, even aliens like me.

Sha's face pops in front of me, scaring me. I jump and yelp. The helper who smiled at me quietly chuckles. I heard that, so I bet my hearing will check out fine.

"I'll now test your vision by putting this cone to your eye. Please don't blink. I will study your eye from my end." She puts the large part of the cone over my right eye and peers into the other end.

Some sort of television screen inside of the cone flashes on and amplifies her eye. I stare into her eye and realize it's purple. My eyes are green, but hers is purple and slowly swirls. No worries about me blinking; I can't help but stare.

She removes the cone. "Very good. We will now check your other eye." She puts the cone to my left eye, and I peer into it. The purple swirling eye stares at me again. I stare back. That really is about the coolest thing I've seen so far. "Very good. You have excellent vision." She tells me in her professional voice.

I guess that's good to know.

I glance at Jordie again. I bet he's impressed with my excellent vision. He isn't; he's still tapping away on his tablet.

"And finally, we will test your hearing." The helpers are busy switching trays again while Sha looks at me. I look her in the eyes.

"Do you know that your eyes swirl and move?" I ask her. "Does that make you dizzy? I mean, seeing movement all the time?"

She stops working to talk with me. "Yes, my species have eyes that swirl. No, it does not make me dizzy. But it lets me see colors and shapes differently than you. When you see me, you see the front of me. I see the front of you and both sides, all at the same time. And you see one color on the walls, I see various colors blending and swirling together."

"You mean there are more colors than I know about? And you can see me from different angles?" I look around the room, noting the flat, maroon walls. Maybe they aren't flat and maroon to her.

She smiles. "Yes, I see things differently than you, but I have studied your eyes, and I believe I understand how you view things. It is a bit limited, but you humans don't seem to mind."

What? I think I should be offended, but I'm too curious to worry about it.

"Now, let's check your hearing. I will place these receptors into your ears. Please raise your right hand when you hear a tone in your right ear.

Raise your left hand when you hear a tone in your left ear. Are you ready?"

Do I have a choice?

She puts the earbuds into each ear and steps back. Without her leaving my side, I suddenly hear a high pitch in my right ear. I instantly raise my right hand.

Right, left, left, left, right… this continues with different tones. Some are high-pitched, some are low-pitched, and some are so quiet I can't tell where the noise comes from. As this is happening, I see a screen built into the far wall that seems to be tracking my hearing. It shows lines and waves moving up and down. I get so distracted that I almost forget to listen for the tones.

After about twenty tones, we're done. "Very good. You are all done." She removes the earbuds and nods at Jordie. Her helpers pack everything up and roll the tray out of the far door where they came in. I watch them leave, and the one alien quickly turns and gives me a cool-person wave before he is out the door. Not a geeky full-on wave, just a quick acknowledgment.

It all seemed to go pretty quickly. I bet all three of these tests only took about half an hour.

I stand up, stretching. "So, there you have it. I have clean teeth, and I bet I have perfect hearing and eyesight." I know that has to impress him.

"That is good, Britt. Everything is in order. Now that you understand it doesn't hurt, you won't have to worry about coming back periodically for your check-up."

I freeze. "What? I have to do this all again? Like a dog that has his yearly check-up? This is what'll happen to me?"

"Yes. I have told you all of this before. You are a pet your owner must bring you here to keep you healthy. There isn't anyone to clean your teeth on Janti." Jordie says this slower, like I should automatically understand it.

I've seen videos of dogs that like to be groomed, but I haven't seen any that like to have their teeth cleaned like I just had mine done. But then again, it wasn't really that bad.

I was fairly happy three seconds ago, but now I'm freaked out again. "I don't want to be a pet," I whisper.

Jordie sits back down in his chair, so he is eye-to-eye with me. "Britt, perhaps you are looking at your situation wrong. Being a pet is not a bad thing. When you stayed with the various families, did any of them have pets?"

I think back. Yes, the Millers had a golden retriever dog; and the Wongs had a short-hair orange cat. Then the Evan's had a poodle, and..."

Jordie interrupts my thoughts. "You have been around pets?"

I nod.

"Did they seem to have a bad life?" He asks.

I think about this. The animals got plenty of food, sleep, playtime, treats, and heaps of love. "No, they didn't have a bad life," I admit tentatively.

"And you will have a good life too. You will be fed and taken care of."

"But will I have love?" I ask quietly.

"Yes," Jordie answers. "Other species do know love."

"Really? Aliens like you love their family? Huh, and here I thought they just invaded other planets and kidnapped people."

Jordie sighs, "Few species invade other planets. Most are peaceful, more peaceful than humans. And please stop referring to every other species, including myself, as *aliens*."

Yep, it didn't take me long to figure out that Jordie doesn't like to be called an alien.

I still enjoy messing with him. But I don't know what to call all species from outer space. The word alien covers all of them. I'll just have to keep it to myself.

Jordie changes the subject. "We have some time before we are scheduled in the hologram room. Would you like to go back to your room?"

I get a choice in something? Just my luck; when I finally get to decide something on my own, my mind goes blank. I stare at Jordie, trying to figure out what my choices are.

"Actually, I think now is a good time to take me back to Earth." Maybe if I say it with enough authority, Jordie will automatically obey.

He doesn't.

Sighing, he simply says, "Britt."

"I know, but it was worth a try." I shrug. "I'm not tired and don't smell bad, so I don't think I need to go back to the room to sleep or shower. Can we see the aliens and spaceships again?"

Jordie smiles a bit. "Would you like to see outer space? I believe I promised you that."

My eyes open wide. "Will I get sucked out and die without any air?" I've heard that there is no air in space, and a human would die out there, so this truly is a concern I have.

"No, you will be perfectly safe," Jordie assures me.

"Well, in that case, heck yeah! Since I'm not getting any younger, let's see outer space."

Chapter 8

Jordie walks me through one hallway after another. Wait, there aren't any pictures on the walls. I bet that's why I keep getting turned around and lost, everything looks the same. "Where are the pictures?" I ask after our third turn.

He understands that I'm talking about the lack of pictures. "Not all species partake in art. Many don't understand the reasoning behind pictures on walls. Some enjoy art, but it's very different for each. There is no way we could display paints from all species that like it and try to explain it to the ones who don't. It's easier to not have anything on the walls."

Huh, I'm not sure I agree with the reasoning. "But wouldn't it be better to introduce different art forms to other species? Maybe they would like it. How do you know? Ms. Williams told us that we need to be brave and try new things. She said we should try to understand people who are not like us rather than ignore them. Some aliens may not understand a picture of a tree, but they might like the colors. And maybe I wouldn't understand their art, but at least I would know about it."

Jordie stops dead in his tracks and stares at me.

What? I look down at my clothes in case I spilled something on myself. Then I look behind me. Did an alien walk up? What?

"Britt, that may be the most intelligent thing I have heard today."

Did Jordie give me a compliment? A huge smile plasters itself on my face.

"This is one reason I chose you to be a pet. You are intelligent and able to adjust to new situations. I'm very proud of you."

And just like that, he takes away the compliment.

I don't want to be a pet. I want to be a good person, but not necessarily a good pet. Does being a good person automatically make me a good pet? My smile is gone, and now I'm confused about how I feel.

Jordie gently touches my shoulder and continues to walk.

I follow him, but I'm not excited anymore. "Jordie." I get his attention. "How long have I been here? Like on this ship or whatever? With no clocks or windows, I've lost track of days. I sleep and eat, but I don't know if I'm on a schedule or not."

"You have been here roughly three Earth days. You are just a little way through your orientation."

"What happens after orientation?"

Jordie stops and looks at me for a long moment. "After orientation, I will take you to the planet Janti to live with your owner," he slowly tells me.

"I'm not an idiot. I wanted to make sure what comes next," I mumble. Now I'm totally offended.

Jordie's voice slightly softens. "I know you are very intelligent. I didn't mean to make you feel any different. Do you truly understand why you're here and not back on Earth?"

Great, he's going to make me say it. I've never actually said out loud that I'm going to be a pet because I think saying it makes this all the more real. "Yes, I understand."

Nope, I'm not giving in yet. I'm not going to admit that my future life is being some alien's cat.

Yeah, this conversation took a huge wrong turn.

Jordie eyes me suspiciously, but he doesn't push me. Instead, he nudges me, "Come, let's go see space."

"This is going to be so cool, as long as I don't die. What is space like? Is it really quiet? Is it all black and nothing else? Well, there has to be more. Will I see stars? Will I see other planets?" I forgot about seeing outer space! I smile and bounce on the balls of my feet.

I am so ready for this.

Walking again, we make two more turns before Jordie stops in front of a door. "This is the same place where you saw the workers that first day. Do you remember that?"

How could I forget?

He continues, "The same rules are in place. Do not cross the yellow line or interrupt those working."

"Yeah, yeah. Rules. Got it. I'm ready!"

We enter the small holding room, and the next door opens to the large hangar area.

Okay, I don't think I'll ever get used to seeing aliens walking around. I get caught up looking at them and barely realize I'm following Jordie along the side wall and towards the back.

I see Stan about halfway across the hangar and do a full wave with both arms over my head. I want to make sure he sees me. He does, and an arm shoots out from his square body and waves back.

I hop up and down and do a little dance.

I'm friends with an alien.

Jordie stops so abruptly that I bump into him. I'm too busy watching everything happening around me to apologize.

Jordie taps me. I ignore it. He taps me again. "A ship is about to enter. The door will open, and you will see space."

That gets my attention.

I was right that first day. The entire back wall is one giant door. Actually, it's two doors that begin to slide apart.

I step backward. If I weren't frozen in place, I would turn and run.

Doors bigger than any building I've ever seen slowly slide open.

I grab Jordie's arm and hold on.

There's a spaceship hovering in front of the door. It's steel grey in color is flat with long wings. I wonder if it will fit inside the hangar without hitting anything else. Once the door is fully open, the spaceship's wings fold under itself, and it glides into the hangar without hitting the edges of the door. As the ship passes the doorway, it goes through what seems like an invisible wall. That explains why we are still breathing. There must be a shield around the hangar that keeps the air and gravity inside. These aliens have thought of everything.

"You are now looking at outer space." Jordie states as he nudges me out of my trance.

I look past the ship, and sure enough, there is outer space.

I could easily pass out.

There are thousands of stars, all blinking, and *right there*.

There were some nights on Earth when the stars seemed closer than other nights, but nothing like this. This is a sight I will never forget.

I walk forward, wanting to stand on the edge of the platform. Jordie stops me before I hit the invisible wall. Maybe it's not invisible to him.

I completely break rule number one and step past the yellow line. I walk to the center of the doorway and stare out.

Absolutely nothing in my entire life has prepared me for this moment

I stand on the edge of *nothing*.

Total and complete nothing.

I've seen the ocean and it goes on forever. This is bigger than that. Bigger than all the oceans in the world.

I'm afraid to touch the invisible wall in case it zaps me like an electric fence, but it doesn't block my view.

The stars blink, just like I see them from Earth. Except there are more stars than I can count. There's a round, green star. "Is that a planet?" I whisper to Jordie.

He stands beside me, looking into space. "Yes, that is the planet Ja'ha'sta."

OMG, I'm looking at a new planet!

I'm stunned, amazed, awe-struck, and every other word I can think of. I can't believe outer space is so real. And I get to see it.

The idea of being a pet is not good, but seeing this almost makes up for it.

"Alright, let's get back behind the line. They need to close the door." Jordie is trying to herd me towards the side wall.

I wish I could stay here all day and stare into the blackness with blinking stars. I finally go back to the side of the hangar area. I'm walking sideways, still staring out into space. I stand behind the line and watch as the doors slowly close. I even stay still a few moments after it closes.

I'm at a loss for words… and that never happens to me.

I look at Jordie, still not able to speak. He smiles, "It's amazing, isn't it?"

That doesn't even come close to describing it.

"Come, let's go back to the room."

I turn in a full circle, looking at the entire hanger.

Aliens, outer space, spaceships, aliens, outer space.

I have no idea why this is happening to me, but it's hands-down the most fantastic thing ever.

I finally follow Jordie out of the hangar.

After a bit, Jordie talks again. "I'll let you stay in your room for a while. You are probably tired. Go ahead and rest, and when I come back, we can see a hologram of your owner."

Wait, what?

I totally forgot that I get to see the alien owner lady. My mind is totally blown. I'm glad I get some downtime first. I don't think anything can top seeing outer space.

At about the same time we get back to the room, my senses return, and I start feeling the reality of how cool it was to see outer space. I turn to Jordie, "That was amazing! We were standing on the edge of outer space. Who gets to do that? Me, that's who! Is it normal to you, or do you still get that tingly feeling? Because I can't ever imagine that getting old. How often do you get to see outer space? Will I get to see it from the new planet? Because I could do that every day."

I'm so pumped that when the door to the room opens, I run inside, do a lap to my bed and back, run around the table, and suddenly stop in front of Jordie.

I jump up and down several times, unsure of how to handle all the excitement.

Jordie is smiling. "It never gets old. Stay here, take it in, and I'll be back shortly."

When he leaves, I have absolutely no idea what to do. I'm too amped to sleep, so I run three more laps around my room. When I'm out of breath, I grab the paper and pencil he left the other day and begin drawing. I draw the aliens. I draw outer space. I draw Jordie.

I keep drawing.

Chapter 9

At least thirty pictures must be laid out on the floor around me. Jordie comes into the room and stops in front of some of them. He bends down and looks at my drawings, "You have been busy."

Yeah, well, what else does he expect me to do?

"Please, pick up your pictures. Do you want to see the hologram of your owner? Her name is Zussta."

"My owner is a female? I forgot that part!" I'm not sure why, but living with a female owner seems better than living with a male. I vaguely remember Jordie mentioning a female owner several times, but it never really sank in. I was too distracted with the whole 'being a pet' thing.

"I know you have already seen aliens, but now I want to show you what your owner looks like. I want you to see who you will live with so you won't be scared when you meet her."

I step back. "So, what's this hologram of the alien like? Is she tall? Can she read my mind? Will I have to protect my thoughts? I bet she'll like me; most people do. Except for Mrs. Morgan, but I think that was more her fault than mine. The guys in the park like me, and Ms. Williams likes me. I have lots of friends at the group home, or at least I did. I'm not expected to wear a collar or anything, am I? Because I absolutely will not. And I probably won't obey orders very well."

Jordie smiles at me. "Let's see the simulation room, it might answer some of your questions. Are you ready?"

Yes... No... Okay... Do I have a choice?

I follow him out the door. Strolling down the hallway, I drag my hand along the wall and close my eyes. I wonder if I can walk straight without looking.

I bump into Jordie. So much for walking a straight line.

Mumbling an apology, I decide to keep my eyes open from now on. Maybe I should start to learn my way around this place.

We turn into an empty room. The walls are dark grey and colorless. What a surprise. "This is the simulation room," he starts to explain. I move to the center of the room to see it all at once. "Please step to your right; Zussta's simulation will appear where you are currently standing. I will be in the next room, and we can begin the simulation. We can hear each other, so you won't be alone."

He walks through an almost hidden door before I can answer or ask questions. I walk to the edge of the room and start touching the walls. Maybe there's another hidden door somewhere. I've always wanted to find a hidden door, like behind a bookshelf or something. I think every street ninja needs a room with a hidden door.

"Hello, Britt. Please pay attention to the center of the room," A strange voice growls from out of nowhere. Like a bear, a lion, or any other scary animal growls. That's what this voice sounds like.

I'm a bit freaked out. Where did that come from? I haven't seen another human around here. Is there a guy who can see everything? Is he the controller? Is he Jordie's boss?

Then Jordie's voice comes over the hidden speakers. "Britt, a narrator will talk you through the simulation of your new galaxy and owner. Please follow his instructions."

A narrator, okay. I stand just to the right of the center of the room. Nothing happens.

I wait. And I wait some more.

I decide to practice my handstand. I can get my legs up, and I can balance for a little bit. I'm working on balancing longer and eventually walking on my hands. One time, I saw a performer in the park who could walk on his hands for a really long time. I want to be able to do that.

I'm on my third handstand when Jordie's voice comes over the speakers again. "Britt, please be still. Here is your owner Zussta."

As soon as he says that, an alien appears directly before me as if it just beamed into place. I scream and jump back. Where did that come from? How did it come out of nowhere? I look up to see if the alien came from the ceiling, but I don't see a trap door.

Jordie's voice tells me, "This is only a hologram of your owner. She is not actually here."

I step forward to touch her. Instead, my hand passes through her. He's right; it's not real. I've never seen a simulation. I know some people who have done virtual games and stuff, but not me. This is a first.

And it's… awesome!

She looks totally real.

I pass my hand through her again.

Then I run through her.

Then I do a cartwheel through her.

"Britt." Jordie firmly says through the speakers. I stop short just before diving headfirst through her. "Please stop that and stand still. This is a simulation of your new owner. I need you to study what she looks like so you will not be frightened when you see her."

I look up at her. "Why would I be afraid of her? You said not all aliens are mean and scary. I wasn't afraid, but now I kind of am. Should I be afraid of her? Will she be mean to me?" I wonder how aliens are mean. Do they yell, or bite, or kick, or do some weird mind trick?

Jordie actually sighs over the loudspeaker. "No, she is very nice. But sometimes humans are frightened when they see a different species, especially one that will be their owner."

"But I've already seen all kinds of aliens, so I'm not afraid anymore." Did he forget that we saw all those workers in the hangar area? I wonder about Jordie's age. Maybe his memory is fading, like the old guys in the park. I sometimes have to say the same thing to them every day since they forget things. But it's okay. I don't always have heaps of stories, and this way, I can double up on the tales. And the guys don't mind. They are happy to hear my stories over and over, and I'm happy to keep telling them.

"Good, you are not afraid. This is what your owner will look like, and I want you to know that. Please describe to me what you see."

Well, that's new. But I go ahead and start describing her. "She is about twice as tall as me." I stop when I see something weird. Even weirder than describing an alien – to another alien.

She has one big eye on her forehead and another on the back of her head.

She has an eye on the back of her head.

A big eye.

One on the front and one on the back of her head.

I can't breathe.

I've seen lots of aliens already, but for some reason, this eye thing completely freaks me out.

She has a blue mohawk that goes from one ear, over her head, and to the other ear. A sideways mohawk. That's a good thing; otherwise, having hair cover her back eye would be kinda funny.

Jordie's voice comes over the speaker. "Britt, what's wrong?"

"Her eyes," I whisper.

This is, hands down, the strangest experience I've ever had. And I don't know if I like it or not. With that thought, the alien turns her head to the side so that I can see the front and back of her head at the same time.

She heard me! I back up until I bump into the wall.

I put my hand over the side of my mouth and whisper again, "Jordie, hey, Jordie. Can you hear me?" I'm in total covert mission mode.

Jordie obviously isn't in covert mission mode because he speaks loudly throughout the room. "Yes, Britt, I can hear you."

I turn my back from the alien owner lady and whisper. "Can she hear me? I mentioned her eyes, and she moved. I thought you said she wasn't real."

The narrator's voice answers this time. "Each hologram understands several programmed sentences. And we knew you would ask about her eyes."

Okay, I feel better and turn back around to face her.

"In that case, then, can I get a closer look at her eyes?"

With that, my new owner squats down. I walk in front of her, staring into that huge eye. Then I circle around to her back and stare into the other big eye. And here is the freakiest part of all, one eye is a blueish-orange color, and the other is purplish-yellow.

Questions pop into my head at lightning speed. "How can she see with her eyes so far apart? Does she see a split screen and two views at once? Like the television shows when they have split screens? Does she see color like I do, or does she see extra colors like the dentist lady?"

The voice answers again. "No, she sees similar to you, just more. You have two eyes but only see one picture, no split screen. She sees one picture, but she sees a 360-degree radius around her. She sees in colors differently than you; her eyesight seems a mixture of colors where you see specific, different colors."

So cool. I wish I could see what was happening behind me.

The alien stands tall again and spins her head completely around! So, the back of her head is looking forward!

Whoa, she just keeps getting cooler and cooler. I wonder what else she can do.

She stands up tall and turns her head to the correct position.

"Please continue to describe what you see," Jordie says.

I take a deep breath and look her over. "Okay, again, she is about two times taller than I am. She has a big eye in the front of her head and another in the back. But she still has a face on the front but not the back of her head. One nose, one mouth. She also has a sideways blue mohawk. She is not soft at all; in fact, she looks like she is in good shape and has muscles. Do they exercise on other planets? Will I have to exercise? I don't like jumping jacks, but I can jump rope all day long. One time…"

Jordie interrupts me, "Britt, please stay in the same conversation. We are talking about your owner."

I nod. "Oh, right, alien owner lady. Well, she's a bit blocky. Her body is more square-shaped than a human body. Not long and lean." Now I'm walking in a circle around her, seeing her from all angles. "Her skin is pearl white but changes colors as I move. It changes from pearly to pink and shimmers. That's pretty amazing. She has two long arms that hang to her knees with a hand at each end."

With this, she holds out her hands to me.

I look closer. "Are those little suction cups on her fingertips?" I ask not expecting an answer. I wish I could touch her hand.

"Yes, she can hold items without closing her hand. It is up to her if an item sticks to her hand or not," The voice answers.

"So, she can control her suction cups. Got it." I like that. Wow, I wish we humans had all these gadgets on us.

I talk out loud again. "Her legs are long but also blocky like her body. Maybe she doesn't run?"

I step towards her, then back up a bit, then closer again. Is she changing colors? I squint at her legs as I circle around her again, and sure enough, the hue of her skin slightly changes. "Why does her skin shimmer and change colors?"

"The skin of the Zobian species appears to change depending on your viewing direction. This is because they see colors differently than you. To them, their skin is one blended color instead of seeing it as a mixture of white and pink."

"What's a Zoboian?" I check her feet. They are smaller than I would have thought for someone so tall. "Why are her feet so small? Does she have trouble standing on them? Does she fall over?" That would hinder a species if they kept falling over.

But at least she would see the ground and the sky at the same time as she went down.

I crack myself up.

"Zoboian is the name of her species. And she does not fall over. Her body balances her appropriately."

Well, wasn't that an all-formal answer? I hope I didn't offend the narrator. Maybe he's a Zobian.

I decide to wrap this up. "Okay, now I know what she looks like, and I'm not afraid. What's next?" I ask.

At this moment, she squats down to my level and starts speaking alien to me.

Chapter 10

Waaah! I jump back and fall on my bum.

It spoke!

She makes the noise again, but this time the voice over the loudspeaker interprets it for me. "She is saying '*hello*.'"

She says it again.

"Um, hello, I guess." Do you answer a hologram?

This time Jordie's voice comes over the speaker. "It's now time to start learning her language. Please listen to the words and try to learn and repeat them."

Oh, we're going right into training. Wow, no break at all. Okay, I guess I'm ready.

The hologram repeats the word, and I try to copy it.

I know I said it wrong the first time I try, so I keep practicing. It feels weird to make a new sound for the first time.

She repeats hello.

I attempt to say hello.

She says hello.

I say it better, almost the same as hers.

She says hello.

I say hello perfectly!

I think I'll be a pro at picking up this language.

Now she says a different word. I wait and see what it means, and sure enough, the voice tells me, "Now she says, '*goodbye*.'"

The hologram says it again, and this time I say goodbye back correctly within two tries. I'm pretty impressed with how fast I'm learning how to speak her language. Well, maybe not the entire language, but I now know a couple of words.

I do a little jig.

I go ahead and take it upon myself to say *hello* and *goodbye* a couple of times on my own. The sounds are becoming more familiar to my mouth.

I stand on one foot and say *"hello,"* then I hop to the other foot and say *"goodbye."*

Hello. Hop. *Goodbye.* Hop

Hello. Hop. *Goodbye.* Hop.

She says a new word, and the voice translates it for me. "She said, *'let's go.'"*

Let's go. I suppose that's better than the command to come. I appreciate that. I wonder if I'll be told to sit or stay. If that happens, I'm not going to repeat it. I'm not even going to learn it.

No, wait, I take it back. I'll learn it, but I won't do it. I'll pretend I don't understand.

Hmmm, I wonder if I can use pretending not to understand her to my advantage. I decide to keep this idea to myself and not tell Jordie.

I smile to myself and repeat after her, *"let's go."*

I can now say *hello, goodbye,* and *let's go.*

I call out, "Hey, Jordie, am I picking up the language quicker than other kids? I think I'm doing pretty good."

Jordie's voice comes over the speakers. "You are doing very well, Britt. You will learn her language quickly. That will make it easier for the two of you to communicate."

He's proud of me, I can tell.

The hologram alien owner lady speaks again. The voice translates it to, *"Stay here."* Well, at least she is not giving me the order to stay like you would a dog. Okay, I'll accept this.

I repeat after her, *stay here.*

I say it a couple of more times. Then put all the new words together.

Look at that; I learned several words and phrases within a few minutes.

We keep going with her saying a word and the voice translating for me.

Good morning.

Good night.

But I start getting mixed up when I try to repeat them all together.

I stop my fumbling and call out to Jordie or the voice, "Can we review the words I know again before moving on?"

They must restart her program, because she says '*Hello*' and runs through the list, with me slowly repeating each one. I want to make sure I get this right.

Before we begin again, Jordie's voice comes over the speaker. "That is enough for today. You have done very well."

Oh, okay. I give a quick wave to the hologram alien owner lady and tell her "*Goodbye.*"

She says goodbye, and disappears as the lights come back on in the room. I kind of forgot I was in a gray room with nothing around.

Jordie walks into the room from his hidden door. "How are you feeling?"

He has never asked me that. I think for a moment before I answer. "I'm doing okay. I'm a bit tired, and my brain is tired too. Sometimes at school, when we tried to learn a lot in one day, it would make my brain tired, and that's how I feel now."

Jordie nods, "You have done a lot today. We will go back to your room so you can relax and sleep." With that, he holds another almost hidden door open for me to walk out.

He leads the way. I'm next to him, but my feet start dragging a bit. I think I'm more tired than I realized. "Are you hungry?" Jordie asks.

I can always eat, that's never a problem. At the group home, we have our meals at a set time. Brekky is at 7:30 am every day, lunch at noon, and dinner at 6:00 pm. We do get a small snack between the meals, but I've never had the choice of when I wanted to eat. It throws me for a bit of a loop. Jordie notices my hesitation but doesn't say anything.

"No, I think I would rather take a nap right now and eat when I wake up." Making this decision is new. I can't believe I've turned down ice cream or anything else I want. But I'm getting more and more tired as we walk. How far away is the room?

"That's fine. You can sleep, and I'll come back with food when you wake up." He says as we reach the room.

I want to be polite and tell him something, like thank you, but that doesn't seem right. "G'night," I tell him instead. I don't know if it's day or night, and I'm too tired to care.

I crawl into my bed and fall asleep before Jordie leaves the room.

Chapter 11

There's a rumbling loud enough to wake me. I'm still mostly asleep, but the rumbling happens again. It's slowly pulling me out of my slumber.

Rumble.

Oh my, it's my stomach. I'm so hungry that the noise wakes me up. That's funny! I'm even more hungry than the time I was sent to bed without dinner at the group home because this girl, Christine, took my headband away and wouldn't give it back. She was taller than me and was holding it high over my head. I told her many times to give it back, and she didn't. So, I punched her in the stomach. When she doubled over, I grabbed my headband.

Of course, it was at that moment when Mrs. Williams walked in.

I tried to explain that Christine had started it, but I still got in trouble. The only good thing is that Christine got in trouble too. We were both sent to bed without dinner.

Yep, I think I'm even more hungry now than I was that day.

I sit up, stretch, and wonder how to tell Jordie I'm awake.

I shuffle around the room for a moment before realizing that I slept in my clothes. I stroll into the bathroom and see more clothes near the shower.

I guess I might as well shower since I'm right here.

I'm used to having a set shower time. I wonder if the alien owner lady will make me stick to a schedule or if I'll have to figure this out on my own. Is that what adults do? Make their own schedules? And what happens if I don't feel like taking a shower? Can I skip a day? Will I be in trouble if I do? In all of the homes I've been in with pets, the humans always set the pet's schedule. But what if the pet didn't like their schedule? Do their humans ever even think about that?

All this runs through my head as the water sprays down on me. If the showers on planet Janti are anything like this, I think I'll shower every day. I don't have anyone banging on the door telling me my time is up. Plus, the hot water here never runs out. Bonus.

I get out, dry off, and put on the new clothes. I choose white pants and an orange shirt. I'm feeling colorful today, so I put on my purple headband.

I still like these pants. I can move, run, and climb without a problem.

Will I have clothes like this on the new planet? What happens as I grow? I'm only ten years old and still have some growing to do. Is there a mall where we can shop for things I need?

I take the paper Jordie left on the table and start making a list of all my questions.

It turns into a long list.

My stomach growls again to remind me why I woke up.

I think it rumbles so loud that Jordie must be able to hear it from wherever he is.

And sure enough, the door swooshes open, and Jordie comes in carrying a tray with food.

"Hello, how are you doing? Did you sleep well?" He asks as he sets the tray on the table.

I slide into a chair and put the bowl in front of me. "Hi. Yes, I think I slept okay. How long was I out?"

I eye the mush again. I wish it looked better.

"You've been asleep for several hours. Your owner understands you need a sleep schedule, so you never have to worry about that."

Um, I wasn't but now I kind of am.

I poke the mush with my spoon. "Do you think the guys in the kitchen could fix me a steak instead of this bowl of nothing? You have all these other cool gadgets, but it seems the way you make food is lacking."

Jordie doesn't look up as he keeps tapping on his tablet-looking-computer-thing. "We developed your food to be sustainable and highly nutritional. And don't forget that it tastes like anything you want."

Fine, whatever. I close my eyes and debate what I want to eat. Maybe some pancakes and sausage. Yeah, a piping hot stack of pancakes covered in butter and syrup. I take a bite and almost moan out loud.

It's so good.

After a couple of bites, I'm finally ready to speak to Jordie. "What's on the agenda today? Oh, hey, I started a list of questions to ask you. Can I go and see the aliens in the kitchen again? I bet I would like hanging out with them." I take another bite, waiting for him to answer.

He sets down his tablet. "What are your questions?"

I finish that bite and start asking. "I like these pants, but can I get some with pockets? And if I can't have pockets, can I have a backpack? Not a school backpack, but a slouchy one. And also, will I get new clothes as I grow? What about other things I need? How will I get them?" I take another bite.

Jordie nods. "I will keep your owner supplied with clothes as you grow. As for other things, I will stop in every now and then to check on you. If you make a list, I can get you what you need. But you'll find with time you'll need less and less Earth items."

I ask Jordie, and he'll get me what I need. Got it.

"About our agenda today, first, we will trim your hair. For the next several days, you will practice the language and learn more about your owner and the planet Janti. Now that you have accepted that you will be living on another planet, you can learn what to expect and what is expected of you."

I pause, spoon mid-air. "What's expected of me? You kidnapped me. If it were up to me, I'd still be on Earth. Nothing should be expected of me."

As humans, what do we expect from our pets? Not to bite and to be potty trained. I can't promise I won't bite anyone, but I'm already potty trained.

"Yes. You will be expected to behave and be behave and do as you are told. Of course, there will be days when you are in a bad mood. But in general, I want you to show good manners and good spirits. No one wants a grumpy pet."

There was that grumpy cat that was famous on the internet for about a week or some short period like that. But I decide not to bring that up. The old guys taught me to pick my battles.

Plus, I can't believe he said that to me.

I lost my appetite.

Almost.

The pancake mush is too good to waste.

"Okay, so the rules are not to bite and be pleasant. Anything else?" I ask in a snarky voice.

Jordi either doesn't pick up on my attitude or chooses to ignore it. "Your owner will let you know of other rules."

What else could there be? Stay off the couch? No begging?

I'm not liking this.

Jordie must notice I'm unhappy. "Please do not overthink this. You have rules that you follow now. There is no difference; there will be different rules, that's all."

I guess he's right; we do have rules to follow. I'm told what time to wake up and go to bed, and I'm not allowed to hit others (well, I'm not supposed to). I have heaps of rules to follow. And as humans, we have rules for our pets. They aren't allowed on the tables, sometimes the furniture, or to bite humans.

Most adults expect me to follow their rules, so having an adult alien give me rules isn't so different.

But that doesn't mean that I'm always going to follow them.

Jordie is still talking. "Let's not worry about it anymore and get your hair trimmed. Once again, I promise it won't hurt."

Why would getting my hair cut hurt?

How does he always manage to scare me?

Chapter 12

We walk into yet another room. How big is this ship? This room is small and cozy, with what I assume is a barber's chair in front of a mirror on one side and a waterfall on the back wall. Do they have water on other planets? Do people of Earth know that there are other planets with water? Jordie sits in a comfy chair off to the side, and a human walks towards me.

I don't buy it anymore; I bet he's not human. But the scary thing is that I'm beginning to accept this.

I think I should still be afraid, but I've seen enough aliens lately that I just take them as they are.

"Hello, you must be Britt." The guy says as he extends his hand for me to shake. "My name is Simon, and I LOVE your hair. Please don't tell me you want it cut."

Okay, alien or not, I like this guy.

I shake his hand as he continues to talk. "Come this way; you can sit here." He guides me to the one and only barber chair. Yeah, I figured that's where I would sit, but I don't want to be snarky with him.

Simon keeps talking as I climb into the chair. "You have fabulous hair."

"Thank you." I finally get a word in. "I like my hair too, but everyone else tries to tame it and make it straight. I don't worry much about it, but I definitely don't want to cut my hair. I wear these headbands."

Simon is duly impressed. "That is the perfect headband. You're lucky to have it. Do you have trouble brushing your hair?" He's picking up my hair and inspecting it from all angles.

"Oh, I can't brush my hair. It gets too frizzy. But I comb it in the shower when I have conditioner in. That's the only way I have found to get the snarls out. And I don't comb my hair every time I shower, just when I think of it." I wish I had my comb with me to show him.

"You are doing exactly perfect. Let me get your hair wet so I can trim it. Don't worry; I won't take any of the greatness away." And with that, he somehow sprays a mist that soaks my hair but doesn't get in my face. I haven't had my hair cut often, but I'm usually a wet mess when the salon lady on Earth is done.

Simon wields a comb and wand. And by some magic, the tangles come out without any pain at all. No pain… I really, really like this guy. He then uses ordinary-looking scissors and begins to trim. Not cut, just trim.

I sit back and relax. "Simon, are you a human? Or are you the same species as Jordie?" Maybe if he's human, he will tell me what spaceship I can hide on to get back to Earth.

"No, I'm not human, and I'm not like Jordie either. I can change to look like any species." He tells me while still trimming.

No way.

"Do you know Stan? Can you look like him? I'm friends with Stan. I saw him the other day in the hangar, and when I waved at him, he remembered me and waved back. He's square, and his hands are hidden until he needs them; then, they poke out of the front of his body. Can you and I be friends? Then I can say that I'm friends with two aliens." Why don't humans have all these amazing abilities that aliens do? The thought of *that's why humans are pets* crosses my mind, but I quickly pretend I didn't think it.

Simon looks at Jordie with his eyebrows raised. Jordie answers him. "Stan is the English name. In his language he is Vay'chet."

Stan isn't his real name? Before I can ask Jordie about this, Simon answers. "Oh yes, I know him. Most of us here know Stan. He's a great guy."

I look at Simon out of the corner of my eye. "If I see Stan, or any of the aliens again, how will I know it's really him and not you pretending to be him?" My ninja-like abilities are kicking in again.

He smiles big and laughs. "I love it! No, I never take the form of anyone already here. I promise, anytime you see me, I will be in this form."

I give a sigh of relief. I should have stuck with my first instincts and trusted him completely. I smile and laugh with him.

"How are you settling in?" He asks.

I'm not sure how to answer that. "I think I'm handling it very well, but I still don't like the idea of being a pet. I want to go back home and to my life on Earth. I mean, I lived in a group home, and I liked it there. I miss the old guys in the park. I don't want to be a pet at all. I don't follow commands very well. And I don't like the fact that I don't have a say in all of this." He asked me, so I tell him the truth.

"Maybe you're looking at this all wrong," Simon tells me as he clips away. "This is an adventure that very few humans get to have, and you seem like you can handle adventure."

I quit breathing for a moment. He's right; I do like an adventure. And Mrs. Williams always said that we may not always be able to control what is happening around us, but we can always control our attitude. Well, almost always. I sometimes have trouble with my actions and my attitude. But I get a general understanding of what she means.

Even though I can't control the fact that I'm about to be a pet on another planet, I can control how I react to my situation. I can accept it and make it fun or fight it and try to get home.

I'm not sure what I should do. I have to think about this.

All the while, Simon is snipping away at my hair. He then sprays it with another bottle, and poof, my hair is dry. "Whoa, how did you do that? It usually takes hours for my hair to dry." I ask in wonder as I touch my hair. And I can pull my fingers through my hair – that's a first. "Where are my snarls? How did you get it soft but still curly and looking like my regular hair, but better?"

Looking in the mirror, I still can't believe that this is actually my hair. I turn my head, looking at it from all sides.

My hair is not all perfect and pretty. It still looks wild and curly, like it always does. "It's my regular hair, but without snarls. You may not understand the importance of this, but the magic you did is huge. At the group home, there was a girl named Wendy. She had perfectly straight, brown hair. She never got snarls and would always tease me about my hair. When Mrs. Williams wasn't looking, I sometimes pulled her boring hair."

Simon lets out a full laugh when I say this. He doesn't scold me for pulling someone's hair, and I keep liking him more and more. "I'm glad you like your hair," he says, still smiling. I can give you some special conditioner to add to what you already use. It will help your hair be free of snarls while still being great.”

Jordie appears next to me. “I’ll take the ingredient and add it to the shampoo and conditioner for her.”

Well, that’s offensive. I turn and glare at Jordie. “I’m not a baby; I can add it myself,” I huff.

Jordie doesn’t even apologize. “I never thought you couldn’t. But since I will supply your owner with everything you need, I will add this to your conditioner before it’s given to you.”

I look at Simon and roll my eyes. “Jordie can be a dork sometimes.” I quietly say.

Simon hands a bottle to Jordie. As soon as Jordie turns around and returns to his chair, Simon smiles big and nudges me. Yeah, he gets it, too.

“Well, beautiful little human, you are done,” Simon says in his normal voice, loud enough for Jordie to hear.

I stand up, not sure if I should hug Simon. I decide a handshake is better. I stick out my hand, and he shakes it. He must have been around enough humans to know we do that. “Thank you, Simon. I enjoyed meeting you. There aren’t many people for me to talk to. Maybe I’ll see you again.” I still want to hug him, but I don’t.

“I enjoyed meeting you as well. I hope you have grand adventures on your new planet.”

Chapter 13

I flop into a chair at the table when we get to my room. "Now what should we do?" I ask. Jordie always seems to have plans for me.

"You have another language lesson later, but you have some free time. Are you tired? I can leave you to sleep?" He asks.

I have free time? And I get to choose what I want to do?

"Does going back to Earth count as what I want to do?" I ask, knowing the answer.

"No, that is not an option. Would you like to stay here and draw?"

I don't need time to think about that. "No, can I go visit the guys in the kitchen again?" I'm much too antsy to sit still. I was never one who could quietly sit and pass the time. There is simply too much to do.

Jordie tilts his head and looks at me quizzically. "Why would you want to visit those working in the food preparation area? That is not a common place for a human child."

What is a common place for a human child on a spaceship in some unknown galaxy? I decide to keep this comment to myself. "They seemed dandy and weren't bothered by me. It would remind me of hanging out with the old guys in the park. Please, can I go to the kitchen again?" I say please to be polite, but I'm defo not begging.

"Dandy? Is that another old guy term?" He tilts his head at me.

I notice he didn't answer my question, so I quickly rush with more reasons why I should go to the kitchen. "Yeah. And I promise I won't bother them. I'll stay out of their way. I can practice my words with them. Do they speak Zobian? Do they know English? Even if they don't, I would still like to hang out with them."

I pause, giving Jordie time for Jordie to consider my request some more.

Jordie lets out a sigh.

Yes, I'm in! But I stay calm and play it cool.

Before I get too excited, he asks, "What is the word 'dandy' you said? I'm not familiar with it."

"It means good. The guys in the park always said that I'm a dandy kid." I like teaching Jordie new words.

"You can go. But only for a short time if you stay out of their way. I do not want to hear that you caused any delays in their work. Otherwise, you cannot go again." Jordie gives in to me.

"All right! Thanks, I promise I'll be good. The old guys always liked having me around and never asked me to leave. So, I know how to behave around adults." I jump up from the table and sprint to the door... and it opens!

I'm so stunned that I don't run away. I turn and look at Jordie in amazement. Did he forget to lock the door? That's not like him at all.

"I believe you understand that you are on a ship and will no longer try to escape. The door will remain unlocked for you. But I need you to be responsible. You cannot be interfering with others and causing trouble." Jordie stands in front of me, looking all adult and commanding. I'm so excited that I don't even laugh at him. Plus, he would probably get mad.

I give him a solemn look back and nod my head. "I promise to behave."

At least to the best of my ability.

He eyes me, not sure if he should believe me or not. "I will show you the way to the kitchen. Come back here when you're done, or I will come to the kitchen when it's time for your language lesson."

Yes! I won, I won, I won! I get to do something I want. I have a say in my situation. If Jordie weren't here, I'd do a little dance.

I walk with Jordie out the door and pay attention to where we are going, so I can find my way back. We turn right out of the door and turn left into the second hallway, and it's the second door on the left. Wow, that was easier than I remember.

Jordie stops before we go inside. His face is all stern and serious. "Again, don't bother the workers or get in their way. I can't imagine what you will talk about since you don't know their language. But here you are. Please behave."

I know this first time is important. He probably won't let me come back here if I mess up. I put one hand on my heart and hold up the other.

"I do solemnly swear to be on my best behavior," and I mean it. I never try to be bad on purpose.

He nods, and we go inside. The aliens pause and stare. I give them a wave as Jordie introduces me. "Hello. This is Britt. She is a human and is on this ship before she goes to her new planet. She was here the other day and has asked to come and say hello to you again."

The aliens don't respond at first, but then they all seem to remember me. The tall blue one with waves on its skin has four hands, two on each side of his body. I'll have to make sure to stay away from his flipper feet; I don't need those crushing me. He opens his mouth wide; it scares me at first. Then I realize he is smiling. I smile back.

There's a yellow one that's about two and a half meters tall, with jewels on its head, and he gives me a slight wave. He only has two arms and two legs, so he doesn't seem too odd. Except that he is tall and yellow and alien.

Then there is a short, almost square-shaped alien. His skin is a dark green color, and he's about as tall as me with purple polka dots. He has long, wavy arms that can reach even the higher shelves.

I look for Stan, but I guess he isn't a cook.

Jordie turns to me. "Britt, this is Kalen, Bjork, and Bodhi." He holds his hand out as he makes the introductions. "Don't stay too long. Just talk for a little bit and then let them work."

I barely look at him, but I nod my agreement and walk into the kitchen.

Okay, so Kalen is the blue alien with waves on his skin.

Bjork has the jewels on his head

And Bodhi is the short, polka-dot guy with really long arms.

Got it.

I'm sure that's not their real names, but it's at least nice to be able to say any name rather than "*Hey you.*"

I know they don't understand me, but I can't help but to talk. It's what I do. "Hi, everyone; I'm Britt, but Jordie already told you that. I'm from the planet Earth. Have any of you ever been there? It's big. Well, at least it's big to me. We have land and oceans and a blue sky. I guess you breathe air like I do since we are all standing here breathing and stuff. So, if you wanted to visit Earth you could do so. Do any of you live where there isn't air? How do you survive?"

I walk between the guys. "What are you making? Can I try something besides the mush Jordie gives me? Not to offend you, it tastes delicious. But sometimes I want something different, something crunchy, maybe." I point to a plate. I assume that's food on it since we're in a kitchen and everything, but it's not like any food I know. It looks like small, red triangles piled on top of each other. "How about that? can I try that?" I ask Bodhi.

He looks at me but doesn't do anything. I point and ask again. "That, can I try that?" I try to make hand signals by pointing and then pretending to eat.

Some of the old guys in the park couldn't hear very well, and I had to talk loudly and use hand signals, but we did just fine.

I point to the triangles and then point to my mouth. He must realize what I mean because he suddenly makes a strange squeak that causes me to jump. I wasn't expecting that at all. He makes another noise that I think means he's laughing at the fact that he scared me. I laugh too. I always think it's funny to be startled.

The laughter must break the ice for the other aliens because suddenly, they are all moving and making noises with each other again.

Bodhi doesn't have a hand like I do, but he has a circle at the end of his arm. As he reaches for the triangle things on the plate, the circle suddenly sucks up one triangle piece. I hold out my hand as he brings his vacuum hand to me and drops the piece of food into my palm.

Shoot, now I have to eat it. What if it tastes terrible? Or makes me sick? Or what if I choke on it? Maybe asking to eat some alien food wasn't such a good idea.

But I can't back down now. I quickly pop it in my mouth before I change my mind. It's crunchy but doesn't taste like anything. Nothing. No flavor at all. I guess I won't complain about my mush anymore.

But I'm nothing if I'm not polite. "Thank you, that was very good." I smile and nod to him and wander around the kitchen.

Bodhi is mixing up a clear liquid. I lean in close to check it out. He makes a very low guttural sound and pokes me in the shoulder. I didn't expect just a deep voice from someone so short. I jump back in case the liquid explodes.

He shakes his foot and pokes me again.

"Hey!" I smile at him. "What's that thing with your foot? Does that mean something good or bad? Are you laughing at me?" I know I'm going to have to learn a new language, but I never thought about learning new body language.

I shake my foot back at Bodhi. He shake-foot-laughs and shoves my shoulder.

Then the one with four hands and waves on its body, Kalen, starts clapping. But the funny thing is that he claps his two right hands together while still working with his left hands. How convenient.

If we were on Earth, I would assume he was stirring something in a bowl. But here, in the middle of space, it actually looks like he is waving a wand over the bowl and the contents are moving on their own. Odd.

This is the strangest kitchen I've ever seen. But since it's a kitchen for aliens I suppose I wouldn't see a microwave and dishwasher. I wander around, touching things, but not actually picking them up. I don't know what anything is, and I don't want to break it. "This stuff is all so cool. What kind of food do other aliens eat? Like what kind of food do you eat? Do you like those triangle pieces? Do they have a taste to you?" I keep exploring and staying out of their way.

It probably only takes me about fifteen minutes to see the entire kitchen. If I knew what all the appliances were, I could spend all day playing with them.

I make my way back to the front with the guys.

I see a huge metal spoon. Huh, I wonder how big of an alien it is to use a spoon of that size. I reach for it, wondering if it's heavy.

Bodhi does his squeak laugh, grabs it before I can, and tosses it to Kalen. Of course, we knock over the plate of triangles, which scatter all over the counter and floor.

Kalen holds the huge spoon over my head. It's like a game of keep-away. His mouth is open wide in a huge smile, so I jump to try to reach it.

Bodhi wraps his long arms around my legs and lifts me high enough to reach the spoon. I grab hold and hang there like I'm dangling from monkey bars.

Bjork is flapping his arms enjoying the show.

We are all laughing, clapping, and foot shaking.

And Jordie walks in.

We all freeze.

Triangle food everywhere.

Me hanging from a large spoon that Kalen is holding over my head.

Bodhi has his arms wrapped around my legs, holding me up.

Bjork stops flapping his arms.

Jordie stares at us.

We stare at him.

He stares at us.

Jordie clears his throat.

Kalen slowly puts me down, and I straighten my shirt. Play it cool, we weren't doing anything wrong, and I didn't break anything. So why do I feel like I'm in trouble? Probably because I usually get scolded for doing things I don't think are wrong.

"Hey, what's up?" See, I'm cool.

Jordie surveys the kitchen and looks back at me. "I thought we agreed that you would not interrupt them as they worked."

"I didn't mean for it to go that far. We were joking and having fun." I honestly can't remember how it all started.

Jordie sighs but doesn't yell at me. "You've been here long enough. We need to go now."

They all understand him too. I think the noise they make is a collective groan. "I know, guys, but I'll be back. Okay? Thanks for letting me hang out with you." I turn and wave when I get to the door.

What an odd site, all three different aliens waving and calling out to me. I can't help but smile.

I just made more friends.

Chapter 14

Jordie doesn't say anything as we walk through the hallways. I'm not sure if that's good or bad. It's good that he's not scolding me, but it could be bad if he is too mad to talk.

About a year ago, I was at school one time, and Brady pulled my hair hard. So, I turned around and walloped him a good one. Of course, that was when the teacher happened to be looking, and I was the one who was in trouble. She tapped me on the shoulder as she walked by me and crooked her finger, indicating for me to follow her. See, I was in so much trouble that she didn't even yell at me in front of the other kids.

So, I don't know if I'm in trouble now or not.

I keep quiet. I've learned to never confess until you're sure what they know.

I can't keep quiet. "Jordie, how long have I been on this ship?" I don't know if I'm accepting the fact that I'm on a spaceship or if I'm still in denial. But either way, I keep going along with it.

"You have been here for over an Earth week. You only have two more weeks before we go to your new home. So, we need to work hard to make sure you are ready."

Only a couple of weeks? Then my life changes again. I have to say, it hasn't been horrible here, but I'm just getting comfortable, and everything will be different again.

I slow down and eventually stop walking.

Jordie stops too. "Is something wrong?" He asks.

"I didn't realize a week had already gone by. The old guys used to say time flies, and I know the school breaks always seem too short, but now I get it. This last week went by fast. I'm kind of getting used to things here. It might be scary to see a new planet."

Jordie seems to understand. I'm not sure if he really does, but then again, I'm not the first kid that he's taken.

"Or," he says "It might be exciting."

He smiles at me, and I can't help it; I smile back.

It is kind of exciting.

We keep walking. In fact, I take the lead to the simulation room.

I guide us straight there without getting lost. I beam up at Jordie; I bet he's impressed with how quickly I've learned my way around. He nods and goes into the next room.

I stand in the center of the room. I've given up hope of finding a secret door and simply wait instead. The lights dim and I move aside, assuming the hologram will magically appear.

It does.

The alien owner lady is standing tall, looking straight ahead or straight behind her, depending on which eye I'm looking at. How can I not laugh at that?

She says the word for hello. I guess we're starting from the beginning again. No problem. I repeat the words we learned last time.

Hello.

Goodbye.

Let's go.

Stay here.

Good morning.

Good night.

"Do you still remember what each word means?" Jordie's voice asks me over the loudspeaker.

I nod. "Yep, I remember them all," I loudly and proudly announce.

Jordie nods, "Then we shall move on. As before, please listen to the words and repeat them."

The hologram looks at me and says another word. The voice follows with the interpretation. *Good.* I attempt to repeat it. I'm getting better; it only takes me twice before I say it correctly. The next word I learn is *Bad.*

Yeah, I'll probably hear that one a lot.

The voice then teaches me how to apologize. Yeah, I guess I'll need that. I truly don't mean to get in trouble, but I apologize when I do something wrong. So, I learn the word *sorry.*

I'm just happy I'm not being told words such as fetch, sit, stay, and get off the couch.

This back-and-forth continues for what seems like an eternity. I'm getting bored. I sit down and start moving my legs through the hologram. It's not like I'm kicking her if she's not real. I do a squat spin with my leg out. I would have taken her legs right out from underneath her if she was really standing here. I don't mean her any harm, but practicing my ninja moves against a hologram alien is fun.

"Britt. I think we are done for the day."

I'm so wrapped up in my next move that I forget Jordie and the other voice are in the next room. I stand and bow to my unsuspecting competitor. Jordie doesn't even question me. The lights go up, and the alien owner lady magically disappears again.

"Sorry, I was getting bored learning a word, and a word, and a word. Can't I talk to her for real? I think I have some of the basics down. I'm ready to learn more. When I was in school, I would pick up on things pretty easily. Am I still going to go to school on the other planet? Will there be other kids my age? Would it be like a puppy daycare where the aliens drop all the humans off for the afternoon, and we play and learn? That would be awesome! Will the other kids speak English? Or maybe we would all speak the alien language."

Jordie interrupts me. "From now on, your language training will be more conversational. No, you will not continue school on the planet of Janti, but you will learn about the Zobian culture. You will probably not see any other humans. There are not many human pets on the planet."

Huh, that's a bummer - no other kids to play with. I hope the alien owner lady is fun or has things for me to do. But I'm not too worried; I always manage to entertain myself.

Jordie leads me out of the simulation room and starts talking alien to me. I didn't realize he knew the language Zobian. Does he know every language? I wonder if that would be confusing after a while. What language does he dream in?

I try to pay attention to what he is saying. I pick up on *"Hello Britt, good morning."*

I answer by repeating it back to him. *"Hello Jordie, good morning."* I add an arm swish and a bit of a bow. It seems so formal to say that I figure I need to act formally.

Jordie keeps talking the entire time we are walking. I don't think he wants me to answer, just listen. Zobian is an interesting language, and it doesn't hurt my ears. I understand a couple of words here and there, and surprisingly, I get the idea of what he is saying.

He switches to English." Next time, I'll show you a hologram of your new planet if you like."

"There's a hologram of the planet Janti? Yeah, I want to see that. Thanks. So, will I see the planet from space? Or will I actually get to see where I'll live? Seeing it from space would be great, but actually seeing where I'll live would be better. You know, to kind of give me the lay of the land."

We turn into my room. "Both," is all Jordie says.

Okay, cool. I sit at the table, wondering what happens next. I grab my list of questions and look them over. I think most have already been answered. For once, I'm at a loss of what to talk about. Jordie isn't saying anything. I tap my hands on the table, whistle a bit, and look around.

Jordie breaks the silence. "I received a message. The workers in the kitchen pass along their greetings to you."

My head snaps around. "Really? They said 'hi?' Please tell them I say 'hi' back and I'll visit as soon as possible. They're a fun group of guys. They let me try some other food, and it tasted like nothing. Even tasting like cardboard would have been something, but this was nothing. So, now I like the runny food you bring me. At least I can have it taste like anything I want. That's heaps better than tasting like nothing."

"Yes, well. You can spend time with them or explore. But please, please stay out of trouble. I'll be back in about an hour." He then switches to Zobian. "*Goodbye.*"

I tell him goodbye back.

Hmmm, what to do for an hour that won't get me in trouble…

Chapter 15

To the kitchen, I go!

When the door opens, the aliens look up and see me, shouting in unison. "Oi!" It's great to have people, aliens, whatever, happy to see you. Sometimes you want to go where everyone knows you. I laugh and stroll in.

"Hello, mates!" I happily go back into the kitchen. They make room for me to watch what they are cooking today. I have no idea what it is, nor do I want a sample, but it's still fun to watch.

They laugh with each other. I may not understand their words, but I know a good ribbing when I see it. They are like the old guys in the park back home; they have an easy friendship and have accepted me.

We are all getting along well when the door opens.

I freeze.

It's an alien that looks like the alien owner lady.

Is she here to get me? I thought I had several days left. Does Jordie know she's here? Is she going to kidnap me? Can you be kidnapped from your kidnapper?

Without a word, I slowly ease behind the polka-dot alien. He understands my fear and helps to hide me. I'm not ready to leave yet, especially without Jordie.

It speaks, and I understand some of the words. "Hello, food, please."

Oh wait, that isn't my alien owner lady, but it is the same species. I think it's here for food. Well, that's okay; I can handle that. I quietly step out from behind my hiding spot. "Hello," I say in the Zobian language

It's funny that even aliens have common emotions, such as surprise. This one looks more like a male. His head spins around to look at me with one eye, then the other, and he steps backward. Maybe he's never seen a human child speak in its language. I give a little wave to show I come in peace. I have no idea why, and I can't pinpoint what makes him different from the hologram I've seen. But I've decided to call him a guy alien.

His skin has a pinkish-pearl hue like the alien owner lady. I see it change as I slowly approach. "Hello," I say again, but a little louder in case he doesn't hear well.

He squats down and gets eye-level with me. I'm a bit freaked out, but I stand my ground. He smiles and speaks back to me. I catch a couple of words here and there. "Hello, how are you, name." This is exactly what I wanted, to learn the language by speaking it, not learn certain words.

I point to myself. "My name is Britt." I talk in both Zobian and English. Zobenglish.

Telling him my name gives me something else to worry about. What if the alien owner lady wants to change my name? I mean, when people adopt a pet dog, cat, or hamster, they sometimes change its name. Not everyone likes the name Fifi… but Britt is a good name. Can the alien species even say Britt? Maybe I'll have to learn the translation of Britt. How will I know when the alien owner lady is calling my name? Will I get in trouble if I don't answer?

Well, now I have something new to worry about.

I bring my attention back to this guy. He isn't scary at all. I want to inspect him closer. The hologram is a great way to see the alien owner lady, but real life is better. I hold out my hand, palm up, asking him to show me his hands.

It's the suction cups that I want to see.

He holds out his hand for me to inspect. I brush my finger over the palm of his hand, and it doesn't stick. I do the same to his fingertips. I poke his fingertip again, and my finger sticks to it. He activated the suction cup!

I laugh and yelp and pull away.

That was weird - in the best way possible.

He laughs too. Look at me, bonding with aliens.

Is this what makes a person a good pet? I'm not afraid, and I can make friends with just about anyone or anything. Bugger, I guess I'm more like a dog than a cat.

Bodhi interrupts us to give the alien the food he requested. He says "Thank you" to Bodhi. I'm happy I understand it. Aw, I'm friends with a polite alien.

"Goodbye," he tells me in his language.

I tell him bye back. As he leaves, he looks at me again with the eye in the back of his head and waves. Man, that eye still gives me the heebie-jeebies. But I don't want to offend him by freaking out, so I smile and wave.

When in doubt, smile and wave.

I try not to giggle as his tiny feet carry him out the door without him tipping over. That breaks the weirdness.

Yeah! I just spoke with an alien in alien!

I turn and look at Bodhi and raise my hand to give him a high five. It must be a human thing because my colorful friend simply raises a hand back at me. We stand there, each with our hands raised.

Good enough for me!

I figure it's also a good time for me to leave. Jordie will be looking for me soon. I stand in the doorway before I go. "Okay, mates, I have to go now. Thank you for letting me visit. I'll be back as soon as I can." None of them understand me, but it's universal to say something as you leave. They all make noise and wave their hands or arms. I take it they are saying *bye* to me.

I walk back, smiling. How cool is it that I'm friends with heaps of different aliens?

Maybe instead of being a pet, I could be a friend.

Pets are friends too. Dogs are great friends to humans. Although humans are responsible for pets, so maybe the pet/friend thing only kind of works.

I bet I could make it work.

Dogs seem to be the perfect pets for humans… maybe a little *too perfect.*

My walk slows.

Why are dogs the perfect pet for humans? Did that happen by accident or was it planned? This thought scares me.

I walk into my room and barely have time to sit at the table before Jordie arrives. Either my timing is perfect, or he knew I was coming back.

"Hello, Britt. How were the workers in the food preparation area today?"

"What? Oh, hi. They're fine" I'm still distracted by my dogs-as-aliens thoughts.

Jordie sits at the table, watching me closely. "You seem unsettled." He states.

"I've been thinking. So, dogs seem like the perfect pet for humans. And I went to a home that had a dog that understood what the grown-ups were saying and would do what they said. Like go get his toy ball, or go to bed, things like that. So, I was thinking… are dogs aliens?"

Jordie stares at me, blinking.

I continue. "I mean, at one time, were they aliens? Did you or someone like you bring them to Earth a long time ago to be pets for humans? You're bringing me to Janti to be a pet, so maybe dogs are originally from another planet, but bringing them here was such a success they stayed." I tap my fingers on the table, still thinking this through.

"No, dogs are not, and never were, from another. Dogs are descended from wolves and are from Earth." Jordie said he would never lie to me, but I'm still not sure.

"I don't know… I believe that a dingo may have come from a wolf, but not a teacup poodle. I don't see that resemblance at all. Or what about a Yorkie dog? they look nothing like a wolf. Although they can be grouchy, that doesn't mean they are related to a wolf. So, you see my thinking? Dogs are just a little *too perfect* as pets, and I'm not sure they really do come from wolves."

I laid out my argument as factually as possible.

I bet other adults would laugh at me, but Jordie doesn't. I like that he takes me seriously. "Please, believe me, dogs are not from another planet. They are creatures of the Earth, the same as humans."

Hmmm… okay.

OMG, I have an even more scary thought.

"Is there a planet out there somewhere full of human pets?" I whisper this because saying it out loud would make it even more real. "Like dogs are popular on Earth, are humans bred somewhere and kept as pets?" This is totally freaking me out.

Jordie rests his hand on my shoulder. It helps keep me from passing out. "Britt, look at me." My eyes are darting all over, but I manage to take a deep breath and look at him. Huh, he had brown eyes. I guess I never really looked. He starts talking again, distracting me from his eyes. "There is no planet of human pets. It has only been recently discovered that humans make good pets on other planets. It means you are very rare and very special." He is trying to calm me down, and it's working. "Please do not worry or imagine such a thing. Humans only live on Earth. Except for the very special ones that get to travel to another galaxy. You are one of the special ones." He looks me dead in the eyes and smiles.

He promised never to lie to me, so I make myself believe him.

I feel much better. "Okay, thank you." I'm not usually relieved when I'm wrong. But I'm glad I'm wrong this time.

All of this thinking has worn me out. I think I've had a full day today: I made friends in the kitchen, spoke with the hologram of my alien owner lady, and realized dogs are really from Earth.

Whew.

I look at the bed, and boy does it look comfortable.

Jordie must see me winding down. "It's time for you to rest. Get some sleep, and I'll come back later."

Yeah, no worries there, mate.

I crawl right into bed without changing clothes. Besides, I wasn't outside playing and didn't get them dirty.

Chapter 16

I nap or sleep. I'm not even sure anymore. It's weird not knowing if it's day or night - but also kind of freeing not having to live by the clock. I eat when I'm hungry, nap when I need a quick refresher, and sleep for hours when needed.

The whooshing of the door opening wakes me up. I stretch and see Jordie has brought food. This must be what it feels like to be a dog or cat. Sleep until your owner brings you food. It's not so bad.

I stretch and get out of bed. Jordie greets me. "Hello, Britt. Are you hungry?"

I wish he would have said either good morning or good evening, then I would know if I should think of brekky or dinner to eat.

"Do they have sunrises and sunsets on Janti, like we do on Earth? How do I know if it's morning or nighttime? Will I have a bedtime and a wake-up time? I usually wake up pretty early anyways." I sit and think about what I want to eat. Maybe I'll have brunch, just in case. Oh, I know. I'll have a breakfast sammie - that covers both breakfast and lunch. I close my eyes and picture a bagel with lots of bacon, some cheese, and an egg. I like it nice and hot. I take a big breath before digging in. Yep, so good.

"You will have a sleep schedule. Your owner understands that humans work best with regular sleep, -but there will not be the twenty-four-hour rotation around the sun you are used to."

So, I'll have a regular sleep schedule; I guess that's good. As much as I like playing outside, I like a good night's sleep.

"So, what are we doing today?" I ask in between bites.

"I will show you a hologram of Janti today." He off-handily tells me.

Oh, yeah! I forgot about that.

I scarf down my food and jump up from the table. I'm ready.

Jordie talks Zobian as we walk to the simulation room. I'm starting to pick out words I recognize and try responding with what I know. This is much better than sitting in a grey room learning words. Jordie automatically goes into the other room. I never know if it's him or the scary alien voice who will be talking to me, but I'm okay with either.

The lights dim. I start to wiggle; I can hardly wait to see this planet.

Stars and planets appear around me. It's as if I'm floating in space. I slowly turn, looking all around me. The alien voice begins. "This is your solar system. You can see your sun and the planets that circle it. There is Earth; I see you recognize that."

I step closer to Earth. I walk around until I see Australia. I've never felt homesick before and never knew I would miss being on Earth. My mouth and brain go quiet.

The scary voice doesn't let me dwell on my loss for too long before it starts talking again. "If you'll look over here, do you see the area without stars?"

I look at the blackness that seems darker than the rest. Is he highlighting something? I walk closer and see what looks like a movement of black on black. I can't figure out what it is.

"This is a wormhole. It allows us to travel from one galaxy to another. You came here with Jordie through a wormhole but you were asleep, and will use one to travel to your new galaxy and planet. Movement through these can be unnerving at first, so I would like to show you what it's like."

We begin to zoom in on the wormhole.

"It would be best if you sit down."

I plop down on the ground without taking my eyes off of outer space. We zoom in more.

I take a deep breath in and out.

The picture moves into the wormhole, and I feel like I'm going with it. This would make a great ride at an amusement park!

We fly into the wormhole.

There is a flash of light and bam! It's as if I'm zooming through a slide. I'm moving so fast that black and white lights flash by me. The ride drops down, turns left, turns right, and then climbs up – all while lights are still zipping by.

I put my hands down to brace myself, trying not to fall over.

The ride lasts longer than I thought it would. How far away is this galaxy? I see a light coming up, like the end of a tunnel. I brace myself.

It feels like we pop out of a tunnel and suddenly stop. I fall forward, even though I'm still sitting on the ground.

I sit up and look around. Is this my new galaxy?

"This is not your new galaxy. We must travel through it to get to another wormhole."

Well, that answers that question.

"This is the galaxy of Trimbullo. If you look to your left, you might see the wormhole we will travel through next."

I look left and don't see anything unusual – except for everything. About five planets are circling the sun, but none look like Earth. I stand up and walk to the pink planet with green swirls. I didn't realize space and planets would be so colorful.

The voice interrupts my exploration, "Let's keep going. Please sit down, and we will enter the next wormhole."

I sit down.

We fly to the left. Now I see the black move again. Hey, I can now spot wormholes. Maybe it's a skill that might come in handy one day.

Zoom! We start zipping through the slide again. If all the planets are different colors, why are the lights in this wormhole only black and white? I forget the question as soon as I think about it. I'm too busy trying to keep my balance and not get sick. I wonder if other humans have thrown up because of all the twists and turns.

We must have been closer this time because I soon see the end of the tunnel. I'm ready this time and don't fall forward when we shoot out and suddenly stop.

Ha! I can do this. I can travel through space. I'm curious if my alien owner lady flies through space, or will we stay on Janti and never go anywhere? What if I get bored? I don't want a boring owner. What if she is old and wants to sleep all the time? Do I have to always be quiet? I don't think I can be quiet every day. And I don't want to be in trouble all the time.

The voice starts talking again. I'll remember to ask Jordie more about my owner.

"This is your galaxy. As you see there is only one sun that the planets circle. Janti is the small, yellow planet with silver marks."

I see it. Janti is in the middle of all the planets, and he's right; it's smaller than the others. By now I'm standing and bouncing on my toes. I'm so excited I can hardly stand still.

"Are you ready to see it closer?"

"Yes!" I excitedly shout.

We fly towards Janti.

Closer. Closer.

Pretty soon, we are moving in the sky, then failing towards the ground.

The anticipation is more than I can handle.

"Waaah!" I yell. I'm not afraid, and I'm not screaming because I'm scared. I simply can't stop the excitement from coming out.

I hold up my hands. "I'm okay!" I call out. I don't want the simulation to stop.

As we glide through the air, I look around. I don't see any water, just kilometers and kilometers of color passing by. Is the ground colorful?

Wait, that's not the ground. That's the trees!

Trees on Earth are tall, and so are these. Maybe all of the trees are tall. Some have a straight trunk and a circle of colorful leaves on top, like a lollipop. Other trees have branches going in all directions and leaves growing every which way. I kind of like those; they seem wild and free.

The leaves are outlined in black with beautiful glowing colors inside. At least, that is what I think I'm seeing. "Can I check out the leaves closer?"

We stop gliding and move into a tree, stopping to let me see the leaves better. I reach out to touch one, but my hand goes through it. Shoot, I forgot this was a hologram. I lean as closely as possible to the leaf. I'm right, it's outlined in black, and the veins inside are black, but each leaf area in between is a glowing color that I can see through.

One tree has leaves that are outlined in black with a deep, glowing, see-through blue. Then, another tree's leaves are outlined in black with a vibrant, glowing, see-through red. The colors are endless, and some I'm not sure I know what color they are.

It's probably the most beautiful thing I've seen in my whole life.

I get to live on a beautiful planet!

I want to see more. I step back and nod. "Okay, I'm ready to keep going," I tell the alien voice.

We float to the ground, which is silver.
This is Janti.
This is my new planet.
This is my new home.

Chapter 17

My new home.

It's scary and exciting at the same time. I always knew that one day I would be adopted and move, and now it's happening.

There are so many questions going through my head that I can't concentrate.

What will my house look like? Will I live in a building or a cave underground? Or maybe in the sky? Or something else? Will I have my own room or only a place to sleep? I've never known a dog with its own room, only a dog bed. Although I did hear of a pig that lived in a house with his own room. Maybe my human bed will be in the living room next to a fireplace. I like to be warm. Will I have toys? Oh, what toys do I want? Maybe a rope swing; that would be fun. How will I get my toys? Is there a human store – like a pet store? Probably not since humans are still rare. So again, how will I get my things? Will I get an allowance and be able to decide what I want, or will I get what the alien owner lady brings home? I bet I'll just get what I get. Jordie said he will bring me food. Maybe he can bring me toys as well. What about treats? Maybe he can bring me chocolate every now and then.

I'm totally lost in my thoughts when the voice brings me back. "This is the area near your new home. Please look around and become familiar with it." I'm in an open area, not as big as a park, but still, an open area surrounded on three sides by glowing trees. And some colorful plant-like objects dot the land. I can't see past the hill on the other side. One day I'll go exploring to see where that goes.

I don't think I'm standing on grass; at least not green grass. The open area is silver-streaked with yellow. I'll be living on a silver and yellow planet.

So, is this like my yard? Or do we live near a park? Now that would be fun. Will I be allowed to run around outside and play? "I'm not going to have to wear a collar and leash, am I?" I ask out loud.

I refuse to wear a collar. I'll be like a cat; they are above such things.

"No, you will not be required to wear a collar," Jordie answers. "But we will speak later about the rules. One is that you do not run away when you are outside."

I forgot about the rules. Whatever.

I begin to walk around. The flowers are similar to the trees, except they are outlined in white with glowing, see-through colors. I can't wait to touch the flowers and climb the trees.

I look at the sky and see the sun in the yellow sky. What is the temperature like? Back at home, we had four seasons: winter, spring, summer, and fall. Does this planet have seasons?

I have so many questions.

But I still don't see a house.

I look again at the distant, rolling hill. The house may be over there. I start walking in that direction when the voice quickly tells me, "Stop!"

I freeze.

"Remember, you are still in the simulation room. I do not want you to walk into the wall." It calmly tells me.

Oh, well, yeah. There is that.

I turn around and walk the other way until I assume I'm in about the center of the room again.

"Is this my yard? Is there a house close by?" I can't stop the questions from coming, but at least I limit it to two for now.

"The Zoboian live underground. The weather is hot and dry, so living below the surface keeps the homes cool." As the voice says this, a large hole opens in the ground near me.

I step forward to peek in.

I see a large object rising towards me. I step back and watch a clear bubble float to a stop in front of me. "To get to your home, you will step into the bubble, and it will bring you to your main living area."

Oh, that is too cool.

I step forward as if I'm entering the bubble. The view changes, and we go down through the silver earth. The ground shimmers silver and yellow. We don't go far before the bubble stops, and I see the inside of my new house. It's smaller than I thought.

The ceilings are high since the alien owner lady is tall. The room is a large square, with a hallway off the back side. It's not much; I was hoping for something grand. Jordie said humans are special so I assumed we are expensive, and I figured the house would be huge. "Is this the entire house?" I ask out loud.

The voice answers. "The Zoboian do not spend much time in their dwelling. Humans pride themselves on large houses and many belongings. Zoboians pride themselves on having less. You will have a place to sleep, keep your clothing and belongings, and store your food and water. But otherwise, the majority of your time will be spent outside."

Perfect, that's how I like it. I don't want to be stuck inside anyways. Imagine all the exploring I can do.

"Where do I sleep?"

With that question, the room changes into a different square. This one is a bit smaller, maybe three meters by three meters. It's an empty room.

Great. I sleep on the floor.

That bums me out, and I slump a bit. It reminds me even more that I'm nothing more than a lowly pet. I sigh, at least dogs and cats get some sort of bed.

Jordie talks this time, "Zussta has asked that we wait to show your room. She has worked hard to make it nice for you and wants your room to be a surprise."

I perk up. "She made a special room for me? That's so nice! Is she happy I'm coming to live with her?"

I can almost hear Jordie smile, "Yes, she is very excited to meet you and have you live with her."

That is so exciting! I bounce up and down. It's like waiting to see your birthday or Christmas present.

"Okay, then, can we go back outside?"

With that, the scene changes, and I'm back above ground. It happens so fast that I almost lose my balance. Again, I'm glad I don't get motion sickness.

Deep colors are everywhere. Not soft colors, not light pinks and light blues. No, these are how I imagine jewels would look.

Colors on trees.

Colors on flowers.

Colors on the ground.

Seeing so many colors hurt my eyes. Sometimes, you need to see soft colors.

I'm getting tired and sit down. Jordie must realize that I've had enough. "Okay, Britt, let's stop for today and go back to your room."

That sounds good to me. I'm tired and hungry.

I take one last look around as everything fades away. The simulation room is boring with its grey walls. I meet Jordie at the exit door, and we walk back to the room together. Even the hallways seem boring compared to Janti. Unless of course the hallways are all different colors to aliens like the lady who cleaned my teeth. But for me… boring.

"Can I get something to eat? When did I last eat? I don't even know what day it is or how long I've been here. Can't I have a clock or something?" Yep, I think I'm getting hangry. When I get hungry and tired I defo get angry - hangry

Jordie doesn't seem to mind my attitude. "Yes, some food will be delivered shortly. You go ahead and eat and sleep, then we will talk about your time remaining in orientation and when you will go to Janti."

We enter my room, and I flop into a chair at the table. Before I can complain, the door opens, and this time a new alien brings my food. I'm too hungry to be happy to meet someone new. But I do remember my manners and thank them for bringing me something to eat.

See, I can be a polite pet.

I take the cover off the dish and close my eyes. I'm hungry for a meal, not treats. I want spaghetti and meatballs with lots of garlic bread on the side. I think about a heaping plate of spaghetti. I open my eyes and dig in. I slurp the mush, pretending it's noodles.

It's so good that I start to hum and rock back and forth. I eat it all, scraping the bowl clean.

Jordie has been working on his tablet and hasn't spoken a word throughout the entire meal. And, as it turns out, I didn't talk either. Wow, I must really be tired. I'm not sure how politely to ask him to leave so I can sleep.

I do an exaggerated yawn and stretch.

Jordie looks at me. "I'll leave you to sleep now. When you wake up, we will discuss what you can expect next. Please write down any questions, and we will go over them."

I know I have heaps of questions, but I don't care about them right now. I smile at Jordie and get up from the table. He also rises and picks the tray up too. "Sleep well," he tells me.

I shuffle to the bed and crawl under the blanket. All my questions run through my mind, but they can wait.

Huh, this is pretty nice. I get to nap anytime I want.

So, if something is going on that I don't like, I can pretend to be tired, and maybe my owner will let me be alone so I can nap.

That's something to remember.

My ninja street smarts are always making sure I have a way out if I'm suddenly in a bad situation.

Chapter 18

The days blend together. I sleep, eat, and go to the simulation room to practice the language. Life is kinda boring when I think of it like that. But I'm not actually bored. I feel like I've been busy for a couple of days. So much so that I haven't even been back to the kitchen to see the guys.

I'm picking up on Zobian words quite well if I do say so myself.

Jordie and I are sitting at the table. I'm eating, and he's pecking away at that tablet. He always has that with him. He looks like those people who can't put down their cell phones. I wonder if aliens can become addicted to technology like humans.

I figure it's best not to ask that. Humans tend to get offended when I say they are addicted to anything.

Instead, I enjoy the food for a while.

"When do I go to Janti?" I garble my question while eating.

"Please finish your food before talking." Is the reply Jordie gives me. Yeah, I know. Ms. Williams didn't tolerate us talking with food in our mouths either.

I finish a couple of bites, wipe my mouth, and try again. "Sorry, when do I go to Janti?"

"We will fly there in roughly one Earth day," Jordie answers while setting down his tablet, giving me his full attention.

It's a good thing I wasn't eating because I start choking on nothing.

Tomorrow?!

We leave tomorrow?!

I turn sideways and lean forward with my head by my knees.

I gulp for air, catching my breath. I don't know if I'm ready to leave tomorrow. I knew this day was coming, but it was always in the future – but now it's happening.

Tomorrow.

I forget about my food, slowly stand up from the table, and start pacing. I have so many questions. I need to say goodbye to the guys in the kitchen. I don't think I have a suitcase to pack my clothes… I don't think I'm ready.

Jordie watches me. I pause in front of him. "I'm not ready." I try to say this firmly, like an adult, but it comes out quiet and squeaky. I clear my throat and try again, but nothing comes out.

Jordie gently places a hand on my shoulder. "I know this can be scary, but I believe in you. You are ready. You are learning the language and have seen a hologram of your owner and planet. With the hologram, you have flown through galaxies and have seen real outer space. You have done very well. You are ready."

I wish I believed him.

Is this what a dog feels like when told he must go somewhere new? I know most dogs don't like going to the vet. At least I know where I'm going. It must be confusing for a dog to be dropped off at a new house and left there with no one to explain the situation to them.

Tomorrow.

If I don't sleep, maybe tomorrow will never come. I know that's not true, but I consider it anyways.

I take a deep breath and decide on a plan. I need answers to questions. That may help me feel *ready*.

I stand tall, addressing Jordie, "Okay, I have a few requests." I hope he notices I didn't say I had some demands; he probably wouldn't like that.

Jordie nods, "What are your requests?"

Great, he's willing to work with me on this. "I have a lot of questions to be answered first. And I want to visit the guys in the kitchen again before I go. I can't finish my food now, but I want to think about what my last meal will be, so please keep food close by for when I'm ready." I feel like I should have more demands than that, but I can't think of anything else. So, I quickly add, "And anything else I might think of." There, that should cover everything.

"I have no problem with any of your requests. Let's start with your questions. Go ahead and start asking now." Jordie moves his tablet and my bowl of food out of the way, making room for us to talk at the table.

I stay standing and fire away:

Me: "You said it was hot and dry on Janti. How hot? Will I be able to go outside?"

Jordie: "It is similar to a summer day in Australia. Yes, you can go outside and breathe the air. The air temperature will not harm you."

Me: "Will I eat the same food? Or will I have treats with texture sometimes"

Jordie: "You will mainly eat this food. There are some treats similar to crackers that you can have occasionally."

Me: "Can you bring me chocolate?" I doubt if I can imagine the mush as good as the real thing.

Jordie: "No, soon your body will not be used to Earth foods, so no chocolate."

Me: "Will I be able to go outside and play?

Jordie: "Yes, your owner spends much of her time outside. She knows you need to run and exercise and will allow you to do so."

Me: "What does she do for fun?"

Jordie: "Zussta is quite active. She will include you in her daily walks and other activities. She also enjoys traveling to new places."

Me: "Will we stay on Janti or go to other planets? Does she have a spaceship?"

Jordie: "It is common for Zoboians to visit other planets, so yes, you will go to other planets in a spaceship."

Me: "Will she be nice to me? What if I do something wrong? Will she spank my bum or my head?"

Jordie: "She is very nice. No, she will not spank or hurt you, but she will let you know if you do something you are not supposed to."

Me: "Does she know I sometimes get in trouble, but I don't mean to?"

Jordie: "Yes. It is actually one of the things that she likes about you."

Me: "How do I contact you if I need something?"

Jordie: "You don't. You are not to rely on me. If you need something, tell Zussta, and she will help you."

Me: "What do I call her? Right now, in my head, I call her *Alien Owner Lady*. Do I have to say ma'am, or salute her, or something?"

Jordie: She is not very formal. You can call her by her name, Zussta."

Me: What will she call me? Do I have to change my name?

Jordie: The Zoboians do not speak English. She may not be able to say your name. She may call you Britt or change it to something different."

I pause. He has answered all the questions I can think of for now. I'm impressed that he didn't get upset by me asking so much. I'm also impressed by my ninja-like questioning skills. I've learned people usually don't have time to lie if I rapid-fire questions at them.

I sit back down. "All right, can you tell me my rules again? I don't want to get in trouble right away."

Jordie smiles; he's probably glad I'm a good kid. "The rules are similar to what you have now. Behave, be polite, don't run away, and do what Zussta says."

Wow, they really are the same rules I had at the group home. Except on Janti, I get to choose my food and my bedtime. I guess I can't really complain too much.

"What if she doesn't like me?" It's one last question that I have. I'm afraid to ask this. Will she return me so Jordie will find me another owner, or can I go back to Earth?

Jordie seriously answers this question. "Do not worry; she will like you. I spoke with her several times and carefully matched the two of you. She is active like you, doesn't mind if you talk a lot, and understands an adjustment period is necessary for you both to learn about each other."

I try to figure out what our relationship will be like. It could be like a kid and a dog being best friends. I used to laugh at the videos of little kids dressing up their dog or cat, pulling them in a wagon, and painting their nails. Maybe Zussta and I will be like that, except she's not a kid. But she's not a human adult either, so maybe we could be friends… with me having rules.

I figure all my questions have taken less than an hour to ask. I shrug, "So, what do we do for the next twenty-three hours?"

Jordie stands up, smiles big at me, and answers in the alien language. I don't understand all of it, but I pick up the words "*kitchen, goodbye, room, food.*"

I assume I get to go to the kitchen and say goodbye to the aliens working there. Then maybe the simulation room one more time. And I get my last meal. Even if I am eating the same food on Janti that I do here, I've already decided it's my last meal. I'm not sure what I want yet, but I have time to think about it. I can snack for lunch and then do a doozie of a dinner.

"So, I can go to the kitchen?" I double check.

He picks up his tablet, stops at the door, and turns to me. "Please don't stay too long, and come back here when you're done saying goodbye."

I agree, and he leaves.

I look in the bathroom mirror. My hair is absolutely all over the place. I wait to shower, thinking I'll do that right before we leave so my hair will be better when I meet Zussta for the first time. I take off my headband and wet my comb down before trying to tame my hair. When it's a bit better; I wander back into my room.

I've grown to like my room here on the spaceship. I wonder how Zussta has set up my room at the underground house. I guess I'll find out tomorrow, so there's no reason to worry about it today.

I might as well go to the kitchen now. I bet if I run as fast as I can, I'll be there in seconds. I stretch my legs and arms. Then hop up and down like I've seen athletes do. I step into the hallway, taking a runner's pose, one foot forward, the other planted like an anchor to push off from. I bend forward, arms and legs ready for running.

Three, two, one. Go!

Chapter 19

I run as fast as I can towards the kitchen. I take corners at full speed and use the walls to bounce me into the next hallway. I'm going so fast that I barely see the doors as they blur by me.

I have to keep my street smarts with me, even on a new planet.

I turn a sharp left and crash straight into an alien.

I totally didn't see it, and it scares the bejeezus out of the both of us.

I fall backward, landing on my bum. I quickly regain my senses and jump up, ready to fight.

See, ninja street smarts.

The alien is still righting itself, probably not knowing what hit it.

That makes me laugh. Can you imagine walking along and BAM! Something runs smack into you! Now I can't stop laughing. The poor thing was probably lost in thought, planning its day, and I come around the corner. By now, I'm laughing so hard I have tears coming out of my eyes.

I finally pull myself together and look at the alien.

It's Stan!

I catch my breath and start apologizing. "Stan! I'm so sorry. I was seeing how fast I could get to the kitchen. I didn't see you. Are you hurt? Are you okay?" I'm looking him over, but I have no idea how to tell if he's hurt.

Stan shakes his entire body like a dog and focuses on me. He quickly realizes that it's me who ran into him and not an enemy or anything. His hand shoots out from the center of his body. I stick my hand out too, and we shake. I take it he isn't hurt.

It's hard to talk when neither of us understands each other's language. I hope he's not mad at me.

He starts talking his language and pats me on the arm. Whew… not mad or hurt.

I wonder if he'll tell Jordie, and I'll get in trouble for running in the hallways. In my defense, I've never seen anyone or anything around here before. How was I to know the one time I run that someone would be here? One time at school, I was rushing to the bathroom. It was during class, so the hallways were clear. I was running up the steps but watching my feet so I wouldn't trip, and I ran right into a grade two teacher. I didn't hit her nearly as hard as I ran into Stan, but she was still upset. I almost got sent to the principal, but she let me go with a warning since I was bouncing up and down due to having to use the restroom so badly.

Maybe aliens don't get angry like humans. I hope Zussta doesn't get angry at me.

Stan gives me a wave and pulls his arm back into his body. He shakes his entire body one more time and walks away from me.

"Goodbye!" I yell. I don't want to leave without saying bye. He turns around and waves again. He must be used to seeing humans come and go.

There, I got to see Stan. But I messed up my running time. I look up and down the hallway. I still want to see how fast I can make it. I bet my chances of running into another alien are zero.

I jog back to my room, stretch again, and get into my runner's pose.

Three, two, one. Go!

I take off again.

I get to full speed, zooming around corners faster than any human has run before. I use the walls to push myself around the corners. I'm a blur to anyone who sees me.

I make it around two more corners and start for the home stretch. Some kids in my school make the fatal mistake of slowing down before they get to the finish line. Not me; I run at full speed past the kitchen door before I begin to slow down.

I bet I broke all records for speed on this ship, possibly even the galaxy.

I pace a bit, getting my breathing under control. I walk to the kitchen door and wait for it to open.

"Oi! G'day mates!" I exclaim.

"Oi!" They all holler back at me. How can this not make me happy? I assume the aliens are smiling. The tall blue one with waves on his body has his mouth open wide, the polka dot one is hopping up and down, and the short one is shaking its left foot.

We are all happy.

"I come to say goodbye. I'm leaving tomorrow. Jordie is taking me to the planet Janti. Have you been there? I saw a hologram of it, and it was beautiful. I'm scared to go but excited to see this new world in real life." They all watch me while they work. I continue, "I sure appreciate you letting me hang out with you. I've never met aliens before, but I'll be lucky if they are all as nice as you."

Still no answers, just smiles.

I try saying goodbye in the only alien language I know. The short alien understands that. He looks at the others and says something to them, maybe translating for me.

They all stop and look at me.

Crud, what did he say?

Then they all come from behind the counters and surround me, tapping me on the head and shoulders. I hear them say the word, *Goodbye*.

They understand I'm leaving.

I smile and spin around, looking at all my new, strange friends. I usually don't get too emotional at goodbyes since I've lived with quite a few families.

But I am glad I got to know these aliens.

I jump and spin around for them. They all clap and raise their voices. They are impressed with my graceful moves.

I don't stay long; Jordie has told me time and time again not to interrupt their work. I say *Goodbye* one last time and leave the kitchen for good.

Walking back to my room, I practice all the words I know in the new language. I think I'm picking it up quite well. At least I know the basics and will be able to talk with Zussta a little bit.

Hello, goodbye, please, thank you, sleep, hungry… I repeat the words several times before I'm back in my room.

I think about what else I need to do before we leave. I grab my bag to pack.

I look in the bottom of my bag and spot the string and flat metal piece I had that first day I met Jordie. The day he took me. I forgot all about my string and washer.

I move to the center of the room and twirl it around until it makes a whistling noise.

I'm happy and sad at the same time.

Change is hard sometimes.

I go back to packing. I start with my bathroom items. I pick up my toothbrush, comb, and headbands. All of which are very important. Next, I pack my new clothes. I tightly roll them, like Ms. Williams showed me. She said rolling my clothes takes up less room than folding them. Or I could just shove them in the bag.

I'm packing the other two outfits when I wonder how they are still clean. Did someone wash them when I wasn't here? Will Zussta wash my clothes, or will I have to?

I sit down on the floor; I still have lots of questions.

I flop backward and lay on the floor, staring at the ceiling. I look to my right and see the paper airplane I made when I first arrived. It's wedged along the wall, almost hidden.

Has it really only been two weeks since I first saw Jordie in the park? Two weeks.

I met Jordie, got kidnapped and taken to a spaceship, met aliens, saw outer space, went to the dentist and hairdresser, saw holograms of the alien owner lady, learned the new planet, made alien friends…

Whew! No wonder Jordie is picky about who he chooses. I bet not all humans could handle this. Does it make me a lot special or a little crazy?

I smile and decide that I might be a bit of both.

Chapter 20

"What would you like to see during your time in the simulation room?" Jordie asks.

What do I want to see? I get to choose? I thought he would have something planned. Hmmm, what do I want to see?

I want to see everything.

"Can we fly through space, land on Janti, and then see the alien owner lady while talking in her language?" I eagerly ask.

We walk into the room, and I take my place just off the center, and Jordie goes through the hidden door. I've never seen that other room, but I imagine it's similar to a newsroom, with computer boards and screens. Or like a control room like I've seen in movies. When people head to outer space, there's always a large control room. Except this time, there is only Jordie and the scary alien in there instead of lots of people. I'm pretty easygoing and don't require too many people to watch over me, just those two are enough.

The lights dim, and the planets appear. I float above the planets I know - there's Earth, and Saturn, and the Sun. I know some of the other planets, but I forget which one is which.

I look between the planets and notice a movement of blackness to my right. I'm learning to spot wormholes. I wonder how many are in this galaxy. "Hey Jordie?" I call out loudly. "How do you know which wormhole takes you to the correct galaxy? Can you take the wrong one and get lost? One time I was walking down an alley and saw a kitten. I chased her down a different alley and then turned down another, and then I was lost. It's okay though; I found my way to the park. But is it like that? Like, you could get lost but eventually find your way to somewhere familiar?"

I scan the space to my left, looking for more wormholes.

"Different galaxies have various numbers of wormholes," his voice comes over the speaker. "I have learned many of the routes from one galaxy to another. But one can also use a map."

Shut up! There's a map? It almost sounds too easy.

We float close to the wormhole. I know better; I sit down, cross my legs, and get ready to zoom through it. My breathing gets faster as we get closer.

And here we go!

A bright lights flash, and I'm zipping through a slide with black and white colors flying by me. I grab my knees and hold on tight. Zoom! Left, and right, and up, and down. I still think this would make a great ride.

When I see the end of the tunnel coming up, I brace myself for the sudden stop. I stop breathing, waiting for it to happen.

Boom, we pop out of the wormhole and slam to a stop. I remember this galaxy from before. "What is this galaxy's name again?" I ask.

This time the scary alien voice answers. "This is Trimbullo. Would you like to look around?"

Wow, I really get heaps of options today. I glance at all the planets, but I don't need to spend much time here since none are mine. "Not today, thank you. I'm ready for Janti."

See, I still remember my good manners.

Now it's a game to see how many wormholes I can find. I see the one we are facing and heading towards. I squint my eyes and search for more.

There's a wormhole to my left. Oh, and another right next to it. it would be easy to choose the wrong one. I might see another, but we enter the wormhole to my new galaxy before I can look too long.

I totally wasn't ready and fall backward as we take off. I know we aren't really moving, but it sure feels like it.

Oh, it's cool to lay on my back and slide through this wormhole. Yep, still only black and white colors on the top of the tube. We don't make as many turns before I see the end.

We pop out and I barely flinch. I'm getting good at preparing for the ride.

There's Janti. I can tell because of the silver streaks on the yellow planet. Now I know that silver color is land. I bet the yellow is a reflection of all the pretty, see-through colors. I stand up and walk closer to the planet. It's a weird feeling that the picture is flying closer as I walk closer. I put my arms out to keep my balance.

"We are now approaching Janti." The alien voice says.

I float closer and closer to the planet. Then we are there and flying through the sky and into the trees. I still like the black outlined leaves with the see-through shimmering colors.

I float through those and land on the silver ground.

The picture stays still, so I start to walk around. I know I can't go far, but maybe me moving in a certain direction will tell the scary alien what I want to see.

Sure enough, the picture keeps going in that direction when I stop walking. I want to see the flowers again. "What is the word for flowers?" I ask.

The alien voice says the word, and I'm able to copy him on my first try. But to be honest, it's a short word and not that hard to learn.

I try talking in Zoboian. *"Many flowers?"* I want to see an entire field of beautiful flowers. The scene turns and heads in another direction. We head over the hill in the distance, stopping at the top.

Whoa! Just below me are flowers as far as I can see and more colors than I've ever imagined. I can't wait to touch them.

I'm ready to see my alien owner lady now. *"Zussta?"* I ask. I wonder what her name translates to in English. Is it a common name on her planet? Brittany is fairly common; that's one reason I like Britt better. I bet her name is a cool and unique name.

I bet she's a cool and unique alien.

Without warning, she appears next to me. "Waaah!" I holler and jump sideways, getting my feet tangled together, and fall over. I can't help but laugh at myself; I think it's funny when people get scared (including me). But really, a little warning would have been nice. For instance, she could have walked up to me through the field. Or the scary alien voice could have said something.

Her big eye blinks as she looks down at me. "Hi there," I say before I realize that she's not going to answer me. Whatever, I keep talking. "I guess we are going to meet in real life tomorrow."

Jordie interrupts me, "Remember to talk in her language."

Oh yeah, her language. *"Hello. Go to you. Fun."* I'm confident that I'll pick up her language fast. I hold out my hand so she will hold out hers. Those suction cups are the coolest. She holds her hand with her palm up so I can examine her fingertips. I nod, and she stands tall.

There, I've done it all. In the simulation, we used wormholes to zoom into a new galaxy. I saw a field of flowers, and I talked with the alien owner lady.

That was a perfect simulation time.

"Jordie? I'm done now. Can we go back to the room and eat? I'm hungry. Not starving but still a little hungry."

The alien lady and everything around me fade, and the room lights slowly get brighter. I blink several times. It's weird that I was looking at a field of flowers, and now I'm looking at a grey wall. I take a big breath, stretch, and wait for Jordie.

He walks out of the secret door, asking, "Ready?"

I nod, and we walk out.

Perhaps dogs would be able to handle going to their new owners better if they had orientation time like this. They could get used to the smell of their owners before being unexpectedly tossed into a new home.

Maybe humans should give the pets treats and toys that their owner will be giving them and get them used to little things like that.

I bet dogs and puppies would like that. Maybe even cats too.

"How are you feeling?" Jordie asks as we walk.

"I think I'm okay, and that scares me." I'm not sure how to say exactly what I'm feeling. "I mean, why am I okay? Shouldn't I be freaking out and trying to escape? The group home has been my only real home, but I always hoped I would leave there and find a place where I really belong. Maybe that's why I'm not in a panic. I'm scared to meet the alien owner lady but a little excited too. I'm nervous, but I want to see everything in real life. Will you be there when I meet Zussta, or will you drop me off on the planet and leave? What if I get lost? Do all the aliens there look the same? How will I know which is Zussta?"

Okay, now the panic is starting to kick in. My throat starts to close, and I begin coughing. I can't breathe, and I might pass out.

Jordie stops walking and looks at me surprised. "What is wrong? Are you choking?" He slaps my back as I have food stuck in my throat. What if I'm on Janti and really do start choking? Would Zussta know how to save me?

Now I really can't breathe.

I'm gasping and sit down. From far away, I hear Jordie saying my name over and over.

"Britt? Britt, breathe. You are ok. Take a deep breath in."

I hear that last order and follow it; I take a deep breath in and let it out. I do that again and again. After the third or fourth breath, I calm down.

My focus clears, and I can hear Jordie again.

"Are you alright?" He asks me while holding both of my shoulders.

I have no idea if I'm okay, so I don't answer him. I sit still and breathe.

What just happened? One moment I was just fine, and the next, I felt sheer panic and couldn't breathe.

"Maybe I'm not as ready as I thought I was," I croak.

"Can you walk? Let's get you back to your room," Jordie says as he softly takes my arm, helping me up, and guiding me back to my room.

Chapter 21

Collapsing in the chair at the table, I have no idea what just happened to me. I think I had a panic attack.

My breathing returns to normal, and I can see and hear Jordie again, so I guess that's good. At least I think I can see and hear him. "Hi." I quietly say.

Jordie watches me with caution and concern, maybe I scared him. "Hi Britt. Are you feeling better? Do you need medical attention?"

Do I need medical attention? I take a quick inventory of myself. I can breathe, I can move my arms and legs, and I don't feel any pain. "I think I'm okay now. I'm beat tired, but okay."

"What happened?" He asks me.

I think back to my last thoughts when he asked if I was ready for tomorrow, and heaps of scary thoughts jumped into my head. "I think I panicked." It's all I can figure. "I mean, I thought I was ready for tomorrow, I thought I was handling this whole situation pretty good, then BAM, I suddenly wasn't handling it well at all."

Jordie nods as if he understands, but I doubt he does. But it's happening to me. Tomorrow, after he drops me off on Janti, he will go back to his normal routine, and I'll have to figure out my new life.

I flop back in the chair and let my head hang backward as I stare at the ceiling.

I pull at my hair.

Sitting up, I take a deep breath. "Okay, I have more questions. Maybe your answers will help me."

Jordie gives me a half smile. "I will always answer any question you have."

"What happens if I get lost? How will Zussta find me? Or if I'm hurt, can she fix a broken bone? I often fall and scrape my skin, and that's not bad. I can handle the everyday stuff; it's the big stuff I need to know that she's ready for. People always want a cute dog or bunny or lizard as a pet, but do they really know how to care for them? Or kids, for that matter? I know adults are screened before they can adopt kids. Did you put Zussta through a good screening process? I think that's my biggest concern. Can she take care of me? Not just hold and pet me, but actually take care of me?"

It scares me even to ask this out loud.

Jordie leans forward and looks me straight in the eyes. "Yes, I did screen her. Yes, she is very capable of caring for you. She understands that you need more than food and shelter, and she is ready to give you everything you need. Most other species are more advanced than humans, and we have the medical services to care for you better than you would receive on Earth. Zussta may not know about every emergency that may come up, but she is very smart and will always find a way to do what is best for you. She will love you and always care for you very well."

"She'll love me? Are you sure?" I slide off my chair and under the table as I ask this.

Jordie gets onto the floor next to me. "Yes, she will love you."

He smiles and gently pulls some of my hair. "Who could not love you and that hair?" I think he tries to lighten the mood in his own awkward way.

But he's not wrong; I do have great hair. And I'm a pretty cool kid too. The old guys in the park always said so. And Ms. Williams always told me how wonderful I am.

So yeah, of course Zussta will love me!

I smile, and we climb out from under the table and sit in the chairs again.

"Are you still hungry?" Jordie asks.

"Now I'm starving!" Funny how a good emotional outburst can make a kid hungry. Jordie taps on his tablet a couple of times, and within minutes, one of the guys from the kitchen brings a tray of food.

"Oi!" We greet each other. It's the blue alien with waves on his body. He opens his mouth wide in a smile. I wave at him, and he raises one of his small hands in greeting. "*Thank you,*" I say in the Zoboian language. He seems to understand and waves as he leaves.

I want a juicy cheeseburger with bacon, lettuce, and tomato on top. I close my eyes, picturing the burger. I would rather pick something up with two hands, but the spoon will have to do.

I slurp my juicy bacon cheeseburger.

So good.

I'm slurping so loud I almost don't hear Jordie talking. "Are you packed and ready to go?" He asks like it's no big deal.

But I'm okay after our talk. I nod and answer between bites. "Yeah. I packed my bag and bathroom stuff. I found my paper airplane; I think I'll take that too. Are you sure you won't forget to bring me more clothes when I need them? Because you know human children keep growing, who knows how tall I'll end up being?" I take another bite. "Speaking of clothes, will Zussta wash my clothes for me? I don't want to be a smelly pet. I don't mind getting my clothes dirty, but then I like them clean again. What if my comb breaks? Can I get a new one?"

Then I have other thoughts. I keep speaking my mind before Jordie can answer.

"How long will it take to get to Janti? Do we have to leave at a specific time? Is Zussta expecting us right at noon or something? Do they even tell time on my new planet?

I pause to slurp some more burger when Jordie jumps in and quickly starts answering my questions. I get it, I sometimes talk a lot.

"Yes, we are taking my spaceship to the planet Janti; it should take roughly two Earth hours to get there. I'll notify Zussta when we leave so you can sleep as long as you need, and we will leave after you are awake and eat."

One more night in orientation.

It seems weird to think I'll be leaving just as I was getting comfortable here.

Jordie continues to answer my questions. "Zussta will clean your clothes, but she may also show you how to do it. And yes, I will bring you more pants and shirts as you need them."

So, I guess this is it. I finish my food and push the bowl away from me. I look around, wondering what to do next. I look to Jordie for any ideas.

"You've had a busy day. Are you tired?"

I'm not sure if he's honestly asking me or if he's hoping I'm tired and want to go to bed. I guess I am a little sleepy. It's like trying to go to bed the night before Christmas – the excitement keeps me awake. But then again, once I'm sleeping, I'll be able to wake up and fly in a real spaceship. Through honest to God space and see new planets.

Now I'm excited again.

"I think I'll stay awake and hang out here for a while. I could draw or something." I shrug my shoulders, not admitting that I'm tired.

Jordie stands, picking up my tray. "All right, but please go to sleep when you become tired. We have tomorrow's schedule planned."

He leaves, and I'm left thinking about my future. Most kids never know what's in store for us. And as a pet, I really have no idea what to expect. Then, add the fact that I'm moving to a new planet. I can barely imagine tomorrow – just think what will happen next week or even next year.

I jog a couple of quick laps around the table. Then I grab the paper and pen out of my bag and sit down to draw.

I draw Zussta. I draw the trees and flowers from the simulation room. I draw outer space.

I want to see what tomorrow brings.

I want to fly.

I think I'm ready to start my new life.

Maybe.

Chapter 22

Today is the day! At least I think it's daytime. But, whatever. Today is the day!

I hop out of bed instead of lounging under the covers. I want to be showered and ready before Jordie comes with brekky.

I'm going to miss this huge shower. Maybe Zussta will have something great like this as well. Do they have showers on Janti? If so, I bet it's a really tall shower. We never had heaps of hot water at the group home. Having so many kids taking showers, it used up the hot water by the time it got to me - unless I woke early and showered first. I did that sometimes. So maybe I'll always have hot water.

I'm dressed and double-checking my bag when the door slides open for Jordie. He's carrying my tray of food and balancing his beloved tablet in the other hand.

"Hello, did you sleep well?" I notice he doesn't greet me with a good morning. If this ship doesn't rotate around the sun, is it ever morning or night, or just always noon? I smile because it doesn't matter anymore.

I'm flying out today.

"Yep, I think I slept well. I feel good." I tell him as I slide into the chair and wait for him to set the food down. I think of dogs waiting for their owner to feed them, and I get it. And having to wait for Jordie to arrive with food kind of bothers me.

"Good." He replies as he slides the tray to me. "We will leave shortly. We have a long ride to get to Janti. Did you pack your bag?"

I give him a quick nod. I'm too busy thinking of what I want for my last meal. Do I want brekky, lunch, or dinner? I want more than snacks or sweets. I close my eyes and picture several different options. Waffles soaked in syrup with bacon on the side. Or spicy shrimp with grilled veggies. Or grilled chicken with pineapple on top and a salad.

I decide on shrimp. I close my eyes and imagine some spicy shrimp. My first bite is fabulous. I love this food. I take several more bites before I remember Jordie is sitting in front of me.

"Sorry," I say after a swallow. "I got caught up in the food." I don't stop eating, but I pay attention in case he has something to tell me.

"Quite alright." See, he's not offended. He probably barely notices me since he's busy on his tablet. Good, I go back to eating. I can taste the spices and the salty shrimp. For the last couple of bites, I switch to a cool, crisp salad with ranch dressing.

Here's the weird thing, I never get full, but I'm never still hungry when I'm done with the bowl of mush. I'm not sure how they figured out exactly how much I want, but it's always perfect. "Hey, Jordie." I get his attention. "Will I be given more food as I grow? In two years, I'll probably need to eat more than I do now. Will Zussta know to give me more if I tell her I'm still hungry?"

He sets down the tablet to talk with me. He's polite that way. "Yes, she understands that you are a young human that will continue to grow and need more food and sometimes more or less sleep."

Why would I need more sleep? Or less? Do adults sleep less than kids? Never mind, I'm not worried about it.

"If you are ready, then we can get set. I'll be back shortly, and we will be on our way. Please have your packed bag ready." Jordie smiles as he stands and tells me this.

OMG, this is it.

I'm ready.

I'm not ready.

I'm ready.

Jordie leaves, and I walk through the room, making sure I have everything. I look in the shower, on the floor of the closet, and under my bed.

Yep, I think I got it all. If not, I figure I either don't need it or Jordie will bring it to me later.

I'm trying not to freak out.

I sit in a chair at the table to wait for Jordie.

I stand up and pace in a circle.

I sit on the bed.

I stand up and pace in a circle.

I'm just about to start doing jumping jacks, which I hate, when the door swooshes open.

I freeze.

Jordie looks all relaxed and casual while my insides are churning from excitement and nervousness. I take a deep breath, hold it for a count of three, and let it out. Okay, I'm ready now.

Without any fanfare, Jordie picks up my bag and looks at me – eyebrows raised.

I stand up tall, straighten my shoulders, and nod.

I take one last look at my room before the door closes behind us. Walking through the hallways, I realize there still isn't any art on the walls. I guess it will take a while for my idea about exposing all aliens to art to come to life.

Now I'm excited and skip next to Jordie. He nudges me, asking "Are you ready to fly in a spaceship?"

"Yes!" I almost shout. Sometimes it's hard to contain my emotions, and they come out loud and strong.

"I can't wait. Will it feel the same as the simulation room? That was pretty fun. I bet I won't get sick. I can handle rides without being sick. One time, a carnival came to our town, and I got to ride the roller coaster and three rides that spun really fast. Pete got sick and threw up, but I didn't. Right after he got sick, he drank water, then ate another corn dog. Boys are weird that way. I would have sat down, but he just kept going. But anyways, I didn't get sick, so you don't need to worry about me throwing up in your ship." I figure he would want to know that.

"Good to know. I would rather you not make a mess in my ship." He sounds serious, but I think he is joking with me.

I go with the joking. "I'm good like that, very polite."

He actually smiles.

We turn into the small holding room of the hangar and wait for the door to close behind us before entering the large area.

I forgot to hang out here. This place is awesome.

Aliens are working, talking in all different languages, and ignoring me. I see the one with spaghetti arms and legs, and the fuzzy alien from my first day here. At least, I assume it's the same guy.

And there's Stan.

I holler and wave my arms. "Oi, Stan!"

He stops, and an arm shoots out of his body and waves at me.

Yep, I'm totally friends with him.

I see the alien that looks like Zussta. "*Hello,*" I say in Zoboian.

He stops and answers me. "*Hello, how are you?*"

Here I am, carrying on a conversation with a space creature like it's a normal, everyday thing to do. "*Good.*" Then I switch to English. "I'm leaving today. I'm heading to your home planet. From what I've seen, it looks beautiful. Maybe I'll see you there sometimes. I may not recognize you since there will be so many that look like you, so you'll have to come over and say hi to me. That would be great to have a friend on a new planet."

He smiles and pats me on the head. Oh yeah, I forgot I was speaking English, and he probably didn't understand anything I said.

Jordie waits, not hurrying me along. That's nice of him. I'm not dragging behind, but I'm not rushing to the spaceship either. I want to see all the aliens before I go.

I look around and behind me, holding onto Jordie's suit coat so I don't run into anything. He walks slowly, allowing me to take it all in.

An alarm sounds, and the huge door begins to open. I stop. That is something I'll never get used to. Seeing that humongous door open makes my stomach drop.

Outer space is right there.

Well, not right there; it is way out there. But it's right there.

Jordie nudges me twice before I can think straight again.

"My ship is over here." He points to a grey spaceship. I guess he is too proper to have a colorful ship.

I follow him to it and watch as a door I didn't notice opens. "You climb in here and make your way to the chair on the right. It will form around you and hold you in place," he says, helping me into the ship.

Climbing in, I automatically take the chair on the left like I would back in Australia. Jordie climbs in after me and taps me on the shoulder. "That is my seat; you sit there," He points to the other seat.

Oh, so in outer space, they sit in opposite chairs, the driver on the left and the passenger on the right, totally opposite of how we drive in Australia.

Interesting. I wonder if they drive on the other side of space as well. Do they have traffic lanes in space? They must have some laws, otherwise they would all crash into each other.

It's one more thing for me to get used to.

I scoot over to the other seat, and sure enough, it tightens around my sides and hips. The seat is snug without being tight and quite comfortable.

Jordie climbs into the driver's seat. The door automatically closes.

He presses buttons on a small dashboard. I don't pay attention; too much happens for me to worry about what he is doing.

The huge door is all the way open, and we are slowly moving towards it. The aliens stay behind the yellow line and walk around us, keeping their distance so we don't run over them. That would suck to have our flight delayed because we ran over someone.

We move closer and closer to outer space.

This is it.

I hold my breath.

We drive through the clear shield of the door and simply start floating in outer space.

I'm floating in outer space!

Jordie taps my arm. "We are about to take off. Remember, we go fast. Are you ready?"

"Yes!" I totally shout. I don't even try to contain myself.

I'm ready!

Zoom! We shoot forward, and I'm pushed back into my seat.

I'm flying through outer space on my way to a new planet and my new life!

I wonder if this is what pets feel like when they're adopted and leave the shelter. They're heading to their new home, scared and excited, not knowing what to expect but hoping for the best.

That's me.

Going to a new home.

Not knowing what to expect but hoping for the best.

Chapter 23

Being in outer space is even better than looking at it from the maintenance area. It's amazing and quiet and huge. I can see forever.

I plaster my hands against the window next to me, looking all around. Stars appear both close to us and far away at the same time. I can't tell the difference between a star and a planet, and I don't care. It all fascinates me.

In the distance, I can just make out the green, blinking planet I saw that day standing in the hangar.

I try to remember to breathe.

Too bad the entire spaceship isn't clear; if it were, I could see above and under me too. Maybe I'll suggest that to Jordie if he ever has to buy a new spaceship.

It feels as if we are floating instead of speeding through space. I don't see a gauge telling us how fast we're traveling. Are there speed limits out here?

I start talking. "Wow, look at all of this. There were nights in Australia when I would sneak out and lay on the ground, looking at the stars. I would imagine what it would be like to be up there, and now here I am. I really can't believe it. One of my teachers, Mr. Jones, said that none of the planets had life on them, but he was wrong. Well, maybe not wrong. There might not be life on the planets that we can see from Earth, but there is life on other planets – faraway planets. I bet Mr. Jones would love to be here now, traveling through space with an alien. No offense. He would be surprised at all the different species on the orientation ship, and that I made friends with several of them."

Jordie doesn't interrupt me, so I continue to talk. "How do you prepare for something you never knew was going to happen? You told me to prepare for today to fly into space and meet the alien owner lady, but how do I get ready for something I've never done before? I think I'm handling this all pretty well. What do you think?

I glance at Jordie, hating to look away from the window. "You are doing very well," he says while steering.

Yeah, I know.

I blow my breath against the glass and draw a smiley face.

I try to lean over to see out his window, but the seat holds me tight, which is probably for the best. I would crawl around looking out all the windows if I could.

Something ahead and to the right catches my eye. I turn and stare. There it is again. An area that's a little wavy but blank, with no stars.

"Is that a wormhole?" I point and ask Jordie.

"Yes, it is. They are sometimes hard to see."

I bet I impressed him. Now I try to find more.

We are keeping to the left of it. "Aren't we going through that wormhole?" I ask him without looking away. Maybe he missed our turn or something.

"No, that would take us to a different galaxy. We want the one up there." He points forward. I look hard until I see it. There it is, a blank space in space. I laugh at myself. A blank space in space. Sometimes I crack myself up.

"I see it," I tell him. I keep looking around while watching us get closer to the wormhole. "Are we going towards it, or is it sucking us in?" I fidget in my seat. "Does a wormhole suck you in like a black hole?"

"We are going towards it. We must hit the wormhole from the right direction and at the right speed for it to take us to your galaxy. We will be entering the wormhole in about five Earth minutes. Do you remember the simulation of what it feels like to go through the wormhole?" he asks, looking at me instead of watching where he's going. But hey, it's not like we're going to hit anything.

"Yep, like a covered roller coaster ride. I went through the simulation a couple of times and never got sick. Remember? So, I bet I'll be fine here too. Do you think we will travel through wormholes when I'm with the alien owner lady? Maybe you can tell her that I can handle going through them without puking."

He laughs at that, but I'm serious. "Yes, I will tell her. But you'll need to talk with her as much as possible to learn the language. Remember to try to speak in Zoboian more than English."

Yeah, yeah, whatever. I know.

The planets and stars seem so close, yet forever away.

I keep glancing at the wormhole as I look around. The closer we get, the quicker my breathing gets.

I must really be huffing because Jordie looks at me with an eyebrow raised. "Are you going to be alright?" He asks. What would he do if I said no? Can we pull over?

The blank nothingness gets bigger, and we are aimed right at the center.

Don't freak out.

Don't freak out.

I'm getting lightheaded.

Don't freak out.

"Britt. Britt." I hear Jordie trying to get my attention. "Britt, look at me."

I tear my eyes away from the blank spot and look at Jordie. "Take a deep breath in, and now let it out. And again." He says to calm me down.

I do this a couple of times.

Okay, I think I'm all better now. "I can breathe again. Did you let the air out of the ship or something?" Maybe he did something, and I really didn't just panic.

"No, there is still air in here. Remember how you liked it in orientation? It is the same. You like roller coasters."

"You're right, I do. Okay, I'm ready now. Are we there yet?"

I start wiggling in my seat.

I am so ready for this.

I'm not ready at all.

I'm ready.

I'm not.

No worries.

We get closer and closer.

Jordie turns to me, smiling. "Here we go."

"Here we go!" I holler back at him.

It is like a ride. We shoot forward and zoom through a tunnel of black and white stripes. The seat holds me in place firmly.

This is even better than the simulation!

"Yeah!" I yell and hold on tight to the sides of the seat. "Yeah!" I yell again.

We bank left, then right.

We are shooting straight ahead when I see the end of the tunnel.

We zoom right to the end and come to a complete stop but my arms, legs, and head keep moving forward. Well, we don't stop completely; just not zooming anymore.

"Whoo hoo! Yeah, now that was fun! Did you see how fun that was?" I'm trying to bounce up and down, but my seat holds me tightly.

Jordie gives me a full smile. "Yes, that was fun." He says like he actually means it.

My heart calms down, and I look around. This galaxy has heaps of planets all around us. I count seven without even looking out Jordie's window. Like our Saturn, one planet is circled with rings.

I'm looking straight ahead at a blue planet, then scan left towards a red one when I spot it, a blank space. "Another wormhole." I proudly point out to Jordie.

"You are getting good at noticing them. Not all aliens can see them as you can. Their eyes see additional colors, so everything blends together."

Whoa, so I can see things that aliens can't. I like that.

He turns the ship a little to the left and we head towards that wormhole. "This next one will take us to your galaxy," he says as he fiddles with the screen between us.

We're almost there.

I can't wait.

I don't want to go.

I don't know if I'm excited or scared. I can't figure out which emotion I'm having right now.

Let's go with excited.

We head straight for the new wormhole.

"Hold on, here we go." Jordie stops pushing buttons.

I hold tight onto the seat again.

Zoom! It's like we immediately go from zero to a thousand kilometers per hour. Black and white stripes fly by us. I'm laughing really loud.

We turn right, then down! I wasn't expecting that, but I love it! Zoom!

Before long, I see the end approaching. This time I'm ready and plant my feet on the ground to keep them from flying forward. It doesn't work; my legs and arms shoot out again.

That was so much fun I can't help but laugh! I look at Jordie, and he is smiling at me.

I keep laughing.

"All right, we are now in your galaxy. There is the planet Janti." Jordie points directly in front of us

I freeze. For a moment, I forgot that I'm about to land on a new planet, my new planet. I'm about to meet the alien owner lady. And I'm going to live here.

As a pet.

I look to where Jordie points. Sure enough, there's Janti. It's almost the same as seeing it in the simulation room, only better.

Or a little worse since I can't get up and walk around, but better because it's real.

I immediately recognize the silver planet with yellow marks.

We're getting closer.

This is it. I'm going to my new planet.

I'm going to my new home.

Chapter 24

I'm looking at Janti, and from far away, it hardly feels like we're moving, but as we get closer, I realize we're speeding towards it. The planet is getting bigger and bigger, and my legs start bouncing with anticipation.

Pretty soon, my entire body is bouncing.

Jordie glances at me but doesn't say anything. Besides, even if he told me to calm down, I don't think I could.

I'm breathing so fast that I'm getting light-headed.

I'm scared.

I'm excited.

I'm happy.

I'm freaked out.

I want to see everything!

I want to be back home.

There are too many emotions inside of me that I can't contain them anymore. Each of my hands grabs some hair on either side of my head, and I pull outwards. I close my eyes and scream, shaking my head and kicking my feet.

"Waaaaahhh!!!!!"

I let all my emotions out.

Jordie watches me but doesn't interrupt. Maybe he realizes that sometimes kids just need a way to release their emotions.

Or maybe he doesn't know what to think.

Or maybe I scare him.

When I'm done screaming, I let go of my hair and take a deep breath. I look at Jordie.

He's looking at me. "Better?" is all he asks.

"Much," Is all I answer.

For once, I don't need to talk.

We descend from space and arrive in Janti's sky, and I can pick out the same trees I saw in the simulation room. They're even more colorful and beautiful in real life. I can't see each leaf on its own, but I remember what they look like. They are outlined in black with glowing see-through colors on each leaf.

We sail past the trees and land in an open area. I get the feeling that I've been here before. It's strange to have seen a place in a movie, and now here I am.

The spaceship touches down softly, and I barely know we have landed. Well, except we aren't moving anymore.

I look out the window and see the hill in the distance. I don't see the alien owner lady anywhere. Maybe she forgot we were coming today. Well, that's disappointing. I mean, I didn't expect her to do a dance or anything, but at least not forget about me.

I turn to Jordie. "The alien owner lady isn't here. Did she forget about us? What if she changed her mind and doesn't want me? Or… maybe she is busy buying me toys and treats." A moment of silence passes, and I'm talking again. "Is she as tall as the simulation showed, or taller? Does she still have the suction cup fingers? Will she show me what's on the other side of that hill?"

Jordie is busy fiddling with buttons on the screen; I guess you have to shut down the spaceship before we get out. Does he lock the doors so another alien doesn't steal his ship?

The seat lets go of me, and I'm instantly up and climbing over it. My foot slips, and I accidentally kick Jordie in the arm. "I'm so sorry. I didn't mean to kick you. I really didn't. I suppose you're going to tell me to sit down and behave. Are you going to give me the command in the Zoboian language to sit?"

I'm not sure Jordie knows what to do with me. He stays calm and doesn't get mad like some of my foster parents did. "No, I'm not going to give you any command. Please move away from the door, and I will let us out."

Wow, why can't Jordie adopt me?! It's great that I never seem to get in trouble. It was an accident, but I still usually get scolded.

Hopefully, Zussta will be as understanding as Jordie.

I move to the back of the ship to let Jordie near the door. Before he opens it, he looks at me. "Remember, don't run away."

"I have no intention of running away. I may want to run and play a bit, but I won't run away and not come back. Scout's honor." I make this promise to him.

He nods, opening the door.

I hold my breath in case I can't breathe the air on this planet.

Jordie climbs out of the ship and waits for me on the ground. I poke my head out and look around. The ground is silver and yellow, and it's hot out here.

Hot like we're in the outback, but I can handle it.

I'm still holding my breath.

Jordie must notice because he tells me. "You can breathe. The atmosphere on Janti is similar to that on Earth. You will be okay."

I guess I have to believe him. After all, he wouldn't bring me this far to let me die right away.

I blow out and take a breath.

Hey! I can breathe!

I smile excitedly at Jordie. He simply shakes his head and steps back, making room for me to exit the ship.

I jump out, doing a perfect landing on both feet, and throw my hands in the air like those people who do gymnastics. Ta-da!

Jordie doesn't even shake his head this time.

I look at him,

He looks at me.

I take off running and yell, "Don't worry, I'll be back!" as I go. I'm not running away, just running around. This time there aren't any walls for me to bump into like there were in the simulation room.

I run and run and run in a large circle.

I keep Jordie and the spaceship in sight. I don't want to get lost the first five minutes I'm here. I've been cooped up on that ship for the last two weeks, and it feels great to be outside again. Granted, I'm not on Earth, but at least I'm outside.

This could be why dogs bolt out of the door of their house; they simply have too much energy from being cooped up inside and need to run.

I sit down and examine the flowers. They look exactly like they did in the simulation; except I can touch them now. The petals, outlined in white with glowing see-through colors, are amazing. I can't help but move my face right up to the flower, staring at it. As I take a breath, I notice I can also smell the flower. It doesn't smell like flowers on Earth. I sit back and then bend forward to smell it again. I can't figure out what the flower smells like. It's almost a cross of flowers and food and a little like smoke from a fire.

I totally didn't expect that.

I stand up and run to Jordie. "The flowers smell weird. See, I told you I'd come back. I wasn't running away. I haven't been outside in like forever, so I needed to run. Does the alien owner lady know that I need to exercise and run? Will you tell her she doesn't have to chain me up? I won't run away unless a monster alien starts chasing me. Then, you bet, I'm running from it. But, in general, I won't run away. I don't know where I would go anyway. But if she is mean to me, I might run away. Will you come and get me if she's mean to me? Why do the flowers smell so strange?"

Jordie doesn't answer any of my questions. Instead, he asks. "Have you got the running out of your system? Are you ready to meet Zussta?"

I'm not sure. I'm not sure if I'm done running, and I'm not sure if I'm ready to meet the alien owner lady. I want to explore the area more. I want to run over the hill and see what's there. I want to meet Zussta.

I want it all.

I make one more lap around the spaceship and stop in front of Jordie again.

I take a deep breath. "Yes, I'm ready to meet her. I thought she would be here to greet us." I glance around again.

I'm facing the hill when Jordie taps me on the shoulder. "Here she comes," he says. It's as if she arrived on demand. Maybe Jordie called her when I was busy running circles around the ship.

I look in the direction he is pointing and see a bubble rise from the ground.

Inside is Zussta, the alien owner lady.

Whoa.

I see her blocky shape in the bubble, but I can't quite tell what color she is. I remember that her skin is whiteish – pink and kind of shimmers and changes color.

I want to see her eyes; the one big eye in the front of her head and the one big eye on the back of her head.

And the suction cup fingers, I want to see those too.

She steps out of the bubble and walks with small steps towards us. As tall as she is, I imagined she would have a longer stride. Maybe it's her small feet that make her walk differently than I thought. But she doesn't walk slow, that's for sure.

As she gets closer, I ease behind Jordie. I'm completely behind him and peeking out when she steps up to Jordie. She talks in her language, and Jordie answers in English. Well, not really English since every species understands him in their language. Maybe one day, I'll start thinking in the Zobian language, and that's how I'll hear him.

"*Hello, Jordie. Welcome to Janti. How….*" She said something I didn't understand.

"Hello, Zussta. Our trip was well. Thank you. I think Britt enjoyed her first ride through space."

Jordie steps aside, fully exposing me to the alien.

Traitor.

I've totally forgotten all manners. I stare at her with my mouth hanging open. I'm frozen in place, not even running.

Well, there goes all my ninja skills. The first sign of panic, and I freeze.

I regain control of myself and shake my arms and hands to make sure I can still move.

Zussta bends down, putting her face in front of mine.

I think she said, "*Hello, Britt.*" But I can't be sure. All I see is one huge eye. Ms. Williams taught us not to stare at people with anything strange about them, but I can't help it.

It's just one giant eye. Right there in my face.

I want to touch it. I slowly raise my hand, finger extended.

Jordie catches my arm before I can poke her in the eye.

My trance is broken; I look at him. He slightly shakes his head, knowing what I was about to do.

I start to laugh. How funny that would have been if the first contact I made with my alien owner lady was to poke her in the eye. I quickly get my laughter under control too.

I bet this is why puppies bite; they see a hand and can't help themselves. After all, they don't have hands.

Zussta stands back up and says something to Jordie.

I tug on his shirt for him to translate. "She says you're perfect."

That totally warms my insides. She likes me.

"She is a little shy right now. Shall we go inside?" Jordie says that instead of thanking her for my compliment. That's okay, I know what she said.

They both turn and walk towards the bubble.

"*Hi, Zussta!*" I yell out in her language. Okay, so my reflexes are a bit slow. I need to pull myself together and work on my ninja street skills.

She looks at me with her back-of-the-head eye, but turns her face forward to me with a huge smile on her face. Well, not as huge as her eye, but a big smile nonetheless.

"*You speak my language,*" she says, happily surprised.

"*Yes, Jordie tell me words.*" I'm struggling to say what I want. "*I say many words.*" I'm about to start listing all the words I know when Jordie stops me.

"Let's go inside and talk."

Oh, okay. We walk to the bubble. They both step inside, but I stop. What does it feel like to walk into a bubble? Can I breathe in there? Will I still feel the air outside, or will it be like going into a house with air conditioning?

There is too much of the unknown for me to step into a bubble all willy-nilly. I know enough to be a little careful. Does the bubble only work like an elevator and go up and down, or will it float away like bubbles on Earth? I'll have to remember to ask Jordie. The bubble isn't floating away now, and it stayed in place when no one was in it, so my guess is that it's similar to an elevator. See, I don't need to ask Jordie everything. I'm pretty smart and can figure things out for myself.

They are waiting for me but don't say anything.

I poke at the bubble with my finger. Instead of poking it, my finger goes into the bubble. I quickly pull it back out, then put my whole hand in the bubble.

My hand doesn't start on fire, so that's good.

I reach my arm into the bubble.

Still okay.

Then I place one leg in the bubble. I stand there, half in the bubble and half out. Zussta and Jordie are still watching me, not saying a word.

This is it. I hold my breath and stick my head in the bubble.

Everything looks the same. I take a test breath. Everything seems okay.

I bring my other arm and leg into the bubble.

I'm standing in a bubble with two aliens on another planet.

I nod to Jordie and smile at Zussta.

She smiles back, and we start to sink into the ground.

"Waaah!" I scream and jump out of the bubble, landing belly-first on the ground. They stop sinking and quickly leave the bubble to check on me.

"Britt, are you alright? Are you hurt?" Jordie is squatting down next to me.

I forgot the house is underground, and I'm a little embarrassed by my reaction.

This is definitely not my finest moment.

I stand up and dust myself off. "Yeah. Sorry about that. I'm okay and ready to try again."

I watch Jordie step into the bubble, and this time I step right in. "I'm okay, really. Let's go underground."

And with that, the bubble sinks into the ground.

This time I stay in it.

Chapter 25

I almost scream but manage to hold it in. I hold my breath as we go into the ground. I know holding my breath is silly, but it's instinct, like when going underwater. I quietly let my breath out so Jordie doesn't know what I was doing. He would shake his head at me.

Zussta keeps looking down at me and smiling. Good, I think she's happy I'm here. I wonder how far in advance she had to order me. Maybe I'm like a Christmas present that she was looking forward to. That's a nice thought.

These ideas keep me distracted as we sink further underground. There isn't much to see as the elevator bubble moves down except dirt, so I'm not missing anything. Dirt on Janti looks about the same as dirt on Earth – just a different color. No creatures or colors or pictures. Just dirt.

The dirt opens into a large open room. Since it's underground, I figured the inside of the house would be dark – like a cave. But nope, it's like a normal room. I'm a bit disappointed. I mean, I wasn't so sure about living in a cave, but now that it's not one, I'm kind of sorry. We have rooms on Earth; this one doesn't seem so special.

They both step out of the bubble like it's completely ordinary. So, I follow.

Stepping in and out of a bubble is like that whooshing feeling you get as you open the door to a store. The whooshing doesn't move my hair or clothes, but you still feel it.

I guess Zussta's style is basic because there isn't much here. To the right is an oversized couch. I bet all the kids at the group home could fit on that one couch at once. And there's an even larger table just past the couch.

She has some sort of artwork on the wall. I walk closer, trying to see the picture. I never imagined I'd see alien art. It's not a picture of a tree or anything I recognize, but I'm pretty sure I'm looking at a painting. It's bright colors in squares that somehow all work together.

"Britt, would you like to come and talk with Zussta?" Jordie interrupts my study of her artwork. Yeah, I suppose he's right; I should be talking with them. I'll have the rest of my life to look at the pictures.

Oh boy, it just hit me.

This is where I live now… for the rest of my life.

Don't panic, be cool. A good ninja can control her fear.

I stand up straight and walk to Jordie and Zussta. Jordie starts explaining things to Zussta and me at the same time – I bet we both understand it in our own language. He starts with me. "Zussta knows that you will need to set up a feeding and sleep schedule. Until you both have a good schedule, you must tell her when you are hungry or tired." He then turns to Zussta. "Britt enjoys being outside and has lots of energy. She will want to run around and explore, but she knows not to run away from you."

He makes it a point to look directly at me even though he was talking to Zussta.

I shrug instead of outright agreeing. He really does make me sound like a pet.

"We will be fine." Zussta is talking to me in her language, and I understand what she says. Thankfully she isn't bending down to me and talking in a baby voice or loud. I hate when people do either of those.

I think Zussta is going to be one of those cool people. She doesn't feel the need to be overly loud, babying, gushing, or anything else with me. And she hasn't tried to pet me or pick me up - another plus for her.

"Yes, we will be fine," I confirm with Jordie.

"Then perhaps Zussta can give you a tour of the house." Jordie steps back and lets her lead the way. She is talking as she walks across the large room; I have to almost trot to keep up with her, which is surprising with her small feet and steps. I'm understanding some words as she talks.

"You -- up--." She points to the couch and a small set of steps. Oh look, she made steps so I can get up onto the couch. That is so nice of her. I know some animals back on Earth aren't allowed on the furniture. I'm glad it's not like that here.

I run up the steps and hop onto the couch. The cushion part is soft, and I sink into it. I could live right here. "Thank you. This is very nice. I don't even need a bed if I can sleep here." I'm speaking English and trying to switch to Zobian. "Thank you. Very nice. Thank you up." I give her two thumbs up to show my approval.

She laughs and answers me. Then I make out the words "more – bedroom -- for you."

I want to see my room! I'm off the couch faster than either of them can imagine. "You are fast," she says and walks towards the back of the living room.

Will my room have a bed? Will it be huge, like the couch or pet size? Where will I put my clothes and other stuff? Do I have a door, or do I lose all privacy? Do I need privacy? There weren't many secrets at the group home; we pretty much knew everything about each other. Plus, I don't know of any dog or cat that has a room with a door they can close.

I try to behave and walk politely behind her, but I'm too excited. I dart around her. *"Britt's room!"* I call out as I pass her and Jordie. There is a hallway with a room to either side. I look left, and this space has large pieces of furniture in there. Not my room. I look right and stop in the doorway.

This room must be mine.

Jordie and Zussta catch up to me, and Zussta sweeps her arm in the doorway with the universal sign for me to go in, so I do.

The first object I see is a flat board floating in the middle of the room. I'm at a loss of what to think of that. It's hovering waist-high. My waist, so I know this is my room. I poke the board thing with my finger, and it swings a bit. I crawl under it, and nothing stops me. I pop up on the other side and walk completely around this odd thing. I don't see any ropes or cables holding it in place.

It's just a floating board.

I look at Jordie for answers. He motions his head to Zussta. I look to her for answers.

"This is Britt's bed."

This floating board is my bed? Doesn't she know humans prefer a soft bed with a pillow and blankets? Maybe Jordie forgot to tell her.

I give it a try. I turn around and gently sit on the board. For all I know, it will fall to the ground, slide out from underneath me, or fly away. Who knows?

The board doesn't do any of those; it gently bobs down, like sitting on a bed. I lift my legs and lie down. It bends and conforms to my shape –

like the most comfortable hammock I've ever been in. I haven't ever been in a hammock, but I bet this is better than any bed on Earth. It's soft and completely cradles me. I roll over, and it changes shape, letting me curl up on my side. Then, from the side, a blanket rolls out and covers me. I didn't even notice a place for anything to go. I look and still don't see where the blanket came from, but I love it.

I change my mind; I like my bed even better than the couch. "Jordie, you have to try this. This is by far the best bed I've ever had. Look, it floats and moves with me. I love this. I wonder if I can jump on the bed, would it move with me? What if I try to jump off? Would it stay put or catch me?" I start to stand on the bed.

"Stop." Jordie uses his firm voice. I stop. "Britt, you cannot jump on the bed here. Please, there is still more to see."

Well, fine then. I'm not allowed to jump on beds back home, so this isn't different. Do the same rules on Earth apply on Janti? That's weird.

There's more? I excitedly swing my legs over the side of the bed and stand up easily. A dresser is against one wall. "Do they have dressers here, or is that for me?" I'm opening and closing drawers before Jordie can answer. Not that it matters; I'm just curious. "And what is this?" I notice a round balloon-looking piece of furniture in the corner.

"The dresser was brought from Earth for your clothing. And that is a bean bag chair. It is from Earth as well, though not very popular anymore. I thought you might like it." Jordie answers me.

That stops me still. "You brought furniture here for me?" That's probably the nicest thing he's done for me.

"Zussta wanted a room for you where you would feel comfortable. She asked me to pick out several items that you would like. It was more her idea than mine," Jordie says. Well, that makes more sense.

"Thank you," I tell Zussta, remembering to say it in Zobian. I lower myself into the bean bag chair. It's squishy but fun. For such an open and bare room, everything here is soft and comfortable. It blends well.

It all feels familiar but in a new place - Earth items on a different planet.

More artwork hangs on the walls. I look but don't dwell on it. There is more to see. I notice a doorway to the left. I try to jump up, but getting out of a bean bag chair is harder than getting out of the floating bed.

I run past them and through the new doorway.

It's my own bathroom.

I've never had my own bathroom. But I guess since I'm the only human here, it makes sense that I have it to myself. A shower is along the back wall, just like the one in my room at the orientation place.

This is a weird feeling.

I don't think about it too much and run back to the room where they are waiting for me. "I'm so happy to have my own room. I was worried I would have a small pillow on the floor, like a dog bed, but this is way better. Is this all for me? The ceilings are high, but I bet it's because she is tall. She has paintings on the wall. Her species must like art. Humans aren't the only ones who like pictures. Everything has bright colors; I've never seen so many colors all at once. Is that because her eyes see colors differently than I do? There is so much to explore. Did you bring my bag inside? I'll put my clothes away later, but I don't want you to forget it."

I don't know what to do. Should I try out the bed again, grab my bag, and bring it in, or run up and down the hallway?

I try to be polite and stand still, but there is too much to look at. I'm bouncing up and down a bit, waiting for Jordie to tell me what's next.

"Let's go back into the main room and talk more," he says to both of us. I'm faster than either of them with my take-off and am in a full run before I get to the hallway. I run across the room, up the steps, and do a belly flop onto the couch.

I brush my hair out of my face and smooth it down, trying to be patient while they sit.

Jordie talks first. "Britt, I want you to talk in the Zobian language as much as possible. Zussta will help you learn. This way, you can communicate with her. You remember the rules: behave, be nice, and don't run away."

"Wait, are you leaving?" It didn't occur to me that he would leave so quickly. Jordie looks at me with that sideways look. I try speaking in Zobian. "Jordie go?" There, I can be good.

"Yes, I will be leaving in a couple of minutes. You are safe, and Zussta will be here. This is your new home now. You will soon be comfortable."

I think that's what he is saying. Instead, all I heard was, "Blah blah blah." Because all I can think about is that Jordie is leaving me here on this planet with an alien!

I stare open-mouth at him. "Jordie go?" I ask again. What I want to ask is if he is really going to leave me here, alone, with an alien.

"Britt, this should not be a surprise to you. We have been talking about this for the last two weeks. This is your new home, and you are now a pet on this planet. Zussta is your owner."

Blah, blah, blah.

Jordie turns to Zussta. "I assume you have the food and water ready for her?"

"Yes, food and water," she answers. Well, at least I have food and water. I guess that's a plus.

"Alright," Jordie says as he easily slides off the couch. "Perhaps you can both walk me to my ship."

I crawl to the edge and then down the steps.

He's leaving me here.

I look at him. I look at Zussta. I look back at him.

He is unfazed, and Zussta is smiling.

I can't figure out what to do, so I follow them to the bubble. I'm in shock and step into the bubble without hesitation. It's kind of fun to rise up and down in a bubble, but shock wins over fun.

We get to the top and step onto the silver ground. I don't trip or fall.

Jordie turns and looks me in the eyes. "You will be happy here. Zussta is happy you are here and will take good care of you. Don't worry; I'll be back to check on you. If you need anything, you tell Zussta. I don't want you to hide in your room. Spend time with her, get to know her, and let her get to know you. She is excited to learn all about you. You are a great kid, after all." And with that, he gives my hair a gentle tug.

That makes me smile. He's right; I am a cool kid.

He turns to Zussta. "This is a bit overwhelming for her, but Britt is very energetic and talkative. She will learn your language quickly; you two will get along very well. If you need anything, please contact me."

I make out part of what she says, *"Thank you -- very good -- we have fun -- go slow."*

Jordie turns to me again. "Remember everything you have learned. This is a good thing, Britt. You now have a new and exciting life."

And with that, he climbs into his spaceship and leaves.

Chapter 26

I look at Zussta.

She looks at me.

Now what?

I'm trying to figure her out, and she's looking at me with the same expression. Well, at least I assume it's the same expression. It's hard to tell with her one big eye. I'll have to get used to that. Her skin shimmers pink and white in the sunlight; I wonder what color it will be when we are inside. I didn't really notice before.

"Ready -- inside?" She asks.

Did she just read my mind? Jordie never mentioned she could read minds. Unless that's what you do when someone leaves, you go back inside. I'll have to ask Jordie next time he comes back. Except, how will I know when he is coming? How will I know when days or weeks have passed?

I follow her back into the bubble, and I step into it without hesitation. We silently slip underground and come out in the main room of her house – my house.

Do dogs ever feel that the house they are in is theirs? Or is it the owner's home? I hope they think of it as their home. And soon, maybe this will be home to me.

Maybe.

I pick up my bag that Jordie left on the floor by the door and show it to Zussta, "I give in room." I don't quite say it right, but she gets what I mean and follows me into my room, talking the entire time.

I can't figure out everything she says, but I pick up words here and there. How do I know if she is nervous like me or excited that I'm here? Probably both.

I would be way excited if I got a new pet.

I've never been in a house when they first bring a dog or cat home. I don't know how to act or what to do. I don't have any toys to play with.

Zussta helps me put away my clothes. We finish too fast. Now what? *"Want to walk?"* She asks me.

Do I want to be outside and exploring? Heck yeah! *"Yes! Walk!"* I answer a little too excitedly, mainly because I'm still not sure how to act.

She walks, and I jog back to the front of the main room and into the bubble. Cool, this is something we can do together.

Something odd crosses my mind. Does she know my name? Can she say Britt in English? Or is she calling me Britt in her language, and I have to figure it out? Or has she renamed me completely? What if she named me something like Noodles?

I point at myself and tell her, "My name is Britt. Britt." I say it again so she understands what I'm saying.

She touches my chest with her suction cup turned off and says something. Crud, she can't say Britt in English. Will I forget how to speak my own language one day?

Will I forget my name?

She taps my chest again and says my new name.

Okay, so that word means Britt. Got it. I'm going with Britt and not Noodles.

We get outside and start walking towards the hill. I finally get to see what's over the hill. I get excited and want to run. *"I not go away."* I'm trying to tell her I'm not trying to escape. *"No away,"* I say and start to jog a bit. I stop and look back, *"No away."* I wonder if she can even run with those little feet.

"You are good. No away." She tells me back. I take that as my cue and start running. I'm running so fast that all of the colors of the flowers start to blend together, but I'm not looking at those.

I must see what is on the other side of the hill.

I come to the top of the hill, out of breath and happy.

There, in the middle of another field, is the most magnificent tree I have ever seen. It's better than anything I've ever imagined in all of my ten years.

It's a tree worthy of its name.

Zussta stops next to me and silently admires it as I am. Even though she probably sees it every day, it's too great not to stop and gaze at it.

"Name?" I ask her and point to the tree. Maybe it already has a name.

"Lamenana," she answers me.

Lamenana, I decide it's the name for a Goddess of Forever Beauty. Lamenana. I could never have imagined something so perfect.

It's got to be at least thirty meters tall, with branches flowing to the ground and colors like I've never seen before. They are vibrant, shimmery, glowing, and changing as I look at them.

I have to get a closer look. I point to the tree again and ask, "We go?" See, I'm trying to show her I'm not about to run away. I still worry she might put me on a leash. But I absolutely have to touch the tree.

She barely gets the words *'we go'* out of her mouth, and I take off running. I'm outside, on a new planet, and it's beautiful!

I run, jump, and turn a cartwheel. The weather is perfect, and I'm heading for the most perfect tree ever to exist.

"Whoo hoo!" I holler as I run. I bet that translates to 'whoo hoo' in any language.

I've always liked to run, and I bet Zussta is impressed with how fast and far I can go. Jordie said she was active, and now she knows I can keep up with her.

I glance over my shoulder to see her running as well.

I almost trip and fall. I've never seen an adult run except on television. And I've never seen an alien run. For some reason, I expect adults to be more… adult-like and not running around like a kid. Do all aliens on Janti run or just her?

I stop and watch her barreling towards me. She's fast for a stocky alien. She runs past me, tapping me as she goes by. I bet she just yelled *'tag'* because that's what I would yell if I tagged someone as I ran by them.

Tag? Game on!

I take off running after her. I'm not quite as fast when laughing, but I'm not too far behind her. She uses her back-of-the-head eye to watch me. I think I even hear her laughing. I try to catch her so I quit laughing and really give it my all. My arms and legs are pumping like a machine, and my ninja skills are kicking in. I notice everything around me, even with my speed: the colors of the flowers, the tree getting larger as I get closer, and me gaining ground on Zussta.

I just might be faster than her.

And then she starts running faster.

Like way faster.

Okay, she wins; she's faster than me. But I'm only ten years old; I bet I'll run as fast as she does one day. I now have a new goal: run as fast as Zussta. I now have ninja skills and athletic training to work on. No problem. I love a challenge.

Zussta is waiting for me when I arrive at Lamenana. I'm huffing, but she barely seems out of breath. I'm laughing and hold up my hand to high-five her. She tilts her head, then holds up her hand too. Not high-fiving me, just holding it up.

Well, if we're going for that look, I throw both hands up over my head. "Yeah!" I let out. She copies me and raises her arms over her head, yelling as well.

Okay, Zussta is pretty cool, and I might like her.

Lamenana reminds me of a weeping willow tree, but even more grand. It's bigger, shinier, and all-around more amazing. Each hanging branch shimmers with see-through colors. The darker colors are on top get lighter as they reach the ground, looking like a waterfall.

Yep, Goddess of Forever Beauty.

I reach out and touch one of the hanging branches. It feels soft, like a kitten, rather than like leaves. That's just odd.

A kitten-soft, shimmering waterfall tree.

Now I want to pet the tree.

Isn't that weird? Dogs and cats like to be petted, and I want to pet a tree, but I don't want Zussta to pet me.

I can't stop myself; I push through the branches and walk underneath until I reach the center trunk.

It's like a secret fort in here.

It's humongous under here.

Light barely filters through the leaves, making me feel like I'm inside a stained-glass window.

I lay down on my back, staring up into the tree. Zussta sighs and lies down next to me. I can't help myself. I start talking in English. "This is so amazing. I've never been inside a stained-glass window. Look at all these colors. Is everything on your planet like this? How do you ever get anything done? I would be under here all day if possible. Well, except when I'm running or exploring places. I like my room and everything, but this is my favorite place on the planet. Not that I've seen much of your planet, but I can't imagine anything being better than this. Do you come here a lot? I bet you do. You seem to like it here too. Hey, do you run a lot? You were fast."

I try to switch to her language. "You go …" and I clap my hands together like taking off fast. "How you say…" and I make the motion again.

"Fast." She says slowly in her language.

"Fast." I copy her. "You go fast."

She laughs. "Britt go fast." She pats my shoulder as she says this.

Yep, she is impressed. We lay there for about two minutes when she finally says, "We go."

I wonder if I can say no. On Earth, when an owner gives a command to their pet, they expect the animal to obey. I'm ready to go back to the underground house, but I'm not sure if I want to automatically do as she commands.

It's a dilemma.

I decide not to start trouble right away. I'll probably do something wrong soon enough. There's no reason to purposefully get in trouble on my first day here.

I bet Jordie would be proud.

This is not a bad first day on Janti. I have my own room, live near the most amazing tree in all of the galaxies, and my owner likes to run.

I'm happy.

Chapter 27

I'm still new to this planet and I've already perfected the words, "How do you say…" because I ask Zussta how to say a lot of things. I can pick up on words fairly well. It's putting them together in a longer sentence that is hard. But I know I'll get it.

I know how to tell her I want to sleep and eat, but what if I want to run or yell? How do I say that? Or if I'm bored and want to go outside? Thankfully, she hasn't gotten grumpy with me asking all the questions. She tells me the word and sometimes uses it in a sentence.

I enter the main room and wait for her to notice me.

I shift from foot to foot as Zussta seems busy with something when I tell her, "I'm hungry."

She wobbles her head and keeps looking at something on the huge table that's in the middle of the main room. Jordie said she and I would establish a schedule, but until then, she would let me eat when I asked. And I'm not bored, I'm actually hungry.

What does wobbling her head mean?

Maybe she didn't hear me. "I'm hungry," I say again, this time rubbing my belly.

She wobbles her head again.

Now I know how a dog feels when he wants food but has to wait for their owner to decide to get up and make dinner for them.

This bites.

My stomach grumbles very loudly. Loud enough that Zussta quickly looks up from the table. "Britt good?"

"I'm hungry," I tell her again. She sighs and stops what she is doing to get me food. If she left it where I could reach it, I'd get it myself.

Speaking of which, where do we eat? I don't see a kitchen table. I'm not even sure I see a kitchen. Zussta walks to the opposite end of the room and taps the wall.

A door opens.

"OMG! I live in a house with secret doors! Things keep getting better and better. I bet all the kids at the group home are still stuck in their small beds and must do what Ms. William says, and here I am on a new planet, in a home with secret doors. At the group home, I always wondered what type of house I would have and what my new parents would be like, but I never imagined this. How could I?" I say all this in English. I have to learn the language. Talking is simply what I do.

Zussta takes out a bowl similar to the one I used on the ship with Jordie. She grabs what I guess is the food mush from the cabinet and pours it into a bowl. She steps back, and the door automatically closes. She then taps another place on the wall and a smaller door opens. She places my bowl inside, and that door automatically closes.

So, I'm basically eating cereal that she is heating in the microwave. Got it.

I didn't hear a ding of the microwave, but the door opens, and she reaches in for the bowl. It must not be hot. I wonder if my friends in the kitchen on the ship went through all of this for me.

She hands me the bowl and a spoon.

I stand in the middle of the room wondering where to sit and eat.

It's a bit awkward standing there with my food.

She points to a corner of this area and there is another bean bag chair. Um, okay, I'll sit there.

I sit down, but it's not squishy like the chair in my room. Instead, it forms around me like a normal chair. I'm about to set the bowl on my lap when a tray pops out of the side and floats in front of me.

This is too cool.

I set the bowl on the tray and smile at Zussta. "Thank you," I tell her. She flashes her suction cup hands at me and goes back to the table.

What's so interesting on the table?

My stomach rumbles again, bringing my attention back to the food.

I close my eyes and run through a list of foods. What do I want…? I'm starving and want a full meal, not a snack. I want pork chops, a salad with ranch dressing, and warm bread with melted butter.

I take a bite, imagining pork chops first. It's perfect.

I eat slowly. There's no reason to hurry when I'm on my own schedule.

I eat the pork chops, with salad in between, and lots of bread.

I finish and pick up my bowl. The tray automatically slides back into the chair. I start to stand up, and the chair helps by gently pushing me up.

I love this place; it has the coolest furniture!

"I good," I call out to Zussta. She probably doesn't want me to leave my bowl on the floor, but I'm not sure what else to do with it. Once again, I'm standing awkwardly in the center of the room, holding my bowl.

She comes to take the bowl from me. I start chatting with her in English. "That was really good. I had pork chops. What do you eat? Porridge like me, or do you have actual food? Do you have fish or meat or salads? Or do you eat a pill that fills you up? What do you like the taste of?"

I already have heaps of questions for Jordie.

Or, I guess, for Zussta, once I speak the language better.

She places the bowl back in the first cabinet. Maybe it automatically cleans it. But, hey, I don't have to wash dishes, so I don't worry about it.

Zussta is studying whatever is on the table again.

I wander into my room, practicing my words as I go. "Yes, no, we go, food, bed, chair, I'm hungry, I'm tired, I sleep, sorry, stop, go, go fast." I'm surprised at how much I've learned. But then I remember I started learning this while on the ship with Jordie, so I guess it hasn't been all in one day.

Now that I see my bed, I realize I'm a bit tired. I sit down, and it moves to hold me. I lay down and wiggle around to get comfortable. I've slept on some great beds and some not-so-great beds, so I appreciate this one.

I'll just rest my eyes for a moment, as the old guys would say.

I must have drifted off because I wake up. That's so weird when you don't remember falling asleep, but suddenly you're awake. I have no idea what time it is or if it's night or day. Then I realize that it doesn't matter. I stretch and continue to lay in bed.

I think I want a schedule. I thought I would love being free to sleep, wake up, and eat whenever I want, but maybe I can set my own schedule. I love the freedom; except I'm learning that I want a set time to do things so I know what's coming. I finally get up.

I check my hair in the bathroom mirror. Wow, the way it's sticking out all over means I must have slept for a long time.

I try to tame my hair, but there is no fighting it. I give up and decide to shower. I don't know how long I've been in these clothes, but I bet they need changing too.

The shower works the same as it did in orientation. I love this shower and could stay here forever. We had to take fast showers that had lukewarm water at the group home. I wonder how long I can stay in here before Zussta tells me to get out.

I'll try.

I use the shampoo-conditioner-soap to clean myself and manage to easily get the comb through my hair since Simon gave me special ingredient in the conditioner. The water is still hot, and I happily stand in the water, simply doing nothing.

Never mind, I'm bored.

I get out of the shower and get dressed.

I find Zussta at the big table again in the main room. It's just above my head, so I can't see what's on it. What's so interesting up there? Maybe she is working on a puzzle. I stayed with a foster family that had a table that was specifically for puzzles. They loved them. They would finish one puzzle, break it up, put it away, and immediately start another. I could never stay quiet in one place long enough to finish a puzzle in one day. And I thought Jordie said the alien owner lady was active. That's why it surprises me to see her in one place for so long.

"Hi," I announce myself so I don't scare her. What would she do if I did? Do aliens jump? Oh, maybe she would zap me with a ray gun. I better not test that theory right now.

Zussta looks up quickly. I did startle her. I don't know how the eye in the back of her head didn't see my coming. "Hello. Sleep well?" I what I assume she says.

"Yes, I sleep good," I reply. But I'm curious about what she's doing at the table. "What on the table?" I ask as I point at it.

She smiles and holds her hands out for me. Does she want to pick me up? Will the suction cups stick to me? I stayed with a family who had a cat that hated being held, and now I kind of understand why. It's a little awkward to be picked up by another species.

But, on the other hand, I really want to know what she's doing at the table all the time.

She is still there, waiting for me to decide.

Pick up or not. See what's on the table or not.

My curiosity wins – I must know.

I walk into her hands, and she picks me up under my arms. She isn't using her suction cups, so it's not too weird. But she's holding me straight out in front of her. Neither of us knows what to do now. She doesn't have a hip to hold me against, I dangle as we assess each other.

Thankfully, she turns me around, holds me around my waist against her with her arm, and shows me what she is working on.

I don't get it.

The entire table looks like a computer screen, but I can't figure out what she's looking at. There are lines and symbols all over.

I move a bit, and my foot brushes the top of the table.

The entire screen changes.

Zussta yelps and quickly pulls me away.

I yelp because she startled me, and now I see I've messed up the screen.

Crud, I didn't mean to make a jumble of the screen. Is it like a computer where she lost all her work? I barely touched it. I just brushed it, really.

She sets me down, and I back away. "Sorry. Sorry." I repeat. How do I explain that I didn't mean to ruin her table screen? It was an honest mistake.

I wonder how aliens scold their pets. Are they like human adults scold their pets and will swat my bum? Or like a kid, will I be sent to my room? I've been grounded by adults on Earth a lot, but this will be the first time being in trouble on Janti.

"Sorry," I quickly say again

Zussta closes her big eye and lets out a sigh. Wow, an adult trying to be patient with me is the same on any planet.

"Britt good." She says with a partial smile.

Hmm, I know better.

She starts tapping the screen with both hands, fingers flying all over. I hold my breath, hoping she can get her work back and I didn't ruin anything.

"Ah ha!" She steps back, smiling. "All is okay!"

Now I'm smiling too.

"Britt good?" I ask. I want to ask if everything is returned to normal, but my words aren't there yet.

"Yes, Britt good," she smiles.

She makes a couple of more taps, then turns to me, asking, "Go outside?"

"Yes, go outside!" Yay, I'm not sent to my room. And yes, I realize I sound like a dog excited to go out. But it's true, I would rather be running around instead of cooped up underground.

"Yes, outside." She clicks off the table, and we bubble up into the open field.

This is much better; I defo prefer to be outside. I've only explored one direction. I tap her and take off, running away from the hill.

Tag!

Chapter 28

I flat-out run as fast as I can. Of course, Zussta soon catches up with me. But she doesn't realize I've been working on my ninja street skills. I hear her feet pounding closer. Right before she reaches me, I zig to my left.

Zussta wasn't able to tag me.

I laugh and stop; she stops and smiles too. "Britt go fast and," She then keeps talking, but I don't understand all the words. Her hands make a motion to the left, so I know she is impressed with my zigging skills.

We walk to Lamenana, the Goddess of Forever Beauty tree. I can see this becoming one of our hang-outs. We walk under the hanging branches and lay on the ground.

I think changing your position gives you an entirely different view. Lying on our backs and looking up through the leaves of the tree makes the world look different.

The colors are this planet are amazing. Australia is a great country, but this planet has colors that I've never seen before. At least I don't get dizzy looking at them. I wonder if they have a separate word for each color. That would have to be about five thousand words. Okay, maybe not that many, but a lot.

One time in school, someone brought a large box of crayons, and they all had weird names on them. Not just red and blue, but Sienna and Robin Egg Blue. It would be cool to have a job where you sit around and think of names for colors.

"We go home?" Zussta asks. It's probably been about a half hour of lying here, so yeah, I'm ready.

Wait, what's in the other direction? We've come to the tree two times now. Is there nothing anywhere else around us?

"No home," I start. "What there?" I ask and point to the open field left of home.

"No much there. We can go look." She says and starts walking in that direction.

Wow, that was easy… I ask, and she shows me. Most times, adults dismiss me and keep doing what they want, but not Zussta. She actually listens to me.

We walk for a while, go over a small hill, and she's right. There's nothing out there.

"We go home," I tell her, satisfied in knowing I'm not missing anything in that direction. "We go fast?" I'm ready to run again.

We take off in a flat-out run.

And then it happens.

I go blind.

It's as if someone turned out the light. Everything is black, and I have no idea where I am or where Zussta is.

I trip and fall.

What happened? Where am I? Why am I blind?

Don't panic.

Don't panic.

"Zussta!" I shriek.

I stand up, hollering. "Zussta!"

I yell again and again.

I turn, and there is a huge eye right in my face. "Wahhhhhh!" I yell and stumble backward, falling on my bum.

"Britt okay. Britt ok. I'm here," Zussta calmly repeats over and over. Oh, thank goodness, it's Zussta, and she's here. I grab ahold of her arm. I need someone to hold onto. "Britt okay," she mummers again.

When I have my breathing under control, I take one more deep breath and step away from her. I can make out her form, but I can't see clearly in the dark. "Britt no see fast." I try explaining. "Why Britt no see fast?" I wish I knew the word for suddenly.

She squints her big eye at me. "You can't see?" She taps my shoulder since she thinks I can't see her. How do I explain this? It's like playing that game where you can't talk but have to act everything out, and the person guesses what you're trying to say. Except with the game, you can tell the person 'yes' or 'no.' Here, I have to hope she understands me.

"Britt no see good. I see Zussta no good. Why no see fast?" I'm holding my hands up to her face to show that I can barely see her.

She points to the sky and is talking. Yeah, it's dark there, too; that's what I'm telling her. Wait, she is motioning that the sun is gone.

Is it nighttime?

That fast?

So, it turns from day to night in an instant? Does the sun suddenly fall out of the sky?

Whoa. That is something Jordie didn't tell me.

Zussta taps me to get my attention. She stands up and asks, "Do you see me?"

I tell her yes. It's not great, but I see her.

She takes three steps backward. "Do you see me?"

I can still see her, but barely. "Yes," I reply

She takes three more steps backward and is gone. Don't panic. I hear her voice. "Do you see me?"

"No, no see," I answer really fast, trying not to freak out.

She quickly steps back into view. Whew, she's still here. I calm down a bit but grab ahold of her, just in case she leaves. She squints her big eye as if trying to figure me out.

I'm ready to go home now. The last time I wanted to be home this quickly was when the Morgans decided to take me back to the group home early.

I want to go back to my Earth home. But even going to my room here on Janti will have to do. I want to go home now.

I stand there, trying to figure out how to tell her this. Thankfully, she gets it. "Should we go home now?" She asks. I sigh with relief.

"Yes, we go. No fast." I don't want her running off and leaving me. I'm so turned around that I don't even know which way the bubble is.

"No fast." She answers. And with that, we slowly walk back to the bubble. I keep her stocky legs in sight just to my right. I wish I could hold her hand.

Wait, this means that she can see in the dark? Maybe she sees like those goggles that can see in the dark, where everything is green. But Jordie said Zobians see differently than humans do. And they see colors differently. That would be so cool to see in the dark. I would barely sleep. The world changes once it gets to be nighttime. Not that I was allowed out after dark, but I would watch out my window. One time Ms.

Williams saw me staring out the window at night. She told me to crawl back into bed, but she wasn't mad at me.

Zussta walks us right to the bubble. How can she possibly see a clear bubble in the dark? Boy, I wish I could see what she sees. We step inside and bubble down to the house. I'm not tired, so I don't need to go to my room. I'm not hungry yet so I don't head to the kitchen.

I have no idea what to do.

I guess this is what staying up past my bedtime is like. But I don't have a bedtime. Without a clock, how can I possibly know when it will turn dark? I have the paper and crayons from orientation, but I'm not in the mood to draw right now.

Wait, I have my string with the metal piece on the end. The one I found the day Jordie took me. I run to my room and find it still tucked away in my bag.

I rush back out and show it to Zussta. "Zussta see." I want to show her how it makes noise when I spin it. She has her back to me, but I know she is watching with her behind-the-head eye. I start spinning the string, faster and faster, until it begins to whistle. I'm hoping she is as entertained as I am. I can't tell since I'm looking at the back of her head. But she opens her eye wide at the sound. She turns around, staring at me.

I smile big to show it's a good thing. I bet it's magic to her.

I keep spinning the string and washer so it keeps whistling.

She comes closer, and I stop. I don't want to hit her. I automatically default to talking in English. "Look, I found this string and washer the day Jordie took me. I didn't know what it was, didn't know it would make noise, but it does. If I spin it fast enough, it makes this sound." I step back and spin it again to show her. "I'm not sure what good it does. It won't save the world or anything, but I like it."

I hold it up to show Zussta. She gently takes it from me, inspecting every inch of the string and washer. Maybe they don't have string or metal here on Janti. It would be like me discovering a new animal on Earth. I would be famous. Maybe I would become a scientist and win the science prize for discovery.

But since I'm here on Janti, that will never happen.

"What is it?" She asks.

How do I possibly explain it when it's not anything important? I shrug. I try talking in her language; I have to get better at it anyways. I start acting it out.

"Britt at Earth, walk." I start walking and showing her how I found it. "I walk. I see." I show her how I picked it up off the ground. "I no understand." So, I turn it over a couple of times. "So, I do this." I tied the string to the washer. "And I do this." And I start spinning the washer again. "I hear!" I point to my ears. I'm trying to tell her I didn't know it would make a sound.

She seems very entertained by me; she is smiling, and her suction cups go in and out on her fingers.

Maybe they come out when she has strong emotions. Oh, that would be bad if my fingers had them; those little suction cups would constantly flare in and out.

I hold it out for her again; she takes it and spins it fast enough to have it whistle right away. But then she goes faster and faster. I step back and duck in case it breaks. It stops whistling at a certain point.

I don't want her to break my string toy.

"No, no," I tell her.

She stops spinning it and looks at me, tilting her head. Thankfully she hands it back to me.

I didn't realize how possessive I am over this toy. But hey, since I own so little, I want to keep what I've got.

I tuck my treasure back into my pocket.

Now what should I do?

You know what? I think I'll draw. I lie on my stomach on the floor and begin to draw what I've seen so far. I draw the Lamenana tree, I draw Zussta, and I even draw Jordie in his spaceship. Creating a masterpiece is a great way to pass the time.

Chapter 29

The days blend into one another. I feel grown up since I get to decide when I sleep and eat, but it messes with me trying to figure out if it's day or night when I'm underground, how long I've been here, and if it matters.

I wander into the main room to see what Zussta is doing, but she's not there.

I freeze. Where is she? Did she leave and go somewhere?

I know it's normal to leave your dog or cat at home when the human has to leave, but they at least tell the pet they are leaving.

Did she sneak out while I was sleeping?

Don't panic. Don't panic.

I stand in the middle of the main room, trying to figure out what to do.

I think back to when the Morgan's left and I explored their attic. I found that sitting on the roof was great.

I've made a decision. I'll explore the house.

I mean, I know the main room and kitchen area. And I, of course, know my room, but that's about it. I've only glanced in Zussta's room. And maybe there's another way out, like a back door. Maybe there's a pool!

Yeah, it's definitely time to explore.

I start in the kitchen area, taking a couple of steps and tapping the wall. Nothing happens. No door and no secret hiding spot. I continue into the main room.

I don't see any outlines of another door, but I check it out anyways. I search behind the couch and see nothing but dirt. Ha, Zussta doesn't clean behind her couch every day. For some reason, that makes me happy. I never understood the need to clean under beds all the time.

I walk down the hall and turn left into her room.

OMG! Zussta is sleeping in her bed!

I thought I was alone in the house and then I see her. It scared me so bad that I almost screamed. But thankfully, my ninja street skills stopped that from happening.

I start to quietly back out of the room but then stop. Maybe I'll explore her room a little bit. I practice walking really quietly. I step heel first since tip-toeing doesn't work for me. I walk gently instead.

I walk around her room, taking it all in. The large bed is hanging in the center of the room. It's like my bed, but, like huge.

I walk all the way around it and crawl underneath it. No alarms go off, so that's good.

I stand up and inspect a large floating box against a wall. Is it like a dresser? As I'm poking that I notice another doorway.

I peek inside and see boxes stacked neatly in rows. Okay, a closet, but what are these? I'm completely inside the closet and still haven't woken Zussta. I wonder how long she sleeps. I decide to make this quick.

Most of the stacks of boxes are too tall for me to reach the top, but there are some single boxes almost as tall as me on the ground.

I gently tap the first box. There is a line all the way around and just below the top. I try to lift, but nothing happens. So, I try pushing on that area, and the top slides over!

I quickly catch it before it falls and wakes Zussta.

Whew, that was close. Again, my ninja-like reflexes save me.

Crud, this top is heavy. I ease it to the ground, trying my best not to drop it. I quickly peer out at the bed. Zussta is still there, not moving.

I stand on my tip toes and look inside the box.

It's interesting to see what people, and even aliens, keep hidden in boxes in their closets.

The box is full, and I can only reach the items on top. I'm expecting everything to be heavy, but the first item I pull out is so light that I almost toss it up and out of my hand.

It's brightly colored (of course, everything is) and about the shape and size of a washcloth, but it weighs even less. I know washcloths are not heavy at all, but this feels like it's not there.

I hold it out and release it, expecting it to float to the ground.

Instead, it falls hard with a loud thud!

What is it with this world? Nothing acts like it does on Earth.

Zussta wakes up.

"What?" I hear her say loudly as she sits up.

I freeze.

Do I tell her I'm here or wait and see if she goes back to sleep?

I wait. I'm standing frozen just out of her line of sight. I hear her moving around in the bed, but it doesn't sound like she is up and walking around.

I stand perfectly still.

After about five seconds, or forever, I don't hear her.

I count to forty, acting like a statue and not moving.

Still… no sound, so I move slowly and peek out of the closet door.

Zussta is standing right there looking at me.

Waaah! I scream and fall backward, tripping on the lid of the box. I try to catch myself, turning and stepping and arms flailing, but there is no stopping this downward fall.

I crash onto the floor next to the lid and the stupid light-weight –loud –sounding washcloth thing.

Zussta stands motionless, watching me.

Crud, I'm in trouble.

"What Britt doing?" She asks. But at least she's not yelling.

I don't know the word for exploring. But I try to explain that I wasn't stealing or anything. "Britt there," I point towards the main room. "No Zussta. Britt see here." And I point outside of her closet, trying to say I saw her in bed. "Then Britt see here," I motion to the closet. "Then Britt see this," I point to the box. "Then Britt see this. What is?" I pick up the washcloth thing.

Again, it's so easy to pick up. "Watch," I tell her. I hold it out and let go. It falls and hits the ground with a loud thud again. "Why loud? What is?"

There are so many cool things in this world; I can't wait to discover them all.

Zussta smiles. "You found a --- It is for --- "

Yeah, again, that explains nothing.

"It's not for Britt."

Yeah, that I understand. I hear that a lot.

She picks it up and puts it back into the box and easily replaces the lid.

"Come, we go out here." Zussta starts to guide me back to the main room. But instead, I turn in the opposite direction. I still want to see if there are other rooms.

"Britt look." I explain as I walk further down the hall.

Zussta waits without telling me to 'get back here' or any other adult scolding expression.

The hallway ends at a wall. No more rooms, no secret door, no pool.

But my exploration wasn't a total loss. I found out that Zussta does sleep, and she has stuff hidden away in her closet.

I shrug. Okay, we might as well go to the main room.

I look around. "I see that? I ask her, pointing at the table. It seems important to her. "I be good," I promise her. I'll make sure to know where my hands and feet are at all times.

She hesitates, which is understandable since I made a mess of things last time, but she then bends down and picks me up. She holds me around my waist, against her, and facing out again. We'll have to figure out a better way for her to hold onto me. But this works for now.

She walks to the table but stops before getting there. Again, it's understandable since I messed it up once already.

Lines and shapes appear on the screen. "What is that?" I ask her.

We start the game of 'guess what I'm saying.' She tries to explain, and I catch words here and there such as, "find, I see, go far away, not sure."

Okay, she is looking for something? Did she lose something? Or Someone?

She shifts me to hold me better. She is starting to hurt my ribs by holding me like this. I squirm a little but make sure not to touch the table.

She must be thinking the same thing because she sets me down. "Wait." She tells me. At least she didn't order me to sit and *stay* like a dog.

She goes into her room and returns with one of the square boxes. I don't understand what she is going to do. She easily carries it, so it's not heavy. I move out of the way as she approaches. She sets the box down next to the table and tells me, "Up."

You want me to jump on that? Or climb up on it? Because I can do that. I get ready to climb when she picks me up and sets me on top of the square. I try to stand gently in case it's soft and I sink into it. But it's okay, the box is hard. I don't sink or fall sideways. Both things are a plus.

I tap one foot on the box, then the other. Yep, it seems stable.

I hop up and down. Then I reach down to touch it. It feels solid.

I sit down and tap it with one hand, then the other. Then I start playing it like bongo drums. I'm just about to start using my feet to keep the beat when she interrupts me.

"Britt." She holds up her hand.

I guess that's the universal signal to stop what I'm doing.

Okay, let's get back to the table.

I'm not quite close enough to see, so I hold onto her shoulder as she moves the box closer. I reach out to balance myself on the table… but quickly pull my hand back at the last second.

"Britt good," I tell her. See, I'm trying not to break it.

She smiles at me. "Britt good."

I stare at the lines and shapes. Maybe I can help her find whatever she lost.

Nope, it all means nothing to me. But she is explaining it again. She points to a circle. "Janti."

Okay, that's where we are. I get excited. "Janti!" We must be looking at our galaxy.

She then points to another circle and says, "Sononi."

That must be another planet. I repeat it back to her to let her know I understand.

She draws a line from Janti to Sononi. "We go from Janti to Sononi."

Wait, what? We? She wants to take me to another planet? And do what? When?

"We go," I slowly repeat after her. "Why?"

I hope it's not like when people bring their dogs to the Outback and drop them off and leave them. I don't want to get left on another planet.

"We look and see --" I miss the rest of her words. I'm just happy she's not ditching me.

Now I can concentrate on what she is saying.

She taps the table, makes lines, and the screen changes to a picture of a rock.

Is that the planet? Now I'm frightened again.

"I find this," she says. I breathe a sigh of relief. I'm not being left on a rock planet.

"How do you say?" I ask her.

"Palabonosabrana."

Pala what?

She repeats herself, but slower this time. "Pala-bono-sa-brana."

I try my hardest to repeat her, and I'm getting good with her language, but that one is beyond me. After three tries, I shorten it. "Pala," I say with authority.

"Pala." She agrees.

Okay, so she is looking for a rock called a pala.

"Why see pala?" I ask. Is it hers, and she lost it? Maybe it belonged to her parents, and it has special meaning to her because it sure doesn't look very important. Granted, it's a neat-looking rock with holes like volcanic rock. But it's still just a rock.

Maybe it has some magical powers.

"There are only 3 pala. It is good to have. And I find other ---"

I'm trying to put this all together in my head. She is looking for a rock. I think there are three of them, and they are good. But she also finds other things, other rocks. Is she one of those people who studies rocks? Or Jordie mentioned that she is active and likes to go rock climbing. And we did heaps of climbing and running the other day. Maybe this is a huge rock that we are going to climb. I would love that!

"We go to pala?" I ask.

She scrunches her face. "No. Pala is small" and she holds out her fingers to show me how big a pala is. It can fit in both of my hands, one of hers. So, it's just a rock. Bummer.

She tries to explain again. "We go Sononi. We see pala. We go home."

So, we're going to another planet to find a rock. Well, that doesn't sound fun at all.

"Britt fast. Britt strong," she tells me.

What? Does the rock run away or something?

"Britt and Zussta see pala." She tries to explain.

Well, now I'm completely confused again.

"We go now?" I ask.

"No, we no go now. First, we go fast, up, down, and far. We will go in three ---."

So, we have to find or pick up a pala from the planet Sononi, but not today. We will go in three something. Three weeks, days, hours?

I'm about to ask more when I hear a strange gong.

I whip my head to look at Zussta. She doesn't say anything but quickly shuts off her table. "We go up. Britt no say pala. No say pala." She is pretty firm about this.

I put my finger to my lips. "Britt no say pala." I solemnly tell her.

She points at me, with suction cups out, to make sure I understand.

I tell her one more time that I won't say anything.

"Ok, we go up." And with that, she picks me up off the box and sets me on the floor. I'm glad she doesn't try to carry me everywhere. I had a foster dad who carried his pet toy poodle everywhere. It was kind of dorky for both of them.

We bubble up to see Jordie standing by his spaceship.

"Jordie!" I holler and start jumping up and down.

Chapter 30

Jordie's here!

"Hello, Zussta. How are you?" I understand him, but I think I understand him in Zussta's language.

"Hello, Jordie. We're good. How are you?" She greets him.

Am I invisible? Or does he address Zussta first since I'm a pet? Well, that's not nice. But I like how she automatically included me. You rock, Zussta.

Jordie turns to me. "Hello, Britt. How are you?"

"Hi, Jordie! I'm doing okay. Zussta lets me run around. She trusts that I won't run away. I run fast, but she still catches up to me. But she didn't know I have ninja street skills and I can quickly turn and dodge her. Did you know there is a chair I sit in while I eat and it forms to my body and holds me there? Then a tray comes out so I can set my food on it. And why didn't you tell me how fast it gets dark here? One minute we were running through the fields, and the next, it was pitch black. I thought something happened and I went blind. It scared me, but Zussta found me. Can she see in the dark? She seemed surprised that I couldn't. And there are so many words that I need to have translated. Do you have a translation machine? That would sure help."

Jordie stops me from saying more. "I'm sure you have a lot to tell me. Shall we go inside?"

He was obviously asking that last question to Zussta because she answers, 'Yes,' and they walk towards the bubble. He quickly changed the subject, but I still have heaps of questions for him. I'm just about to get angry when Zussta stops and looks back at me. "Britt good? Britt come?"

She's concerned about me. Okay, I'm not quite as mad anymore.

Jordie is in front of us when Zussta whispers to me. "No say pala."

She doesn't want me to mention the pala to Jordie. I wonder why. So, who do I stay true to? My owner, who I have to live with from now on, or Jordie, who can help me if there is a problem? Is the pala illegal or dangerous?

I figure I'll keep her secret for now and then tell Jordie if something actually happens. Ms. Williams used to tell us that we need to know the entire story before we tattle on someone.

Okay, it's decided. I won't mention the pala.

We bubble down, and they settle on the couch while I climb the steps and sit on the couch too.

Jordie talks first. "I stopped in to check on the both of you and see how things are going." He looks at Zussta first. "How is Britt doing?"

Why doesn't he just come out and say it? He's asking if I'm behaving like a good pet.

Whatever.

"Britt is very good," Zussta tells him. They keep talking, but I tune them out. Will I always be treated like a second-class citizen? Like a pet? I don't like this. I may be a kid, but I'm still important. I want to tell them how I feel, but I don't think now is the best time. Instead, I'll sit and ignore them.

"Britt," Jordie gets my attention. "How are things going with you?"

Oh, now you think I'm worthy of talking to. "Fine." Is all I say. He sits back and tilts his head, studying me. He probably has no idea how rude he was acting and doesn't know why I'm upset. I forgot how abrupt he can be.

"I have a question," I tell him. "Actually, I have a lot of questions. But first, how long, in Earth time, have I been here? And why are you here? Not that I don't want you here; it's good to see someone familiar. But I want to make sure I'm not in trouble."

"You are not in trouble. I told you I would stop in from time to time to check on you. And make sure you and Zussta are getting along and to ask if you need anything. I will stop in more often in the beginning, but soon you won't need me anymore. And you have been here roughly five Earth days."

Five days already? Did I sleep and eat that often already?

Huh, I heard the old guys in the park used to say that time flies when you're having fun. I must be having fun. Or maybe not going to school throws my days off? I used to lose track of the days during the summer.

Jordie and Zussta are talking about what she and I have been doing. She is saying the same things that I already told him, but I guess it's good that we have the same story.

I tune in partway through a conversation, and Zussta is talking. "Go with Britt," and "Britt goes fast."

Is she telling him what a great runner I am?

Jordie turns to me. "Britt, Zussta says you are able to run fast, and she would like to see what else you can do. She enjoys hiking, running, and other activities. She would like to sometimes take you with her. Are you up for that?"

"Heck yeah! I love to do all of those things. I mean, I've never been rock climbing before, but I've climbed all sorts of fences, garbage dumpsters, trees, and on house roofs." I try to think of what else I've climbed in my years.

Jordie talks before I can keep going. "Yes, I know you are very good at various activities. That is one reason I thought you would get along well with Zussta. How are you getting along with her?"

I shrug. "Fine, I messed up her table once, but she didn't yell at me or spank my bum. I didn't mess it up too badly, so she was okay. I like that we go outside and run and play tag. And she feeds me when I tell her I'm hungry. We haven't held hands or anything, and we're still trying to figure out how to pick me up and hold me. She doesn't have any hips to set me on. And she hasn't hugged me yet, which is fine; I don't know her too well yet. Do the Zobians hug? I'm only ten years old and would like some physical contact. Not too much, but some is okay. And I think the suction cups on her fingers come out when she has a strong emotion. And when it got dark so quickly, she came and found me right away and calmed me down. We're learning about each other."

He turns to Zussta and translates everything I just said. Oh, that reminds me, I need to know more words. I can ask him rather than try to guess what Zussta is trying to say.

As soon as he stops talking, I speak up. "Jordie, can you translate some words for us?" I quickly ask so I don't forget. I hate when I forget things and remember after it's too late.

"Yes, we can do that. How are you doing with your room? Do you like it? Do you need anything?"

Do I need anything? I need everything. But I actually can't think of what I need right now. "Does she have enough food and water for me? The blanket for my bed is still perfect. I'm sure I'll grow out of my clothes soon. Can I have a backpack? Not a big one that covers my entire back, but one of those smaller slouchy backpacks? I still have my headbands, but maybe you can take a picture of one so you know what kind to buy for me if I lose or break one. I'm very particular about my headbands, not all of them are strong enough to hold my hair. And I sometimes get bored, can I have something to do? Like a book to read or a game to play? But I suppose it can't be an electronic game since they probably don't have batteries here. So, yeah, some sort of game would be nice. Or more color crayons and paper. Unless Zussta has some games that I can play." I guess I thought of several things I might need.

"You will be brought back to the orientation ship every six Earth months, remember? We will give you new clothes, clean your teeth, and groom your hair at that time. But yes, I will bring you a backpack, take the specifications for your headband, and bring you extra ones. We can ask Zussta if she has something entertaining for you to do."

Oh, the specifications of my headband… so formal. I let it slide and don't tease him (out loud). But I have to go back to the orientation ship? I'd forgotten about that, and I'm not sure how I feel about it.

"What are some words you would like me to translate?" Jordie puts me on the spot again. Of course, now my mind goes blank.

"Maybe the things we will do? Words like 'climb, down, swing, walk, and jump.' And other words like 'find, lost, and work,' and whatever other words she might want to tell me." Jordie looks at me sideways but doesn't ask why I want to know those words.

Plus, it's frustrating that I can't tell her what I want to say. I suppose it will get easier as time goes on.

So, for the next while, Jordie and Zussta teach me even more words. It wears me out, but it's easier than trying to guess what she is saying.

Probably half the afternoon goes by before Jordie stands. I think that is the universal cue that he is ready to leave because both Zussta and I automatically stand too.

"I have enjoyed my visit. I'm happy to see that the two of you are getting along. Life will continue to get easier." He is addressing us both. At least I'm included this time.

Zussta answers him. "Thank you… good see… Britt good…"

I answer him too. "It was good to see you, Jordie. I never thought I would actually miss you. Not in a bad way; I'm just saying it's good to see you. Thanks for teaching me more words."

We bubble up, and I wave goodbye as Jordie climbs into his spaceship.

He takes off, and again, Zussta and I look at each other, wondering what we should do now.

"I no say pala," I tell her.

"Britt didn't say pala." She smiles and raises her arms in a victory pose we did on my first day here.

Yay! I throw my arms in the air as well.

Chapter 31

Zussta brings me outside, but I'm not exactly sure why.

"Britt help?" Zussta asks.

Sure, I'll help. Help do what?

She removes her backpack and begins moving some big poles that remind me of tree trunks. I doubt I can pick it up, but I try. Nope, too heavy for me. So instead, I guide her. Even though she has an eye behind her to see where she's going, I still stand behind her and wave my arms like I'm holding flags in each hand. "This way, slow, slow, a little more. Stop."

That's one log in place. She points to the pile where there is more. "Okay, good. More."

What in the world are we doing with large logs? Is she building a house above ground?

"What is it?" I ask her.

She answers, but I have no idea what the word she says means. She says it slower as if that's going to help any. I shake my head and shrug.

She guides me to one end of the first logs she placed. "Britt up." Okay, I stand on the log.

"Britt go fast." She says.

Go where fast? Across the log? Do you want me to run across the log?

"Britt go?" I double-check as I point to the other end of the log.

She smiles and nods while pointing.

I don't go fast, but I walk the log, arms out and balancing like a pro. I get to the end and turn around, smiling. I walk back, a little faster this time.

Zussta is smiling. "Good."

I only walked on a log, but hearing her say I did good is still nice.

So, I try a bit faster. I speed-walk to the end of the log and speed-walk back.

Zussta is still smiling, so I try again, but faster still.

I'm getting good at this.

After a couple of more tries, I can run from one end of the log and barely stop to turn around and run back.

Who knew a log could be so much fun?

"Okay, more," Zussta says pointing to the pile of logs again. I guess it's time to get back to work.

After we arrange three more logs, we stop for a break while she reaches into her backpack and pulls out some rope.

"What is it?" I ask again.

She sits beside me, using some of the words she and Jordie taught me. "It is for run, jump, climb."

Like a swing set? Is Zussta building me a swing set? That's so nice of her!

She continues with the building. She stands three poles tall and ties them together like a teepee. And then she does it again about 3 meters away.

Yep, it's looking like a swing set.

But then she lays down more logs to the ends of the first ones, making it very long.

Now she starts to dig under some logs. I'm back to helping. I know how to dig.

I've worked up a good sweat, but it feels good to be building something.

I'm not so sure it's a swing set anymore. The structure has logs going over a hole, a rope hanging down, and logs to walk on.

It feels like we have been working for about twenty hours when she finally stops. Wow, she is defo a strong alien. Okay, it's probably only been about four hours, but I'm exhausted.

I flop onto the ground, lying among the flowers. If I turn my head, I can see them close up. The white outline with the vibrant see-through colors is still beautiful. I don't think I'll ever get bored with the plant life here.

"Britt good; we go home," she finally says.

Oh, thank goodness. Yes, let's go home. I wonder if there is a way to carry me because all of the muscles in my entire body are about to give out. Maybe she can roll me like a log.

I laugh at myself and flop over onto my stomach, then roll onto my back again.

Zussta tilts her head at me.

I smile and roll again and again. I can't help but laugh at how much fun this is.

Maybe I could roll down the big hill someday because rolling on flat land is a bit hard.

I finally stop and stand up, brushing myself off.

"Britt okay?" She asks, confused but smiling.

I give her two thumbs up. "Britt good."

She tilts her head and looks at my thumbs. Oh yeah, I forget that we speak a different language, and she may not realize that thumbs up are good.

Never mind, I put them down. "Britt good," I confirm again.

We start the trek home. It's great having an open field right outside the house. On Earth, I lived in the city and didn't have an open place like this. It's no wonder dogs love running through fields.

I slow to a walk and practice talking with Zussta. "Fun today. Zussta strong and Britt help." I can't wait until I can carry on a full conversation. But I think I'm getting better. It's only been about a week, after all.

"Yes, Zussta will finish. Then we run, jump, climb. Britt is fast."

She's going to build more? When? Will she leave me at home, or can I help? But why did she say she would finish, not we would finish? I thought we did good together.

Now I'm all confused again.

We are almost to the bubble when my stomach lets out a loud rumble. I clasp my hands on my stomach and look at Zussta in shock. I didn't realize how hungry I was. Hard work will do that to a person. I suppose it will make a dog or cat hungry too, but maybe not aliens.

"I will feed you," she says as we bubble down.

We get into the house, and Zussta heads into her room. I stand by my eating chair, waiting. I thought she said she would feed me.

She comes back into the room. "Are you hungry?"

"I'm lots hungry," I tell her. "I'm lots hungry and could eat all. Maybe two. I'm lots hungry."

She stops and looks at me sideways. "One meal first."

I never stopped to think whether a dog wanted more food when I was at any of the foster homes. The owners fed the dog and walked away, letting it eat. But what if the dog wanted more? I never heard anyone ask their pet if they wanted more. I guess owners just assume they know best. But how could she know what is best for me when we are still getting to know each other? I think I know what is best for me.

I stay polite and keep my thoughts inside to myself.

Instead, I start thinking about what I want. Something hearty. Maybe steak or lobster. Oh, I know – a thinly sliced steak sandwich with cheese and onions. I saw it on television once and always wanted to try it.

Wait, how will I know what taste to think about if I've never had one?

No worries, I can imagine what it will taste like. And if I don't imagine it right, I'll choose something else. Ms. Williams always taught us to be open to change and be able to shift plans.

Zussta puts my food in the cabinet and walks to her table. She flips on the switch and begins tapping and reading things.

Um, hello? I patiently wait for her to come back.

My food must be done by now, but she is still working at her table.

It's times like this that I'm reminded that I'm a pet.

I clear my throat to get her attention.

"Oh, Britt. I'm sorry, I forgot." Zussta jumps up and grabs my food out of the cabinet.

I get comfy in my chair, and she sets my bowl on my tray. I close my eyes and picture the steak sandwich with onions and melted cheese. I can almost smell it.

I take a bite.

Oh yeah. I have a great imagination because this is so good.

I finish the bowl of gruel in record time. I could eat more. I guess I'm not terribly hungry, but I can always eat more. I look up to tell Zussta, but she is busy at the table again.

I guess I'm done eating.

I'm not sure what to do with my bowl; she usually puts it away.

I stand up, holding my bowl. "I'm done," I announce.

She looks up as if she has forgotten about me. "Oh, I will take that." She takes the bowl and puts it away.

I take a deep breath… and smell myself. Oh, I smell bad from all that hard work. Do aliens have a sense of smell?

"I smell bad. I need shower," I tell her.

She smiles. "Good, yes, you smell bad." She nudges me as she says this.

Wait, is she teasing me and giving me a hard time? I smile back. "Yeah, well, not my bad. You make me work lots." Then I tease her. "Maybe you shower too." I plug my nose.

"Waaah!" She pretends to be offended. "I don't smell. Humans shower a lot because they smell." She tugs a piece of my hair, joking as she says this.

"Oh, aliens smell." I keep my nose plugged. She doesn't smell, but I'm not telling her that.

She laughs and chases me into my room. I collapse on the floor, laughing as she taps and bumps me. I don't think aliens know humans are ticklish, and I'm not telling her. As a street ninja, I know never to tell my weakness.

She stops and looks at me with a soft smile. "We had a good day."

I agree. "It was a good day. I like to help. We make run fast and climb." I'm working on saying full sentences instead of only broken words.

She helps me up, and I head into the bathroom while she goes back to the main area.

I set the shower to hot and step inside. I love hot showers. I use the shampoo-conditioner-soap on my hair and try to comb through it.

I stay in the shower for a long time, never running out of hot water. It's the little things, such as a hot shower, that make life great.

Stepping out of the shower, I remember how exhausted I am. I climb into my hanging bed instead of going back out to Zussta. I hear her come in and check on me, but I'm too wiped out to even open my eyes.

She places a hand on my head. "Sleep well, Britt."

And I'm asleep before I can answer.

Chapter 32

I slept so hard it feels like I was out for several days. I wake up and go into the main area. Zussta is on her couch, so I climb up beside her. I'm slow to wake up, so I sit there staring straight ahead. She taps me lightly on the back. "Hello. Did you sleep well?"

I'm still not sure I'm awake, so I guess I slept well. I nod and scratch my head. I fell asleep with my hair wet, and I'm sure it's quite the spectacle.

Zussta tugs at my hair. "Your hair is all over. Why is it all over?"

Pretty much, yeah. "Sometimes I sleep, and it goes like this."

She gasps and sits back, her front eye opening wide.

What? What did I say?

"What does it do while you sleep?" She looks like she wants to touch my hair but is afraid to do so.

It's much too early for me to understand her fear. But then I understand and have to laugh with a snort. She must think it comes to life while I sleep. "No, I do this," I show her that I roll around in my sleep. "And my hair gets like this." I try explaining.

She understands and is relieved. I would be freaked out, too, if my hair came to life while I slept.

"Wait, I'll be back." I jump off the couch and run to get my comb.

I climb back onto the couch and show her my comb. "This helps. I try to keep good, but I sleep when it was wet. Now it big." I show her how I try to tame it.

"I will help." Zussta takes the comb from me. I usually take care of my own hair, but I guess she wants to try. I turn my back to her and scoot closer so she can comb my hair.

She's a bit rough at first, but I show her how to be gentle with the snarls.

It's nice to have her help with my hair.

Then it dawns on me.

She's brushing my hair like an owner brushes their dog.

Now I'm uncomfortable. I don't want some alien grooming me.

But is it really so different when an adult human helps brush my hair?

Well, now I'm confused.

Is being a kid a lot like being a dog?

It's too early for these deep thoughts. I stop overthinking and let her comb my hair. But not too much; otherwise, my hair gets full of static and stands straight out.

I show her how to put my hair into a ponytail or a braid. She starts talking while playing with my hair. "We will try to see the pala. But first, we run and climb more. I want you good."

We have to run and climb to get to the pala? I guess I'm okay with that. "I run fast and climb. I run and climb on Earth. I like to go fast. Some humans go slow. Maybe Jordie have me here I run and climb."

"Yes, I think you make a good pet." She says.

I don't like that, and I pull away from her. She tilts her head. "Britt okay?"

How do I explain this? "Humans have pets, not be pets."

She stops and looks at me. Then a huge smile comes across her face. "Humans have pets? That is good! I would like to see that."

"Jordie did not let me bring one." I never asked. But then again, I didn't know I was coming here. And I don't have a pet.

She turns me back around and combs my hair more. "Why Britt become a pet?"

"I not want. Jordie take me, and then I was in sky, and now I here with you. I never say to be a pet."

I expect her to be shocked and outraged, as any human would be. But she isn't either; it hardly seems to faze her.

"On Earth, do pets say to be with you and be a pet?" She asks, pulling my hair into a ponytail as I showed her.

I freeze. I never thought to ask a dog if it wanted to be a pet. It was just so.

Dogs and cats are pets. Humans don't ask if they want to be; we simply buy them. We adopt pets – and I wanted to be adopted… this is all too confusing.

I don't answer, and Zussta doesn't seem to mind. She keeps talking, "I happy when Jordie got a pet for me. I like you, and we are good."

I like her too.

I decide to change the subject. "You see in the dark? Remember? We run then it got dark. How do you see?"

"I just do. And Brint not. And Britt no have these on your fingers." She shows me her suction cups; I still need to learn the word for those. "And you only have eyes here and not here." She is pointing out that I don't have an eye in the back of my head. "How do humans not get hurt? I know why humans are good pets - you need help."

I try to stay polite. "No need help. On Earth, we have pets. We can do a lot." I want to say we solve problems, but I can't find the right words.

"Yes, Jordie told me that on Earth, humans are good. But you still need help."

"I'm hungry." I'm not, but I don't know what else to say. I totally don't like this conversation anymore.

But she believes me, and we get up from the couch. I'm not terribly hungry. I think I'll just imagine a peanut butter and banana sammie. I sit and wait in my chair while she prepares my food. I wish I could prepare it myself. Maybe when I'm older, Zussta will teach me.

"What are we going to do today?" I ask as she sets my food on the chair tray. I dig in before she can answer.

"We make yesterday. I add more. We go see."

She added more to the logs? That's great. I may not know what she is building, but I'm excited anyways. Maybe I should be worried, but I'm not. I trust Zussta.

I finish my brekky (okay, it was just creamy gruel) and run to my room to get ready. I change my clothes – happy that I always have clean clothes without doing laundry, and put on my headband.

There, I'm ready.

Zussta is not in the main room; she must be in her room getting ready too.

I wait for her.

And I wait.

And wait.

The excitement is wearing off, and I'm starting to get bored.

I wonder how fast I can run from the main room to my room and back. At the Morgan's house, I ran around the inside of their home fast. I bet I can do that here.

I stand with one hand touching the door to the bubble elevator.

Ready. Set. Go!

I zoom across the room, down the hallway, and into my room. I don't stop. I do a left-turn lap around my bed, and head back out my door, down the hallway, and to the outside door.

I bet I did the entire lap in five seconds flat.

I need to ask Jordie for a stopwatch or a timer.

I catch my breath.

Ready. Set. Go!

I take off running again; through the main room and down the hallway. But this time, I run around my bed in the opposite direction. It feels weird going to the right. I think I lose time. I make it back to the outside door. Yep, definitely slower.

Okay, the lesson learned is that I'm faster when I turn to the left.

Good to know.

I'm set to go one more time when Zussta walks into the main room. She sees me in my running stance and squints her big eye at me. "What are you doing?"

"Running." I mean, that's exactly what I'm doing.

"In the house?"

"Yes."

I'm trying a new approach. Be direct, and don't explain myself. Usually, I would tell her what I'm doing and why, but I want to see what happens when I say very little. I don't think this will happen often, I like to talk, but it's another good experiment.

I'm always testing my street ninja skills.

She tilts her head and stares at me. I smile, showing her I'm a good girl.

She shakes her head. "Are you ready to go outside?"

"I'm ready!" I shout. I also jump up and down a bit and do a little dance. Yeah, I'm ready.

Zussta bends down to talk to me face-to-face; or big-eye-to-face. "I want to show you this. Do not run ahead. Stay by me."

I step back. Well, now I'm afraid. Did she build something that's going to hurt me? Will it take me away from her? I glance at my bean bag chair, thinking I'd rather stay home now.

She sees my fear and laughs. "It is a good thing. I think you will like."

I look at her sideways, not sure what to believe anymore.

"You will like it. Let's go."

And with that, we bubble up.

Chapter 33

We get outside, and I stay by Zussta's side. I want to show her that I don't always take off running. I can behave. I defo don't want to be put on a leash.

As we get closer to the building site, I see she has done a lot of building onto our logs. How long was I asleep? There's a wall, rope swings, and tunnels.

What is this?

Zussta stands tall and proud, and I want to be excited. I try to smile big, but I don't quite understand what I'm looking at.

Zussta must see the doubt in my eyes because she tells me the word for whatever she built. Yeah, saying an alien word I don't understand doesn't explain it.

I shrug.

"Umm… it's great?" I try to be happy.

"We work together. To run, climb, and jump." She points to each area as she says it.

I get it!

It's an obstacle course!

I look up, smiling big at her. "We run and climb and jump!" I tell her, letting her know I understand. She smiles and pats me on the back.

Zussta designed a homemade obstacle course. Here's how it is supposed to work. We start at a full run toward a wall. She boosts me up and over and then easily climbs over herself. Then we run side by side across some planks that I pretend are over a canyon. Next, there is a tube that I drop and crawl through while she jumps over. We run on more planks; this time I picture it being over a lake of crocodiles. We jump and grab a rope and swing across what I pretend is a lake. And run as fast as we can to the end.

I run until I can't run anymore.

We go home and come back again the next day and the next day. We spend the next several days training.

We climb walls, run on skinny planks, and I crawl into small spaces that she can't.

It takes me a while, but we work well together and finally can run the course side by side.

Running the obstacle course with Zussta is great. I've heard people say that they have bonded with their pets. I never knew what it meant, but maybe that's what is happening here. We are learning more about each other and bonding.

And as the days go by, I'm starting to understand her words better.

"Okay, let's go fast on the course. Do it all, and go fast. We go together."

We line up at the beginning of the course; I've run it so many times that I'm not afraid. I have taught her about countdowns. "Three, two one, go!"

I take off as fast as I can. We get to the wall at about the same time. Since she is taller, we have it worked out that she helps me by pushing my bum to help me get to the top of the wall faster. We get to the top, and I run across the plank, and she is on my heels. Since she is heavier, the plank sways, but I've learned to use my arms to balance through the motion. I then drop down and crawl in the ditch under a log as she jumps over it. I grab the rope that hangs from the teepee and swing across what I pretend is a canyon (it's just space above the field), and she long jumps over it. We both do a full-out run to the end of the field. Pushing hard, I run as fast as I can.

I pretend I cross the finish line first – and the crowd goes wild!

I look at Zussta; at least she is breathing hard, too. I feel a special kind of happiness when we finish this race.

We both throw our arms in the air. "Yeah!"

I didn't realize I would become close to an alien by running and working out, but I like it. It's as if she understands my ninja street smarts.

She pats me on the back. "Let's go home." I'm beat, so I don't argue with her. I've seen videos of dogs sassing back to their owners, but I don't think I should do that yet. Plus, I'm too tired to stay outside any longer.

At home, I take a shower and change my clothes. I use my comb in the shower and the special spray from Simon that gets the tangles out of my hair. It takes a while, but that's okay since I never run out of hot water. Zussta has never knocked on the door and told me to get out, so I'll stay here and linger a bit – because I can. I never met a pet that liked showers or baths, but I sure do.

I assume she showered, too, because when I come to the main room, she is already there, and looks refreshed.

She is at the table again. We have set up small containers as steps for me to climb onto the box next to the table. This way, she doesn't always have to pick me up.

I'm always careful not to bump the screen.

I can easily pick out Janti and Sononi. She has zoomed in on Sononi and is looking at different places on the planet. "You find the pala?" I ask.

"No, we go to look for it soon. You help?"

Of course, I'll help. Just the thought of traveling to a new planet is exciting. I wonder if it will be all colorful like this one. Or maybe it's all one color; that would be weird. Imagine a world where everything is the same color. It would be like people who wear the same color pants and shirts and are all matchy-matchy; I bet they would like a planet like that.

Oh, back to the pala.

"Why you find pala?" I ask again. She tells me again, and this time I understand more.

"Many want the pala. I find and give to them. They give me --- ."

I almost understand. I get that the pala is hidden, and she wants to find it. But I don't know what it does or what others will give her for it. On Earth, people would give money for something everyone needs. Do they have a currency on Janti? Is it the same in the entire universe? Do they have a money exchange place, like banks? Not that it matters to me; I don't have any money – I'm only ten. But once one of my foster moms gave me five dollars to go into the store all by myself and buy candy. That was fun being able to browse and pick out exactly what I wanted.

Maybe they trade items and not money.

Okay, she trades the pala for something she wants. And many people want the pala.

Is it valuable?

Maybe the pala is money.

Wait.

Wait.

"What Zussta do all day?" I ask, looking at her sideways, wondering if what I'm thinking is correct.

"I find pala or more. Then I give to them, and they give me --- ."

What?! What do they give her? Jewels? Money?

OMG... My owner is a treasure hunter!

Chapter 34

Zussta is a treasure hunter!

That's why she had me running the obstacle course; at least, I hope that's why. Maybe she wants to take me with her when she searches for the pala!

OMG, OMG, OMG, I can't even begin to contain my excitement!

I need to run. "Up, go fast, happy!" I'm spouting off any words I can think of to tell her I need to go outside and run. She understands my words, but probably not why I'm freaking out. We quickly bubble up.

I instantly take off running over the hill and towards the tree. Zussta keeps pace and runs beside me.

I get to be a treasure hunter!

I've prepared for this my entire life!

I've kept myself active by running, climbing trees, and crawling under fences. I know to watch behind me. I'm quick. And not much scares me… I always knew that one day I would need my street ninja skills. Some of the kids at the group home would tease me for always climbing everything I could, and I got into trouble with adults more times than I could count. But it all paid off; here I am.

A treasure hunter!

An alien treasure hunter.

I'm in a full run as I throw my arms in the air and let out a whoop. I'm yelling and laughing as I look at Zussta. She is laughing and throwing her hands in the air as well.

Whoo hoo!

I reach the top of the hill and jump the first part of the way down. I don't even fall as I land; I keep running and running. We reach the Lamenana tree, and I finally stop, breathing heavily.

"Zussta pala find!" That's the best I can do to explain why I'm so happy.

"Yes, find pala and more." I think she understands why I'm so happy.

"I go fast, jump, climb. I help find pala!" I understand why she wanted a human pet; she needs someone to help her with treasure hunting. I don't think Jordie could have picked a better person for the job.

The table in the house must be one giant map. That's why she studies it so often. Maybe it's a pirate's treasure map. It's all starting to make sense now.

And here I thought she wanted a kid to keep her company.

Being a treasure hunter is much better than being someone's teddy bear.

I'm about to be a treasure hunter.

Does Jordie know what she does? I bet not. I bet that's why she told me not to tell him about looking for the pala. Would he think it's too dangerous and take me away from Zussta? Would I be sent back to Earth or to another alien? I don't want another alien. I like Zussta and want to be a treasure hunter with her.

But what if I could choose to go back to Earth? I liked the group home and Ms. Williams, but I'm not sure I want to go back there and be in the mix again, waiting for another family.

I decide not to dwell on that and think more about being a treasure hunter.

We lie on our backs under the tree. I have so many questions. "I help find pala?" I ask, double-checking that we are thinking the same.

"Yes, you help find pala. You little, go under, I go over." In the obstacle course, she had me crawl under logs; now I see why. I can fit into the spaces she can't. I'll definitely be an excellent addition to make us a team. "Are you happy?" She asks.

Umm, yeah. Couldn't she tell? "Yes, I happy." I want to ask her when we will leave and how far away we have to go. Do I need different shoes or clothes? I guess if I do, she'll get them for me.

I gaze up into the tree, admiring the colors and light and marveling at how I got here. Usually, I don't have much control over my life; but training to be smart and fast finally paid off. My self-training gave me the opportunity to be here. At first, I didn't think being captured by an alien to become a pet was good, but now I see it as something special.

It's crazy how things turn out.

I'm about to be a treasure hunter. With an alien.

I squint my eyes, and the colors of the leaves blend together. The branches move and sway, and the colors shimmer. There are so many colors that I don't know the names of them all. There are heaps of shades of reds, purples, greens, blues, and the white and black between them - the Lamenana tree. I never want her to tell me the real meaning of the name of this tree. I choose to think of it as the Goddess of Forever Beauty. Just as I begin to calm down, I remember why I am excited.

I'm about to be a treasure hunter!

I have a purpose.

I remember some animals on Earth seemed happiest when they had a purpose with their family. Like a police dog had a job and a purpose. But then again, some were content to sleep in the sunbeam on the floor. I guess it depends on the pet.

I, for one, want a purpose.

Now I'm set on learning more. More words, more of the language, more of the land, and more training on the obstacle course.

I want to tell her I'm ready to train for this. Crud, I so need to learn the language better. That's goal number one, learn to talk with her better. Once I make up my mind, I will do it. Ms. Williams always said I was a very determined girl, and she was right. When I want something, I give it my all. The old guys called me a real go-getter.

And I want to be a treasure hunter.

I twist towards her. "Zussta teach me words, go fast, climb?" I want her to know I'm fully onboard and will work hard.

"Britt go fast and climb. We will do more. I will teach you words."

I look up into the tree again. I'm proud that she knows I already run fast and can climb. I won't let her down.

"We go home?" She asks.

Yeah, I'm ready. We begin my language lesson on the way home. She is talking non-stop. The best way to learn is to start listening and trying to answer. I repeat what she says, even if I don't understand everything.

We bubble down and walk to the table. I use the steps to get to the top of my box so I can see.

I study the lines, circles, and boxes, beginning to understand it all a little bit more. She shows me the planets again, and then we zoom in on Sononi. It has land and water. I first thought the pala would be in a cave because that's where movies show treasure is hidden, but now I'm not so sure.

She is pointing to water and land. She makes a motion above the ground. Are there treasures hanging in the sky? Now that would be interesting to see. I can't rule anything out, I mean, I'll be on different planets, so anything is possible. Maybe Sononi doesn't have gravity, and everything is just floating around.

I'm going to be a treasure hunter!

I listen closely as she explains the trip from Janti to Sononi. She points to another planet. She taps it, opening it up and showing oceans of water. More water than land. "Oonala." She says. Okay, that's the planet of Oonala. "Oonala first, then Sononi." We must have to make a stop on one planet before we head to Sononi. I'm not sure why, but okay.

Zussta talks to me, answering my questions. She isn't dismissing me or talking down to me. I feel so grown up.

"Britt smart. You know more?"

Is she asking if I want to learn more? Yes, I want to learn it all. "Yes, I know more."

And with that, my first lesson begins. She shows me Janti and all the planets around it. So, this must be our solar system. There are other planets: Deeenee, TruTri, Glenerd, Zaranti, Chi'Chu'Ci, and others. Oh, this is cool that I'm learning these.

As much as I hate to admit it, it's good to learn again. Not that I miss school, but I kind of miss learning. I have trouble sitting still in school, but finding out about the planets I'll visit is different – this kind of learning is cool.

My stomach growls loudly, reminding me that I haven't eaten for a while. Zussta laughs at the sound as I clasp my belly. It seems like a good time for a break.

I jump off the box and follow her to the food area. She opens the secret doors again and prepares my food. I plop down into the cool chair that forms itself around me. As she hands me the bowl, the side tray appears. I close my eyes and decide what I want.

I want spicy grilled shrimp and corn on the cob with lots of butter and salt.

I take a bite, and the shrimp is perfect. I wish the food was sometimes crunchy, but when it tastes this good, I don't care. And I can almost feel the butter dripping on my hand as I imagine the corn on the cob. I bet it tastes better since I have such a good imagination. My teachers in school were always scolding me for daydreaming. Daydreaming isn't bad, but they wanted me to listen to them.

I finish my food and hand the bowl and spoon back to Zussta. We wander into the main room and sit down, her on the big couch and me in my bag chair. She is still constantly talking to me.

I begin to drift asleep.

I'm going to be a treasure hunter!

Chapter 35

The days come and go. I'm on a mission to prepare to be the best treasure hunter in the universe. Well, the best after Zussta. I'm always working on my ninja skills; now I just have to add treasure-hunting skills. Even though I'm not sure what those skills are. I figure it's running, climbing, balancing, ducking, and just being aware of my surroundings.

And the language. I'm getting much better at speaking Zobian.

I've heard people say the best way to learn a language is just to start talking with someone, and pretty soon you start to pick it up. I guess they're right. Plus, I have no one to speak English with, so Zobian comes out automatically. I'm finally learning to speak in full sentences.

It's so much easier to talk when I know the language.

I like that Zussta talks with me. Whether we are having a conversation or not, she talks and talks. I think the language is really starting to sink in.

And I already know all the planets in our solar system, and I'm learning about the other solar systems and even galaxies. Having wormholes to take us places means I have to know about more than just this planet.

I think it's early one morning, or at least I've just woken up. I stumble into the main room not even bothering to brush my hair first.

Zussta is on the couch typing on a tablet that looks like Jordie's. She smiles brightly at me when I sit down. "Hello, Britt," she says. She is much too cheery for me just waking up.

I mumble a hello in return.

She goes back to typing on her tablet. I take this time to study her a bit more.

I get her attention and point to her hair. How often do you get to touch an alien's sideways, blue Mohawk hair?

She sits on the ground and lets me touch her hair. I lightly tap it on top, then try to poke my finger through it. It's very soft and surprises me that it can stand straight up. I thought it would be stiff due to of lots of hairspray or something.

Okay, I'm done with that.

I use both hands to scratch my head, stretch, and fall back. It's got to be morning if I'm feeling like I'm barely awake. Zussta is talking to me and trying to teach me more of her language, but I don't even know my own name right now.

I hear the words Sononi and Oonala and start to pay attention.

"We will go to Oonala. We need a --- before we go to Sononi."

What? Are we going somewhere? Today? Are we taking a spaceship? Do they teleport places?

Now I'm awake.

"What?" I ask so that she will repeat what she just said. "We go?"

"Yes, we go Oonala. Water on Oonala, need a ---" She is explaining to me.

I don't know if she means the water I drink is on Oonala and we need some or if she is talking about the oceans of Oonala. I hope she means the ocean because it scares me to think of running out of water to drink already.

"When we go Oonala?" I ask her. Because I'm totally game for going today. I wonder if we will see more aliens. Maybe like the ones I saw during orientations, or even different.

"We go today. Then home today." She tells me while still looking at the table.

I get to fly in a spaceship again. I need to get ready!

I run into my room, shower quickly, and choose my white shirt and yellow pants to wear. Am I supposed to dress up for this? It doesn't matter since all of my clothes are basically the same. I bet if I needed to wear something different, Zussta would give me new clothes.

I'm showered, dressed, and back into the main room in record time. See, living with lots of other kids had an advantage; it taught me how to get ready fast.

"I'm ready," I announce.

Zussta laughs and claps her hands (suction cups in). "Britt ready fast."

I can't deny that.

"Britt eat?" She asks. Oh, yeah, it would be a good idea to eat. They probably don't have human food on Oonala.

I settle in my chair while she makes me a bowl of gruel. I say that in a teasing way. I like that I can pretend it's anything I want. She sets down the bowl and a cup of water. I close my eyes and imagine pizza. I love the greasy pepperoni pizzas that are cut into squares. Those are my favorites. Not that I would turn down a regular cut pizza, but since I can choose – I choose squares.

I try not to scarf it down, but I'm excited to go. I'm not sure if Zussta is ready to leave, but I'll be ready when she is. I take a deep breath, slow down and savor the pizza. This is so good that I'm a bit sad when I finish.

"More, please?" I hopefully ask her. I'm not very hungry, but I still want one more piece.

Zussta's one eye opens wide. "More?" She confirms.

"Little more, please," I confirm. I hold up my thumb and first finger to show a little bit.

She debates. Crud, I don't like being told I can't eat more. I bet this is how dogs feel when they ask for a treat, and their owner tells them no. It's frustrating.

But she agrees and fixes me a little more.

"Thank you!" I let her know I have manners so that maybe she will keep saying yes in the future when I ask for more.

I savor one more piece of pizza. It's perfect and hits the spot.

She puts my bowl away and I look to her, hoping we can go now.

I'll wait near the bubble.

Zussta is studying the table again.

I'm trying to be patient.

I rock back and forth, from one foot to the other.

Then I start to hop from one foot to the other.

I hop twice on one foot, then twice on the other.

Next, I jump three times on my right foot and three times on my left foot.

Then I jump straight up and down, trying to see how high I can go.

I don't think I could be on a basketball team, but I jump pretty high. I try touching high on the wall. I wish I could leave a mark so I can practice and see if I'm getting better.

I jump and slap the wall. Jump and slap the wall.

Jump and…

"Britt!" Zussta yells.

Crikey! She scares me so bad that I fall to the floor. I check my heart to make sure it's still beating. I get it why the old guys would say it almost gave them a heart attack; I think mine just stopped.

"What are you doing?" She asks firmly.

"Um, jumping." I thought that was obvious. I go on to explain, "I wait quietly here for Zussta." I was minding my own business, waiting for her. If I had a game or coloring book, I could have been doing that.

Zussta starts laughing. "You are not quiet."

Oh, yeah, I guess she heard my hand slapping the wall.

I start laughing too. "Sorry." I shrug to let her know I didn't realize I was interrupting her. "I'm ready to go to Oonala," I tell her.

"Okay, okay, let's go." She turns off the table, walks into her room, and comes out wearing a backpack. I can't wait for Jordie to bring me mine.

"Let's go." That's all she needs to say, and I'm already at the bubble waiting for her.

We bubble up. I stop and look around. I don't see a spaceship anywhere. I walk in the direction opposite from the hill because I know it's not that way.

Zussta stops me and holds me still. We are surrounded by blue see-through flowers, but she bends down and grabs one that is red. I didn't even see the different color.

She pulls it, and the ground in front of us moves.

I jump closer to her and grab her leg. What's happening?

Zussta taps my head. "It's okay," she says.

A spaceship rises out of the ground in a clear bubble.

She has an underground garage!

I look up, smiling at her. She smiles at me, but having a spaceship rise from the ground must be normal for her.

I get to ride in a spaceship. I start bouncing up and down on my toes and singing in English. *"I get to ride in a spaceship, just like the aliens. I get to fly through the sky. We are going to another planet in a spaceship. La la la."*

Zussta stops in place and stares at me like I'm crazy. And that's hard to do with just one eye. "What are you doing?" she asks.

I'm getting asked that a lot today.

Does she mean singing or bouncing? Probably singing since she has seen me bounce and jump. Is my voice that bad? Or maybe they don't sing. How can someone not sing? Seriously?

"I was ---." I say 'singing' in English. They probably don't have a word for it. "I use words this way, and it makes me happy." How do you explain singing?

She turns back to the spaceship but still watches me with her back-of-the-head eye. She opens the door. "Ready?"

I peek inside, debating where to sit. The ship is similar to Jordie's but a little different. It's the same shape and grey color, just bigger. But then again, she is bigger than Jordie. The seats look huge. I hope I'll be able to see out the windows.

I crawl in, settling into one of the two seats. She climbs up and tells me to move to the other seat. Fifty-fifty chance and I choose wrong.

I crawl into the other seat and wiggle around until I'm comfortable. I can't see out the window. I ease up onto my knees and can see better. I hope she will let me stay like this. I want to see where we are going.

Zussta closes the door, and a T-handle comes out from the dashboard in front of her. She pushes buttons and looks at me. "Here we go."

I squeal in happiness.

Here we go!

The ship takes off straight upwards, not forward or backward, but straight up like a helicopter. I plaster my hands against the window, looking down at all the colors.

I'm still kneeling, but the seat holds me in when I try to stand up and look out the front window. Oh, well, at least I'm kneeling.

We rise until we are in outer space. Then the ship turns in a flat spin, and we move forward.

I'm in a flying spaceship! This is so exciting! I can't help but bang on my legs. It's better than banging on the window.

Zussta smiles at me and keeps driving.

We have been zipping along for about five minutes when I spot a wormhole out my window. "Zussta," I get her attention. "Look. How do you say?" As I point at the movement of nothing.

"How do you say what? What do you see?"

If I knew the word, I wouldn't be asking her.

"That black spot, it go somewhere else." I finish in English. *"See, the wormhole."*

She keeps looking out my side window but doesn't know what I'm pointing at. Maybe she doesn't see it. Never mind, it's almost out of sight anyways.

I'm frustrated. I look forward and we are heading for another wormhole. "There, another!" I point straight ahead. "That. That go somewhere else." I try explaining again.

"You can see the mabo?" She quietly asks.

If a mabo is a wormhole, then yes, that's what I see. She doesn't? Are we going to get sucked somewhere else? Does she know we are heading into it?

Now I panic.

"Mabo! Mabo!" I start hollering.

Yes, mabo is good." She is telling me through my panic yells. I breathe a bit.

"Mabo is good?" I double-check.

"Yes, see." She points to a funnel shape on her screen. Oh, it's showing her the location of the wormhole, but she can't see it in real life out of the winder

"You don't see it?" I ask, pointing ahead again.

"No. You do?" She asks in amazement.

"Yes. Right there."

We regard each other for a moment. So, she can see in the night but can't see wormholes. Interesting. She is probably thinking the exact opposite about me. I can see wormholes but can't see in the dark.

"Hold on," she finally says.

I quickly sit down on my bum and hang on for the ride.

Chapter 36

Black and white flashes through the window. I don't need to look to know how it happens. The seat holds me still as the ship zips through the wormhole, banking right and left. I hold my arms up like on a carnival ride.

Whoo hoo!

"Hold on; we are coming out," Zussta tells me.

I look around but don't see anything to hold onto. Well, now I freak out a bit. I'm still searching for something to grab when it feels like the ship instantly stops. My feet and hands go forward, but the seat holds the rest of my body tight. These seats should be in every car on Earth. it would keep people from getting hurt in a car accident.

When I can finally move again, I get back onto my knees and peer outside. The planet's colors are different here. But the most fantastic part of this place is that it has three suns. I didn't realize that was possible. They're not close together, but there are definitely three suns.

Zussta steers the ship to the left, and in front of us, a dark blue planet comes into view.

I assume blue means water, so hopefully, she was talking about a water planet earlier today and not needing water to drink.

Another mystery is solved.

As we get closer, I see small, yellow splotches that must be land. Good, I was wondering where we were going to land. Maybe the ship can land on water or even go under it.

Instead, the ship heads to land.

This must be Oonala. It's not as colorful as Janti. But it does have an ocean, so that's cool. We land, and I'm busy looking around as Zussta gets out a different backpack. She opens the door and helps me climb out.

Opening her bag, she brings out a clear plastic sheet of paper. She then wraps the flap of the pack around itself so it's closed, and she puts it on the front of her instead of her back.

Everything is different from what I'm used to, even how aliens wear backpacks.

"We go down into water. We go to the ---. I need another of these and a small one for you." Zussta explains as she points to and adjusts her backpack. Or should I call it a front pack?

Wait. Are we swimming underwater?

I start backing away.

I don't swim.

I grew up in a city, not on the beach.

I'm still shaking my head 'no' and backing away when Zussta notices my fear.

Squatting down to my level, her big eye is all serious, and she asks, "Brit swim?"

"Kind of." I shrug. I don't know how to tell her I can float and splash around, but I don't think I can swim too long underwater. Plus, I don't know how far we have to swim. What if I can't hold my breath that long?

With that thought, I start to hyperventilate. Just the idea of not being able to breathe makes me not able to breathe.

Zussta holds me gently by the shoulders. She gently rubs my arms up and down in an attempt to calm me. My breaths slow down, and I'm not dizzy any more.

"It is okay. You'll be okay. This let you breathe in water. I hold your hand."

What does she mean 'I can breathe in water'? Can I breathe the water on this planet?

She readjusts my headband so all the hair is pulled back. Then she shows me the clear plastic sheet. "This go on your face." She wobbles her head at me.

She then starts at my forehead, pushing the edge of the clear sheet against my skin, and eases it down around the rest of my face.

I hold my breath.

She presses around the outer edges to make sure there are no pockets where water can enter.

I still hold my breath.

She checks the sheet around my forehead, down the side of my face, and under my chin. That one big eye is checking me out all over my face. Then she notices that I'm not moving.

"Breathe." She quickly tells me.

I'm not sure I can.

"I promise you can breathe." She is trying to convince me. I still don't quite believe it, holding my breath this long is hard.

I let my breath out in a gush.

And then breathe in.

It works! I can breathe!

Everything on Earth taught me not to put plastic over my face, and now Zussta covers my face with plastic and I breathe. I don't know if I'll ever be able to understand all these new rules of life.

I take a couple of more breaths, in and out, with no problem. And the plastic doesn't fog up, either. Again, another great invention we need on Earth.

I look around to see if this thing makes everything blurry. But no, I can see and breathe just fine. I try talking, saying the words I know: "Hello. Hello. Run. Fast. Up. Down. Boogaboo. Boogaboo." The last part I say in English

Zussta laughs. "I can hear you just fine."

Well, this changes everything. I'm not afraid if I know I won't die.

I have heaps of questions about magic mask. "It work only in water? Or on land with no air too?"

Zussta is impressed with my brilliant question. "Good thinking. It good in water or on planets with no air."

Whoa.

Before I can ask more questions, she stands up. "Are you ready to go? We start here and go not far under the water. I take your hand."

We walk into the water. When we get about waist deep for me (barely to her knees), I bend over and put my face in the water. I automatically hold my breath at first. Then I work up the courage and try to breathe.

It works! I can see and breathe with my face underwater!

I look up to see Zussta smiling back down at me.

"This is amazing! I can see underwater. Are there fish in this ocean? Are they big? Will they eat us? Or maybe just me since I'm smaller than you? How long does this face thing work? Can we reuse them?" I forget I'm saying this all in English.

I have more questions, but Zussta stops me from talking more. "Let's go. I tell Britt everything as we go."

Okay, that works for me. We walk a little further out, and I start to doggie paddle. Zussta is still only waist-deep in the water. She reaches out and holds my hand with her suction cups out. I thought having all those suction cups on my hand would feel weird, but it doesn't. It just feels like she is holding on tight. I feel better about this.

She pulls me further out. When ready, she looks at me. "Okay, let's go down."

I dive down and start kicking. I think I'm swimming pretty good, and she is right next to me, watching to make sure I'm not freaking out, and, maybe more importantly, pulling me along.

We swim next to each other for about ten seconds when I see a huge dome on the bottom of the ocean.

As we get closer, I see aliens walking inside the dome.

It looks like an entire city down there.

Things keep getting weirder and weirder as the day goes on.

She pulls me towards a door. When we get there, she presses a button, and the door slides open. We swim inside a small room. She presses a button, and the door closes. Then she swims to the other side of the small room and presses a button next to another door.

The water begins to drain.

Okay, I get how this works. It's a holding room in between the ocean and the dome.

As the water drains out, and I'm paddling on top of it as it goes down, I realize that Zussta doesn't have a plastic face sheet on. "Zussta breathe underwater?" I ask her.

"No, I not breathe a long time." She answers as she rearranges her frontpack and checks me over. "Britt okay?"

"Yeah, Britt good." Well, I am doing alright until the next door opens, and I see really tall, blue aliens with big flipper feet.

I take a step back into the small room. I'm not sure I want to be out there with them.

Zussta sees my hesitation and kneels in front of me. "It's okay. You stay close to me. These are Mari, and they are nice. No one will hurt you. Stay close."

"Mari no step on Britt." And I'm serious about that.

She looks at me, "No step on Britt," she agrees. "There is air here for you to breathe. We take off the face shield." She says this as she gently peels the shield away from my face. It doesn't hurt like a band-aid does. I barely feel it coming off.

She stands up, and I place my hand on her leg.

"Ready?" She asks.

It's not that I'm afraid of aliens. I saw heaps of different aliens walking around the orientation place. And I made friends with the guys in the kitchen. But all these aliens are the same, and we are the odd ones here.

We step out into what reminds me of a marketplace, and no one seems surprised to see me. Have they seen humans before? I expected everyone to point and stare at me. Some of the aliens smile and point, but it's not like I'm stopping traffic.

Interesting.

And then I look up.

I'm in the opposite of a fish bowl.

I know I'm underwater, but I forgot that fish might be in this water too. Several yellow fish with long bodies swim by… and they each have two heads.

I just saw fish with two heads.

I can't stop looking up and around. Bright fish and silverfish are calmly gliding overhead.

I could stay here forever watching these creatures.

Zussta taps me to get my attention. "Ready?"

I tear my eyes away from the top of the dome and keep my hand on Zussta's leg as we turn right and start walking among strange-looking blue aliens.

I have to admire her confidence.

It's a good thing I'm holding on to her because there is so much to see.

It's almost as if we are in a marketplace.

There are separate stores or stands, and each one has its own dome. So, no matter where we are, we can see the water above us.

Then there is the merchandise in each stand. I don't know what are toys and what are normal Mari daily items, but I want to touch it all.

And it's noisy down here. I thought it would be quite underwater, but not in this marketplace. Aliens are talking, and kids are yelling.

Yep, it's a regular marketplace, similar to the one in Sydney, but different in that we are on another planet, and I'm looking at blue aliens with blue stripes down their bodies.

So yeah, similar but totally different.

My head begins to hurt.

I look up and see more crazy-looking fish swimming above us.

When I look back down, what I assume are kid aliens run by us, pushing a ball back and forth. It floats slowly and gracefully between them instead of the kids having to throw it. I want that toy.

I begin to ask Zussta if I can have a floating ball, but I freeze.

And then I see him.

I see a human boy!

Chapter 37

A human. I see a human.

A boy.

A human boy.

I freeze. Zussta feels me let go of her leg. She stops and comes back to me. She looks down my line of sight and sees the human boy as well.

"Do you know that human?" She asks.

That strange question almost snaps me out of my trance. She must wonder if all humans know each other. I shake my head 'no' but keep staring.

"Another human." She whispers.

I'm more surprised than you are, lady. I think to myself.

The boy turns and sees me. He freezes too.

It's not a contest, but we are definitely having a stare-off. Or we're both too freaked out to move. I wasn't sure if I would ever see a human again, and now I see one already. Who is he? Is he a pet? Where is he from? Does he speak English?

I bet he's wondering the same about me.

I raise my hand to say hi, and he gives me a small wave back.

It's like a movie where we slowly walk towards each other. Zussta is watching closely. Hopefully, ready to save me if this goes terribly wrong.

We're like cats circling each other, deciding if the other is a friend or not.

"Hi?" I say, sounding more like a question in English since I don't know what to say or how to act.

"Hi." He answers me in English too, but he looks at me like I'm a unicorn or something he's never seen before. Maybe he was born on this planet and has never seen a human.

"I'm Britt. Are you a human?" It may seem like a weird question, but Jordie and Simon both look human and aren't, so I think it's a totally justified question.

"Yes, are you? My name is Marco."

"Yes, I'm human and speak English. OMG, I had no idea if I'd ever see another human again, and now here you are! Do you live on this planet? They call me a pet, but I'm not really one; at least, I say I'm not. I live with Zussta over there, on the planet Janti. I was hanging out in the park one day and met this guy who turned out to be Jordie. He said he was a Finder and took me to be a pet. Isn't that the strangest thing you've ever heard? Zussta brought me here to find a bag that wraps closed. She said she needs another. I have no idea what she means, but then again, I usually don't understand all of what she says. I'm still learning her language. I was worried I would forget how to speak English, but here we are, talking and everything."

Marco looks overwhelmed, so I try to stop talking so much.

He reaches out and pokes me on the arm. "I was checking to see if you're real. And you are," he begins talking. "I was taken by Jordie, too! Wow, I wonder how many of us there are. I make waterproof bags. Maybe they are the ones she needs. My owner, Jutte, first made them and taught me. But then he was killed, and I still make them."

I gasp and step back. His owner was killed? "Do you live alone?" I guess dogs and cats have to live alone on the streets sometimes. Does that happen to humans? Do we become strays?

"No, I live with another guy, an alien; he's a friend of mine," Marco assures me.

Whew. I don't want to live wild on the streets of Janti.

Zussta steps up to us. "Is everything okay, Britt?" She is protective of me, and I like that.

I have to think for a moment to answer in her language. "Yes, all is good. This is Marco; he is a human pet too. He makes bags, his owner not here anymore."

Zussta looks sideways at Marco, clearly not believing that he makes the bags. "Does he now?" She asks but doesn't wait for an answer. "Well, let's go inside and look at the bags."

Zussta puts her hand on my back and guides me into the store. I'm glad Marco follows. Zussta and the shop lady begin talking.

I turn back to Marco and speak in English. "Where are you from? Are you from Earth?" Who knows, there might be humans on other planets.

"Yes, I'm from Earth. I lived on a small island off Central America. Where are you from?"

I know he means both planet and country. "I'm from Earth too! I lived in Australia."

"I can't believe I'm talking with another human! How old are you?" He's as curious about me as I am about him.

"I'm ten. How old are you?"

He hesitates for a moment, which is odd. "I think I'm thirteen. But since we don't have birthdays here like we did at home, I'm not even sure anymore. How long have you been with your owner?"

I never thought about birthdays. He's right. How will I know how old I am? Does it matter? I won't be going to school or graduating, so I guess age might not be so important. "I think I've been with Zussta for about a month."

"Ah, a newbie." He smiles. "I've been on this planet for about a year, I think. I lose track of time now. I make bags and sell them. I swim here on my own. Or with the help of the sea dragon!"

I give a snort laugh. "A sea dragon?" I'm not sure if I believe him. At home, boys always made-up big stories to try to impress each other or the girls.

"No, really, the dragon likes me for some reason. So, he lets me hold on to his spiny points and swims me down here. Not all the time, only when he's around. Most of the time, I don't see him."

It suddenly gets quiet in the marketplace. I look around and notice all the aliens have stopped and are looking up.

So, I look up.

A sea dragon floats over us, looking down and directly at Marco.

There is a dragon, like, right there.

His blue scales shimmer in the water as he passes by. He is totally huge, as all good dragons should be. Each scale is almost as big as me, and each one has a bit of a different color blue, but they all blend together so well.

And he has ginormous claws that should frighten me, but I'm too much in awe to be afraid.

"Did you summon him?" I whisper

"No," he answers quietly, watching him as well. "They call him The Old One."

Marco pushes my shoulder to get my attention. "Do you want to meet him?" he excitedly asks.

What?

Meet a dragon?

Heck yeah!

I switch to Zobian. "Zussta! Look! Marco say he friend with that. And I can see it close. Can I go? Pleeeeeease."

"Absolutely not!" She fires back. She has never been so firm with me.

"But he is friends with Marco. It's okay." I explain.

The shopkeeper must understand Zobian because she speaks up. "It is something special. The Old One likes the little human. Your human would be safe."

I send a silent thank you to the shop keeper and turn expectantly to Zussta. She still looks unsure… but at least she isn't completely saying 'no' again.

She finally sighs. "I must go with you. Britt be safe."

"She said yes!" I holler at Marco who takes off running.

I chase after him, and Zussta is right behind me.

We make it to another outside door. Marco jumps and slaps the button to open the first door and steps in, waiting for Zussta and me.

Once we are all inside, he jumps and slaps the other button to fill the room with water.

"Zussta! Britt no breathe!" I totally forgot that I can't breathe underwater.

Zussta expertly places the shield on my face, and I press the edges around to make sure it's tight. Marco watches us. "What is that?"

It's so I can breathe underwater. Zussta can hold her breath for a long time, but I need this. Where is yours?"

Marco leans in and inspects my shield. It's weird to have another human's face right in my face, but I hold still. "I don't have one, I hold my breath."

I turn to Zussta and speak in Zobian. "Marco no shield. You have more?"

Like a true parent, she quickly whips out another face shield and applies it to Marco's face.

"Push all around to make sure it's tight." I give him tips.

I kind of feel like an expert; I'm talking in English with a human, in Zobian with an alien, and explaining how to use a face shield to breathe underwater.

His shield is barely on when the room is full of water. Marco flails for a bit, still holding his breath.

"It's okay," I tell him. "Breathe. I promise it works."

His eyes look franticly at me, so I take his hand and take a deep breath in. He relaxes a bit and finally takes a small breath. He smiles and begins to breathe normally.

"This is great! Let's go before The Old One leaves."

And with that, he pushes and swims his way out of the room. I try paddling, but I'm not very good, so Zussta takes my hand and pulls me along as she follows Marco.

The sea dragon must sense us, because I see it make a slow turn in the distance and come towards us.

It gets bigger and bigger and bigger…

I'm not so sure about this anymore.

Zussta actually seems hesitant as well.

But not Marco. He is smiling and floating in place, waiting for the dragon to come to him.

Crikey this thing is huge. I imagine his teeth are huge too.

I quit breathing.

The dragon looks at Marco as it glides by. Its scales shimmer in the water, as if the light comes directly from them.

It's mystical, magical, magnificent… and every other great word I can imagine. I didn't know that something so amazing even existed.

I automatically have respect for this huge creature. It's no wonder the aliens named him The Old One. He has the feel of ancient ancestors.

He turns again, passing so close that I reach out and touch him.

OMG! I just touched a dragon!

I look at Zussta, who also has her hand out, running it along the dragon as he swims by. She looks at me with the same huge smile that I have.

We both look at Marco, who is watching us. He smiles and taps the dragon. It seems to understand and swims away, disappearing into the blue waters.

Zussta makes a motion to go back to the door. I forgot she is still holding her breath. "Marco, Zussta needs to breathe."

He forgot too. He quickly swims down to the door, with Zussta and me close behind.

We are barely in the holding room when he slaps the button, closing the outer door and letting the water drain out. Zussta swims to the top, taking a breath as soon as she can. Well, now we know how long she can stay underwater.

"That was… awesome!" I start talking in English. "The dragon swam right to us. Well, to you, but we were there too. I didn't know dragons were real, I thought they were only in stories. How did you make friends with him? How did he know how to find you? This is something I'll never ever forget in my whole entire life. And you get to swim with him all the time? How do you ever stay on land? I would move into the water. I'm not that great of a swimmer, but I could learn. Sydney is on the coast, but I didn't go to the ocean very often. One time Jilly went swimming and was gone all day with a family. She said she swam so much that her fingers began to wrinkle. Is that true? Do your fingers wrinkle? The dragon had so many colors of blue. I didn't know there were so many different kinds of blue."

Marco looks to Zussta for help. He must not be used to hearing one person talk so much.

Zussta touches me on the shoulder to get my attention. "That was something," she says, amazed.

Yeah, that was something! I'm so excited, but I try to stop talking and enjoy the silence as we walk back to the shop.

"I need a bag." Zussta reminds me.

Oh yeah, we did come here for a bag.

"You stay here," she tells me firmly.

"OK, I stay here," I reply in Zobian.

Marco stays with me.

This kid is amazing! He's a pet but independent and swims with dragons!

We talk some more. "Did you go through orientation with Jordie? I've already been back to the spaceship for a haircut and checkup. Did you meet Stan? He's a square alien who likes humans." He starts with the questions.

"Yes! Yes! I went through orientation and met Stan! And I hung out with the guys in the kitchen. They were funny. Did you meet them?"

Marco laughs. "No, I spent a lot of my time in the hangar and studied the aliens there. This is so cool to be talking to you."

All too soon, Zussta interrupts us again. "Britt, I have a bag for me, but not for you. And it is true, he does make the bags. We go now."

"I have to go." I sadly translate to Marco. "Hey, do you think you can make a bag small enough for me? She thinks I need one, and I'm a little worried why. But if I need it, I guess I need it." I don't tell him that Zussta is a treasure hunter. I'm not sure if I'm supposed to let others know.

Marco stands tall, and his face lights up. "Sure, I can make a bag for you. Jutte made one for me, and it's great. I'll get started on it tonight. It takes a little while, but not too long. I'll have it done soon."

I translate this to Zussta. She opens her one eye big and smiles. "Tell him 'Thank you'."

"Thank you," I repeat to Marco. "So, maybe I'll see you around again one day. Wow, another human!" I'm so happy I could hug him. But I don't.

"I know, right!" He agrees with me. "Okay, bye." He waves as Zussta pulls me back to the doors to leave.

I'm walking backward as Zussta gently pulls me along. When Marco is out of sight, I finally turn around and walk forward. "Zussta see that? It was another human. He talk to me. And he make a bag for me. Another human - I'm not all alone!"

Zussta stops suddenly, pulls me to the side of the aisle, and squats down to my level. "Britt never be alone. I will always be here. I care for you very much. I hope that you will know that. I will always be here for you."

Well, now I feel bad. "I know. I not mean it like that, I know I'm with you and not alone."

And then she hugs me.

For the first time, Zussta hugs me.

I hug her back.

And everything just might be great.

Chapter 38

Soon we are cruising along in the spaceship. Before she can answer, I'm pointing. "Look, another mabo!" I can barely make out the spot of nothingness, the wormhole, but I definitely see it.

Zussta is impressed with my ability. "It's good that you can see them. Please keep pointing them out to me, and I'll look on the map so we can see where they all go."

Oh, I now have a job. I like that. I plaster my hands and face against the window, looking for more wormholes.

"How about we look for the pala today? Are you ready?"

Heck yeah, I'm ready! This is bonza that we are hunting treasure. "I've been training my whole life for this."

Zussta tilts her head and glances at me sideways. "But you young? You're whole life not very long?"

Why does everyone say that? Just because I'm young doesn't mean I'm not amazing. "Well, yeah, but I've still been training since…" I hold my hand flat above my hip, "since this tall. Maybe not a long life, but my life." My voice is clipped and short.

"You are right," Zussta quickly says.

I'm not mad, but I sometimes get frustrated with adults. "That's okay; you not know. How old Zussta? Britt young, is Zussta old? Marco's owner died. You not die, right?"

"No worry, I be here for a long time. Jordie said you do not have care people. Is that normal for human children?"

It doesn't bother me to talk about my lack of family, so I'm not hurt by her question. "Maybe normal, maybe not, but it happens. I don't remember my adults. And I be with other kids have no adults too, so it was normal for me. But many human children have adults."

Thankfully, Zussta doesn't give me that sad voice and head tilt that most adults do when they find out I'm an orphan. I hate pity. "Well, now you have me, and I am happy I have you. Britt happy?"

"Yes, you are nice and a treasure hunter, so yay. I never find treasure. But I walk and find great stuff. I see things good."

Zussta agrees. "I know; you've been training your whole life for this."

"Right!" She so gets me.

"Mabo there," I warn her. I don't need to yell each time I see one anymore.

She checks the spaceship computer. "Yes, that one we want. It will take us to Sononi."

"Where the pala is ?" I'm picturing hidden rooms and jumping over waterfalls. Oh, this is going to be a grand adventure.

"I'm not sure; that's why we go look. I study the maps, and the pala may be in lots of places. It's not easy to find. That and it…" She said a new word that I don't understand. What? What does the pala do?

Ms. Williams said that anything worthwhile was worth working for. Maybe that includes the pala. I bet it's not sitting out in the open. Do we have to dig for it? "But you not know where?" This worries me a little bit.

"No, no one is sure where."

I guess that's why it's a treasure – and we have to hunt for it.

"Hold on." She says right before we enter the wormhole. Zooming just doesn't get old. I love flying through here with the black and white flashing past. We bank right and then go nose down. Now that I wasn't ready for! I shriek and throw my arms out, but thankfully the seat holds me in. I'm not used to falling straight down, face first. Thankfully, we fly flat and soon are spit out the other end. Whew, that was a wild ride.

I sit a moment, trying to get right again. I take a deep breath and look at Zussta. She's looking at me with a wide-open-mouth smile.

We both burst out laughing! That was awesome!

I throw my arms up. "Yay!" She throws both arms up in victory as well.

Once we calm down, I look around. I'm amazed at how many different-looking planets there are. "Do all planets have air on them? Can we go anywhere?"

I see eight, nine, ten planets. Ten planets around the front of the spaceship, but far away. One is purple… what kind of life lives on a purple planet? There is a yellow and green planet, two that are completely yellow, and one that is red. Don't we have a red planet in our galaxy? I'm lost in the idea of ten new worlds and forgot I asked her a question.

The front of Zussta's face is looking out her side window, but she looks at me with her back head eye. "No, few planets have air. Sononi no have air for us, but it's okay."

It's okay? What does she mean it's okay? "I need air," I tell her, trying not to panic too much. I don't want to die today. "Zussta, I need air. Did Jordie tell?"

She turns and looks at me with her front eye. "No worry, the face mask will let you breathe on Sononi."

I squint at her, not sure I'm ready to put my faith in a thin piece of plastic over my face to save my life. "Trust me. I not let you get hurt." I can see she is trying not to laugh, which angers me more. It's not funny that I am careful with my life. I glare at her harder.

She stops laughing. "I promise; you will be good. I just got you and not let anything bad happen to you."

"Why you want a pet? Did one day you think *I want a human*?" I guess I never thought about why she wanted me. Well, not me specifically, but a human pet.

She pauses before answering. "It is only me. Not many Zobians want to treasure hunt with me. Most live no fun lives. I like to do more. I want a pet to go with me. Humans make good pets and maybe go with me on treasure hunts."

Wow, that is probably the most honest anyone has ever been with me. I suppose it's easy to open up to a pet. I used to make confessions to the dogs or cats at my foster homes. I didn't think they ever cared what I was saying, but I feel honored that she spoke honestly to me. But then again, she may think of me as nothing more than a pet that she can say anything to.

Who am I going to tell?

My emotions flash between liking that she trusts me and being hurt that I'm nothing more than a new puppy to her.

Before I can dwell on this odd situation for too long, Zussta turns the ship and points us toward the purple planet.

Ohhh, I get to see the purple planet!

"We are close to Sononi. We land, and you stay in your seat. I'll get ready and help you with face shield. Stay close to me, do not go away."

Why would I go away and risk getting lost on a foreign planet?

We get closer and closer to Sononi. For a while, purple was my favorite color. But now I like coral best, but purple is pretty. So, I'll probably like this purple planet

We fly to the planet, and all the air – or not air- is purple. On Earth, the astronauts see blue, and it's the water. But here, the purple is in the sky and all around us. Everything is purple.

A spaceship is directly in front of us!

Zussta yells '*boakma*,' and swerves hard so we don't hit another spaceship. We are both breathing hard, me from fear, her from anger. "Why is he here?"

I think she is talking to herself because how would I know why he is here?

I don't even know who he is.

Now is a good time to be quiet.

Zussta glances at me. "Another treasure hunter, and he not nice. Listen to me. You stay close to me. Do not let him at you."

She says this with such fierceness that I'm terrified of that alien. Maybe I should wait in the ship.

She is concentrating on her flying. We move in one direction, then quickly turn and fly another way. I glance at the ship's computer screen and see the other ship close behind us.

Zussta mumbles *boakma* over and over to herself. I wonder if she is saying a swear word. "Fine," she says to herself, "if you want me, then let's go."

I don't like the sound of that.

She nose-dives straight down, and I see land coming up fast. I push back into my seat, still keeping quiet. At the last moment, she pulls up and, bam, we land on a purple planet.

Huh, look at that, the ground really is purple.

She quickly grabs my face shield. "Come here." I don't ask questions. I lean forward and let her press the plastic around my face. As she puts her shield on, I press the edges around mine again. I'm not taking any chances of not being able to breathe.

Zussta quickly puts her face shield on, too.

"Stay down. I be right back," she snaps at me. I obey and slump down.

Maybe treasure hunting isn't as happy-go-lucky as I thought it would be.

Chapter 39

I'm slouched down in the spaceship, but I can't seem to stop myself from crawling into her seat and peeking out the window. Her big square body is storming towards the other ship. She is almost there before the other guy gets out. She's quick and fierce.

A pure white alien climbs down from his ship. Now, I've seen a lot of aliens in my day, I hung out with some strange-looking guys in the kitchen, but this guy is weird. He has two heads that are way too small for his body and four arms. I squint to see. and he has three eyes straight across each of his heads. I've never seen this type of alien before, but my time on the streets taught me how to spot bad guys - and this is one slimy-looking creature. And by Zussta's stance, she doesn't like him either.

This spaceship must not be soundproof because I can hear them arguing. I can't make out what they are saying, but it certainly isn't pleasant greetings.

I quickly duck down as the scary alien glances at the ship. I don't think Zussta wants him to see me, and that scares me again. I cautiously peek out the window just as Zussta gets to the door. I scoot over and wait for her to talk. That's one thing I've learned - if someone is angry, let them start talking first.

She mutters to herself as she gets into the ship. I wait. She takes a deep breath and looks at me. "That is Jama, and I don't why he is here. He following us. He want to find the pala without doing the hard work to get it."

And then she says '*boakma*' again, and I assume it's a swear word in the Zobian language. I try hard not to giggle but swear words are funny in any language. Adults usually try to censor their words around kids, but then again, no one thinks to watch their language around pets.

She relaxes and smiles at me. "He says he go, but he will watch where we go. We will have to go different way to lose him." We watch as Jama's ship flies away.

Okay, it's game on again.

She tells me our plans. "We have to go there," she points to the left. "But we go that way first. Are you okay to walk?" She is pointing to the right.

I nod but don't speak. I don't want to interrupt her. I'm confused where we're going. But no worries, I'll just follow her.

"It be dark and you maybe not see, so hold onto me. It be hard walk. Do you remember we did running and jumping?"

I nod again.

"Today we will do that. Maybe not find the pala today; but find another place to look. And run fast and jump together."

Yay, we get to run a real-life obstacle course. She seems to be done talking, so I start nervously chattering. "That alien was scary, but I'm okay. I can run and jump and swim. This shield good. And if we swim, I can kind of do that too. Maybe need help. A little scared of the dark. Can I hold onto something or only your leg?"

I don't know the Zobian word for a torch. A torch would sure come in handy in the dark.

She wobbles her head and looks around again. "Are you ready?"

"Yes!" I shout. I don't mean to, but my nerves and excitement can't hold back my voice. I'm scared and excited at the same time.

Zussta opens the door and gets out. I take a deep breath, happy to know that the face shield is on tight. She fills her waterproof bag with some stuff from the back of her ship and straps it onto the front of her body. It looks backwards, but I don't correct her. I'm kind of proud that a human made that bag.

She holds her hands out, and I let her pick me up and set me on the ground. I look behind us to make sure Jama isn't still here. I don't see him, but that doesn't mean he's not around.

This is not a barren planet like our moon. Not that I've ever been to the moon, but I've seen pictures, and it looks empty. Not this place. It's a purple forest, but these are not normal-looking trees. The plants are about three meters high and fluffy. Instead of individual leaves, the entire plant looks like a cat that went through a clothes dryer. Fluffy.

I reach out to touch one. It's solid! So, it looks fluffy but isn't… so weird.

Zussta grabs a rope from the back of the spaceship and closes the door. "Here, hold this." She hands me one end of the rope while tying the other to her backpack/frontpack thing. This will come in handy and is much better than a collar and leash. At least she didn't tie it around me.

"Come on, we go."

She doesn't waste any time.

She ducks down a bit to stay hidden in the plants and walks fast. I have to trot to keep up with her. We head to the right, and I have to keep dodging the trees. But I do well and keep up with her.

I trot while Zussta simply walks in this direction for about ten minutes when she makes a sudden turn. I bet we are circling back now. I look at the purple sky but don't see the bad guy anywhere. It makes me uncomfortable not to know where he is. It's like when you see a spider, but then by the time you get your shoe off to kill it, it's gone. I hate that feeling. I know he's out there somewhere.

We head in the new direction for about twenty minutes, and I'm starting to wear out. I'm strong, but I can only run for so long. I give the rope a tug. "Zussta, I'm tired."

She stops to let me rest. "Okay, you are doing very good for being so small." She gives my hair a slight tug.

I stand up straight and smile. I'm glad she's impressed with me.

She reaches into her bag and pulls out a round container and hands it to me.

I patiently hold it, ready to give it back if she needs it.

She tilts her head. "It's water. Are you thirsty?"

I'm so totally thirsty, but this isn't a glass of water. It's a round red ball with no opening. Does she know that the water I drink is a liquid? I turn it over in my hands and look to her for help.

"Here, let me show you; do this." She points to a spot that is barely a shade lighter. She probably sees it as a completely different color. She blows a slight breath on the ball.

Sure enough, a spout pops up.

"What happens if lots of wind? Will we lose all the water? I might need more, I very thirsty. And what about this on my face; how does water go to my mouth?"

"Push here," she taps behind my right ear. "Hold your breath. Drink. Let go when done."

So, pushing behind my ear drops my face shield? I'm not sure I like the sound of that.

"It's okay; you try. I here for you."

I guess this is when the whole trust thing kicks in. I have to trust that she doesn't want me to die.

I take a deep breath and press the spot behind my right ear. I hold the spout up to my face, and it passes through the shield and to my lips. I quickly gulp the water. It's cold and the ball holds more than I thought it would. I stop drinking and quickly let go of the spot by my ear.

I'm afraid to try to breathe. What if I did it wrong?

"Breathe," Zussta tells me.

I try to take a breath… it works! I'm able to breathe again.

I ask Zussta, "It only open a spot by my mouth, or it open my face?" There is a lot to learn when it comes to alien technology. How does the shield work? How much water does the ball hold? I wonder if this is how cats feel when they try to get a treat from inside a puzzle toy. They have to figure it all out.

She doesn't answer, but that's okay; I know I talk a lot, and adults don't always answer me.

I hand the ball back to her and pick up my end of the rope. "I'm ready again."

"We almost there. You do great, but it not always be easy. I help you, but I know you can handle it." She picks up her end of the rope and begins her fast walk. I'm trotting behind her before I can answer.

Treasure hunting wasn't meant to be easy. I suck it up and don't complain. I usually try not to complain too much, not like Anna. In school, she whined and complained all the time. It really got on my nerves when she started with the drama - and she did it a lot. I vowed never to be like that.

I keep trotting behind my alien owner through the purple jungle with the fluffy-looking trees.

Zussta stops so suddenly that I run straight into her.

Oof, I almost fall backwards, but she catches me.

Through the trees, I see what looks like an opening to a cave high above the trees. It's so small that Zussta will probably have to crawl through it. In the movies I've seen, the cave openings are usually huge. But not this one.

"What is this? How do you say?"

She says a word that I assume means '*cave*'. Ok, now I know the word for cave. One day I'll know all the Zobian words.

We hike almost straight up the mountain until we get to the top.

"We go in. Are you ready? Hold on and stay close." She says as she hands me one end of the rope

Yeah, you don't have to tell me twice. It's too bad she doesn't have a torch so I can see her, but I'll be fine.

I've trained for this my whole life.

We go in.

Chapter 40

Sure enough, Zussta gets down and crawls through the cave opening, but I can walk into it just fine. Sometimes being small has its perks.

I can still see a little bit when we get inside. Well, I can see a little way around me and around the opening. Zussta stands up straight, so it's larger than it looks from the outside.

She looks back at me. "Do you still hold the rope?" She asks.

"Yep." I hold it up to show her that I've wrapped it around my wrist and am holding it in my hand. I wish I could see in the dark like she can. But I notice it's not completely dark in here. I look up and notice small openings in the ceiling, letting small streams of light through. It's not enough for me to see very far, but it's better than being in total darkness.

Total darkness is the stuff of nightmares.

I shiver and start thinking happy thoughts before I freak myself out. Pretty flowers outlined in white; pretty leaves outlined in black; the colorful planet; the beautiful tree, Lamenana.

Zussta walks further into the cave, and I'm close on her heels thinking happy thoughts. I look around but don't see much. I can tell a wall is close to my right, but I can't see the outline of the wall. Hopefully, my eyes will adjust soon, and I can see a bit better. I look over my shoulder and take one last look at the opening of the cave.

Thankfully I don't see the bad guy. Maybe he didn't see us come in. We walk deeper into the cave.

"Is the pala in here?" I loud whisper to Zussta.

She answers back in a normal voice. "I don't think so. But we maybe find where it is."

Like clues? Are we looking for clues?

"I be looking for something?" I want to be helpful.

Zussta stops and tilts her head to me. "Can you see inside?" We are still learning how we each see items and colors.

"Well, no, not very good," I admit. But there is a little bit of light so that I can see close to me, but not far. "If you tell me what to look for, I can help. I not ever see a pala is. Is it big, like me, or big like you?"

I want to do more than just follow behind her hanging onto a rope. I'm better than that.

I have skills.

"I tell you later. But now, we look for what not normal here. The pala was here one time, but then it move. We have to find where."

Well, I could probably spot odd things in an Earth cave, but who knows what's supposed to be in an alien cave? I don't let her know my dilemma.

Yeah, that's actually me. I'm out of place on this planet.

Again, I keep that to myself.

"Okay, I watch," I confirm my commitment to help.

I notice a shift in the light.

The opening is quite far behind us now, but I spot a movement of a shadow back there.

"Zussta! Maybe Jama here." I move closer to her legs.

Zussta stops. I assume she is using the back eye to watch the opening. She talks in a hushed tone as well. "Why you say that?"

"The light move." I'm whispering because I don't know how well that alien can hear. Maybe he doesn't know exactly where we are.

"Good job," she whispers back and moves us deeper into the cave, but closer along the wall this time.

I grip the rope tighter and stay close to her. I see some light up ahead. My eyes are adjusting to the low light, and when we get closer to the next area, there is another small hole in the ceiling. These must be air holes. But who would have lived here?

Or what would have lived here?

And why do they need air holes if there's no air?

They must be holes to let light in. That makes more sense.

I see we are in a large, open area. "Whoa." I stop and stare in wonder.

Zussta stops as well. "I have been here before, and I like it every time." She agrees that this place is amazing.

I bet about a hundred people could easily fit into this room. It's ginormous.

I look around but don't see anything out of place, at least nothing that seems totally weird. But I double-check. "I only see walls. What you see?"

She scans the large room. "I see nothing. We keep going."

We walk around the outer edge of the room until we find another path. I'm glad we kept near the wall. Walking in the center of that cave would have left us out in the open, and I've learned that's not always a good place to be.

It gets darker as we leave the big room, but not pitch black yet. I look up and notice small openings about every ten meters.

Yep, something definitely used to live here.

A shiver runs down my spine.

I walk closer to Zussta.

Zussta pauses. "Are you okay?" She checks with me.

I actually am doing okay. "I'm good," I answer. "Small lights help me see," I say as I point to the ceiling.

"Good, we keep going."

I didn't know turning around now was an option. I guess if I got hurt or totally freaked out, she would have no other choice but to take me back to the ship.

I glance back again but don't see anyone.

There are tunnels that turn off from this main route. I really hope she knows her way and isn't lost. We pass those and take the third tunnel on the left.

I still have a hold on the rope, but I'm looking everywhere. I see the holes in the ceiling, and the walls are dark. I veer left and reach out to touch the wall. It's rough but not sharp. And thankfully, it's not soft and fuzzy either – that would be gross.

I start to giggle at the thought of a fuzzy cave wall. But hey, anything is possible on other planets. Ms. Williams once said to expect the unexpected. But how is that possible? How can you expect something that you have no idea about? That would be like knowing the future. It's not possible. Why do people say things like that? Why not say, '*Be ready for some really weird stuff*'? Now that I can understand. I have no idea what the really weird stuff would be, but I know not to expect normal cave walls on a purple planet. So, these normal cave walls seem wrong.

Maybe I should stop touching them.

I hear an echo.

I can't figure out what the original sound is or what the echo is, but I hear an echo. It's as if a sound happens, and then it immediately happens again and again.

"Do you hear that?" I ask.

"Yes. What do you hear?" She asks. I don't know the alien word for echo, so I default to a normal answer.

"I don't know. But I hear something- and hear something - and hear something." I get quieter as I say each '*something.*'

Since Zussta and I see colors differently, I wonder if we hear differently. Or maybe I hear better than she does.

"There is another room. You like this. Maybe we see things." She doesn't slow down with her walking, but her back-of-the-head eye is making sure I'm still here. "Do you still see movement behind us?" She looks at me and then back down the way we came.

"No, I not see anything." I know it doesn't mean he's not there, but I'm hoping it means exactly that. I don't want to run into a mean alien while we are deep in a cave.

I see a glow ahead. Not a bright light, just a soft glow.

What would cause an echo and a soft glow?

Zussta doesn't seem afraid, but I hold the rope tighter.

The walls open further ahead. Here comes the next room. I'm a bit excited since Zussta said I'll like this next room. We stop at an entrance to a huge area. You could fit several football fields in here, and the stands, and all the screaming fans. I mean, this place is even bigger than the place with all the spaceships at orientation.

We are standing on a ledge overlooking a huge open area…

And a lake.

Chapter 41

There is a lake.

In a cave.

And it's beautiful.

The water is crystal clear and a mixture of swirling blues and greens.

I look up and see many small air holes.

That explains the glow.

I'm speechless.

Zussta nudges me. I look up and see her smiling down at me. "Do you like? There's more."

There's more?

I smile back. This really is cool.

We walk forward, standing on a ledge overlooking the ground below and the lake. There is another level of rocks around the water, but I'm not sure how we are going to get to the lower level. By my calculations, we are probably ten meters up. I look for stairs or a ramp of sorts. I don't see either.

"We go there? How we get there?" I'm pacing back and forth, looking for stairs.

Zussta smiles. "We go down." She says as she points straight down.

We climb down?

I get down on my hands and knees and look over the edge.

Hmmm.

Zussta turns around, lies on her belly, and scooches her legs over the edge.

Okay, I guess we're climbing down.

This is my first real-world test of my ninja street skills.

"I know you can do this. I go first, and then you. If you fall, I will catch you."

I tie the rope around my waist as she starts down first. When she is about half way down, I turn around, and lie on my belly. I scoot backwards until my legs are over the edge and use my feet to find a ledge, or a hole, or anything. I poke my feet around and find a small step.

Okay, I can do this.

I slowly make my way over the ledge.

I'm doing it!

I feel for a hole with my other foot, then I find places to grab hold of with my hands. I look down and see Zussta directly below me. She is looking up with her one big eye, smiling.

I keep climbing down.

I'm slow, but I keep moving.

Hand lower, foot lower, hand lower, foot lower.

Zussta calls to me. "I'm down. You do great, Britt. I'm here, but you can do this."

She believes I can do this.

I believe I can do this.

I try not to get too excited and keep my focus on the wall.

Hand lower, foot lower, hand lower, foot lower.

I feel Zussta hold my waist. "Okay, you here. I got you."

I let go, and she sets me on the ground next to the lake.

I look at the lake, then up the wall I just climbed down, then at Zussta.

"Yay!" She throws her hands up over her head in our victory stance.

"Yay!" I holler back with my hands up high.

I've always been proud of myself when I would climb fences and find new ways to get to the park, but it's nice having someone else proud of me when I do something like scale down a wall.

I untie the rope from my waist and let it fall to the ground. Zussta releases her end as well. She still has her water bag on her front, but she doesn't put the rope away. I suppose we will need it to get back up and get out of the cave.

I walk to the edge near the lake and look down. The water is only about a meter below. And then I see it. Since the water is crystal clear, I can see the bottom… or at least what's sitting on the bottom.

I see colors everywhere. Reds, blues, greens, yellows… all sparkling from the small beams of light.

Is that the treasure?

Did we find the treasure?

"What is that? Is that the pala?" I ask without taking my eyes off the jewels.

We're rich. Like, beyond all our dreams rich.

"No, that is not the pala."

She says it so matter-of-factly that I'm let down. So, they are just colored rocks. Or, maybe they're jewels.

I can hardly breathe looking at the diamonds, rubies, and other precious stones.

I tell her my thoughts. "Those are special on Earth; many humans want them. Too bad you cannot bring to Earth."

She looks like she doesn't believe me. "Colored rocks are important to humans? Why?"

Well… I'm stumped. "I don't know; I just know they are." But now I'm second-guessing things. Why do humans consider colored stones to be treasures? She's right. Rubies don't *actually do* anything. But the entire planet of Janti is the color of jewels, so maybe that's why they aren't impressive to her. Everything looks like jewels.

"We not here for the stones?" This whole place is confusing me.

"No. The pala was here. We see if we can find where is now."

"Why we not ask who took it?" It seems pretty easy to me.

"Because the *vibo* not tell us." She simply answers.

What was that word? *Vibo*? I shrug my shoulders to show her I don't understand. So she curls her fingers and makes a scary face.

Monster? We're looking for something owned by a monster?

That doesn't sound good.

"Will we have to take the pala from the vibo? Or it go away? It stay with the pala or put it somewhere else?" I shakily ask. I like to know what I'm walking into. Ms. Williams always said that if you have all the information, then you can make a better decision. I need to know if we are going to be sneaking up on an alien monster or if we can waltz in there and pluck the pala from the ground. Sneaking treasure away from a creature sounds exciting… until you actually have to do it.

She is still glancing around the cave when she answers me. "Maybe both. The vibo may be there or not." She shrugs like it's no big deal.

Okay, maybe the vibo isn't as scary as I was thinking. She doesn't seem to be afraid. I don't think she's afraid of anything. Maybe it feeds on grass and flowers. I can handle that.

I'm wondering what a clue might look like when I get that weird feeling that we are being watched. I look around, at the water, at the entrance to this cave room, and I don't see anything. But the feeling doesn't go away.

"Zussta," I whisper out the side of my mouth. "I think we are being watched." I try to act calm and cool.

But not Zussta.

She spins in circles and yells out, "Who's watching us? Who's out there?"

Well, alright then. I guess the other option is to call out the stalker.

Yep, she isn't afraid at all.

The mean white alien, Jama, steps into the doorway. I was right; he has been following us. But then again, Zussta figured he would.

He is looking down at us with a slimy smile.

I ease behind Zussta.

They start talking loudly in a different alien language. I don't understand the argument, but he seems to say he will find the pala first - or take it from Zussta if we find it first. I think Zussta is telling him that's not going to happen. At least, this is what I imagine they are saying. For all I know, they're talking about the weather.

Then it hits me. How are we going to get out of here? We have to climb up the wall to the ledge in order to get out. And the alien guy is blocking the way.

Oh, I'm not liking this.

I bet Zussta can easily climb the wall, but I can't. She's making motions for him to come on down with us. Good, that would put us on even ground. I like the way she thinks.

Maybe I finally have a mentor and don't have to learn everything about ninja skills on my own.

Jama is pacing back and forth on the ledge, and Zussta turns, facing him each time. I keep scooting behind her legs as she swivels.

And that's when I notice the writing on the wall.

There are symbols and pictures low on the wall across the lake. I can't see it all, but I can see most of it. It's about at about the height of my knees. Good thing Jordie checked my eyes and said I have good eyesight.

I don't want to interrupt the argument to tell Zussta, but I don't want to leave without making sure she sees it too.

Should I say something or stay quiet?

Yeah, I'm not good at staying quiet.

"Hey, Zussta," I interrupt by tapping her leg. "Maybe on wall say where the pala is."

She stops yelling at the mean alien guy and quietly asks me. "What is on wall?"

She's quiet, so I know to be quiet, too. I start to point across the lake. "Over there…"

"No point!" She hisses.

I quickly put my arm down. Got it; we don't want the mean Jama to know what we're saying. "Across the lake. Low down on the wall. See?" I quietly ask her. Maybe the bad guy understands Zobian.

Zussta doesn't look. Instead, she goes back to yelling at the guy. But he knows something is up and stops pacing.

With my toe, I secretly draw one of the symbols in the sand. She looks up at the ceiling, but the eye in the back of her head sees the symbol. She quickly steps on it, erasing it.

We need to figure out how to get rid of this guy before he sees the writing.

But then again, maybe the writing doesn't say anything.

It's not knowing enough that frustrates me.

Chapter 42

Zussta storms to the wall, quickly scales it, and stands in front of the alien guy, yelling at him before he and I even know what happened.

Wow, she is fast for a stocky alien!

And totally not afraid of anyone.

I'm standing here all by myself, watching my alien owner lady argue with another alien. I've never been in this situation before, and I'm not sure what to do.

Do I stay still? Do I move to the side of the cave near the wall so I'm not standing in the open? Do I start to climb up the wall? Do I cry?

I choose to move to the side of the wall; I don't want to be standing in the open, being all vulnerable. And I'm fighting not to cry.

I'm scared.

What if he hurts Zussta? Then what happens to me?

I sniffle, and a sob sneaks out. Zussta hears me.

Without thinking, she quickly scales down the wall again. She comes to me and squats down to my level. "What happen, Britt?"

I haven't cried in front of her yet, so I get it that she doesn't know what's happening. "I'm scared." I quietly tell her.

She uses one of her fingers without the suction cup to push on the spot behind my ear and the other hand to brush away a tear.

I hold my breath.

"Do your eyes have water when you scared?"

I use my sleeve to wipe my nose.

She lets go of the spot, and I can breathe normally again.

I take a deep breath and stop the tears. "Yes, scared or sad."

"I'm very sorry I scare you." She says as she hugs me and continues to talk softly." It's okay. He and I talk loud but never hurt each other." Then she mumbles to herself, "At least I haven't hurt him *yet*."

That makes me laugh a little. She smiles, stands up, and turns to Jama. But he is gone. Huh, maybe a kid crying scared him away.

"Stay here. I go see where he is," she says and stands up, looking down at me. "You okay to stay here?"

I nod. "Yep, I'm good now. Really. Sorry about that, Britt scared, but I'm okay now. I not afraid for long. One time…"

Zussta interrupts me before I can tell her about the time I heard scratching on my window at night, but it turned out to be a tree branch and not a flying monster. "Tell me later. I'll be right back."

I stand up straight, my crying over. I'm not scared, and I don't feel bad anymore. Zussta is not going to get hurt.

Zussta climbs the rock wall and strides out the doorway, turning left.

I don't think anything scares her.

I see her walking past the doorway, checking the other direction. Before long, she is back. She smiles at me and climbs down to me. "He gone. Now, what you see on the wall?"

Oh, we're back on that. Good. This time I point. "Right there, see, pictures on the wall. Maybe words?"

She looks where I'm pointing. "I no see. Show me."

She steps back and lets me take the lead. There is a small ledge around the lake to the other side. The path is a regular size for me, and I can easily walk it. Zussta has to turn sideways and carefully walk the ledge. I see the suction cups on her fingers out as she holds onto the wall.

Those really do come in handy. Suction cups on her hands are handy. I laugh at my joke. Man, I'm funny sometimes.

I regain control and wait for her to get across to the other side before leading her to the wall. "Right here." It's plain as day. I feel weird for being so obvious.

"You see pictures on wall?" She asks.

"You don't?" I ask back.

We're still figuring out that we see things differently like she can see in the dark and I can't. But now, this is the second time I can see something she can't. First, it was wormholes; now, it's secret writings on a cave wall.

I stand tall and explain what I see to her. "It starts here," I motion to the entire area without touching the wall. "And it goes to here." I walk to the end of the symbols.

"Interesting," she says more to herself than to me. She is moving around and looking at the wall from different directions. She gently touches the wall with one finger but doesn't smudge the writing. I tell her this. And she looks back and forth from me to the wall. "You made picture on the ground. Was that it?"

"That was one picture I see. There are more."

"Can you draw what you see?"

I feel like I am helping and am important. I like this feeling.

"Sure." I crouch down, look at the wall, and then draw what I see. It's harder than I thought it would be because I'm trying to get the symbols just right. I don't want to put down the wrong words and have it say something completely different. With my luck, I would send us in the opposite direction of where we need to go.

I assume this is a clue, not just some random child's drawings. What if it's the creature's kid drawing on the wall? It could be a picture of a tree and a flower, and we would run off searching for that specific tree or flower.

I'll draw what I see and let Zussta tell me what it means.

I use my finger to copy the symbols carefully. I sometimes have to go back and fix what I have outlined in the sand, but I'm confident that I copied the top row of symbols correctly.

I stand up and stretch. "That's only some of it; there more," I tell her. "Can you read? What does it say?"

I step out of the way and let her circle in front of my drawings. She tilts her head from one side to the other. She studies it more. "You draw more; this not make sense." She says while still looking at the symbols on the ground.

I get down and start copying the second line of symbols. Maybe aliens don't read from left to right. Maybe they read from top to bottom or skip every other drawing or something strange like that. That would explain why it doesn't make sense.

I sometimes forget not every species is the same as humans.

I take my time and slowly copy each picture the best I can. Now I'm also trying to make sure to line up the drawings with the one above it.

I have to draw it exactly as I see it.

I finally finish and stand up. "There. That all I see."

"Hmmm…." She studies it again. She walks back and forth, sometimes crouching down to get a closer look, then standing back up and walking around it all again.

The suspense is killing me!

"Well, what it say?"

"It says we have to look in the …" She tells me while still studying the ground.

"What is that word? Where we go?" I'm telling her I don't understand the meaning of the word she said.

"Like this," she draws a bumpy circle in the sand. "Like this in the sky."

Clouds? Is she saying clouds? "We have to look in clouds?" I question her. Maybe I wrote it down wrong. I double-check my writing with that on the wall. Yep, it's all the same.

I guess we have to look in the clouds.

She stands up and wipes all my hard work away. I get it; we don't want the scary alien to see it. "We go to clouds."

She says it so matter-of-fact that it almost sounds like a natural thing to do.

Almost, but not quite.

Chapter 43

"We go out a different way. Jama no follow us," Zussta tells me as we turn in the opposite direction of the way we came.

I'm not sure I like this, but she didn't ask what I wanted. So, I follow her. This must be how dogs feel, I doubt humans would ask their pets about decisions such as which way to go.

I look around for clues on the walls along the way, but it's too dark for me to see much. I kind of like holding onto the rope to follow Zussta; this way, I don't have to pay close attention to where we are going. I look all around, taking it all in.

I'm on a purple planet in a cave looking for treasure. I bet all the kids at the group home would be jealous if they knew where I was. Well, except Mary, she's afraid of everything, she probably wouldn't like being here. But that's why Jordie chose me and not her; I can handle this.

While I still don't like the thought of being a pet, I am a bit proud that I was selected to be with Zussta. Jordie knew I would do well.

It must be because of my ninja street skills.

I got mad skills.

I laugh at my joke and almost trip over my own feet. Zussta stops and looks back at me. "Are you okay?"

I can't admit that I'm making silly jokes to myself. I play it cool instead. "Yeah, I'm okay. Can I have water, please?"

She hands me the strange little ball, and I wonder if there is any water left in it since I drank a lot last time. I turn it over until I see the spot that is a little lighter in color. I push the area behind my ear and blow. Sure enough, the spout pops out again. I hold my breath while I drink. Somehow there is still water in the ball.

When I'm done, I push the spot again to close the shield.

What if my face shield doesn't' seal back up again? Is the air is made of acid burns my lungs? Is there any air that I can breathe?

I take a small breath.

No worries, I can breathe again.

I like all the new gadgets that Zussta has. Face shields, little balls of water, and the bubble that takes us through the ground and to her house… our house.

Zussta stops, and I almost bump into her again. I gotta start paying more attention, or at least not walk so close to her. But I don't want to be far away either.

I look around her legs and see what has stopped her.

Nothing. I see only the cave tunnel with light holes from way up.

"What's wrong?" I ask.

Zussta takes a deep breath. "I have never been this way, but I know about it. Remember jumping and running? This is what we have to do here."

Here? Like the obstacle course here? I still only see an empty tunnel.

Zussta turns around and squats down to my level. "We have to work together. Zussta help Britt and Britt help Zussta. Sometimes we go fast, sometimes we go slow. Okay?"

Well, now I'm a bit freaked out.

This is it, a true treasure-hunting adventure, in a real cave, on a strange, purple planet.

OMG. OMG. OMG.

I look into Zussta's one big eye. I can do this.

Really, I can do this.

"Okay, but I no see anything ahead. What do you see?"

She doesn't have to turn around to look down the tunnel; she uses her back-of-the-head eye to explain it to me. "Some places we walk, some places you fall down. Do not fall down."

Um, I wasn't planning on it.

"You step where I step. Do not go to the side." She stands up. "And still hold the rope, just in case."

Just in case? Just in case I fall into a huge hole?

OMG. OMG. OMG.

She looks down at me. "You training for this your whole life," she says in a serious voice.

She's right. This is exactly what I've been training for.

I can do this.

"Okay. I'm ready. I step where you step."

Zussta takes a step forward, and I have to jump to get to the same place. We do this six times. She steps, and I jump. Step, jump. Step, jump.

I look down and the ground shimmers just like when it's really hot outside, and it looks like the ground is shimmering and moving. That's what I see.

I want to reach down and touch where the ground shimmers to see if it's moving or not there. But I can't stop, otherwise the rope will pull me forward.

She stops, and I stay put. I'm further away from her than I like. She takes one step to the right. "Jump here, next to me."

I jump where she says.

"Good. Now let go of rope." She doesn't tell me why, and I don't ask. I figure I will do exactly as she says, when she says.

We're no longer in a cave tunnel. Here it's open to a huge hole with only a ledge along the wall huge hole.

She wraps up the rope and puts it inside her frontpack. When she bends down and looks me in the eye, I know it's important. "This be hard. Listen to me and do as I say. Do you see rocks?"

I couldn't see why the floor was shimmering, so I understand the question. We have to figure out what each of us can see. "I see rocks at walls." I point to either side.

"Yes, we go to side, but we go fast. When I say run, you run. When I say stop, you stop. No questions."

I nod. I got it.

"Move here." She points directly next to the wall. I stand there.

"We run together. Like at home, we run and help each other. Ready?"

I'm ready.

"Go fast!" she yells, and we both start running.

I'm watching above and below me, and I'm watching her.

I run balancing on a small strip of rocks.

I jump over a gaping hole. I don't look down.

"Down!" She yells.

I drop, and a beam of light shoots over me. What the heck was that???

"Run!" She yells again.

I jump up and run.

I run across a wide bridge while she has to balance behind me.

There's a tall ledge at the end. I pause, and she grabs me and hoists me up.

It's so high that she can barely reach to the top, so she pushes my bum, and I fly upwards, grabbing the ledge. I pull myself up and move out of the way. She grabs the ledge and pulls herself up.

There's no time to relax.

"Down!" She yells again.

I drop to my belly just as another beam of light shoots over me.

I have no idea what it is or where it comes from, but I sure don't want to get hit by it.

"Go, go go." She helps me up and pushes me forward.

I take off running again.

We are running side by side, yelling out what we see.

"Down." She says.

There are three beams of light going from one side of the cave to the other.

"Yes," is all I have time to say.

I drop and crawl fast under the beams while she jumps over them.

"Hole," I say as I see a gap ahead.

"Yes," she answers.

I do a running long jump over the gap, and she barely hops over it

"Side," she calls out.

I skirt to the side and run along a small path. It's too small for her, so she has to jump from one side to the other. Right side, jump to the left side. There is barely enough ground for her feet to catch.

But she is good and makes it without a problem.

We keep running.

"Swing," she says, pointing to a purple-hanging vine. I see a regular floor, but I don't question her. While still running I jump, grab the vine, and swing as far as it will let me.

Zussta runs hard and long jumps with all her might.

I see her land and then begin to lose her balance.

I'm almost to the other side and about to let go of the vine. "Hold on!" she yells.

I hold on tighter.

I don't swing as far as she jumped.

I see the ground around her shimmer and move.
She falls backwards.
Down into the ground.
And disappears.
OMG. OMG. OMG.
Zussta fell into the ground!

Chapter 44

"Zussta!" I holler in a panic.

"Zussta!"

There's no answer.

My swinging back and forth starts to slow down. Pretty soon I'll be stopped over what I assume is a large hole in the ground. It's where Zussta fell. It looks like the ground, but it has to be one of those places that look like rock but there's nothing but a big hole. Because I know Zussta didn't fall into the actual ground.

I have to figure out how to get to the other side. But even if I can swing far enough, Zussta said I wouldn't make it, and I completely trust her. If she couldn't make it, then I couldn't either.

I do like the old guys taught me; it has worked before. Stop and look around. Don't panic. Take a moment to figure things out.

I look down at the shimmering ground. The walls of the cave aren't too far away. Maybe I can swing to the side, but I'm not positive about the ground there either.

I look up.

The vine must attach to something.

I start to climb up.

Thankfully, the vine isn't wet and slippery. I use my feet to wrap around the vine and push and pull myself up. It's like climbing the rope in gym class.

I keep hoping Zussta will reappear and rescue me. "Zussta!" I holler every few climbs.

Climb and call out; that's all I can think to do right now.

I climb for what seems like an oddly long time, or maybe I'm just scared and tired. Either way, I don't like this.

"Zussta!" I keep hoping to hear an answer, but it's so quiet all I hear is my breathing.

"Zussta!"

I finally make it to the top.

The vine hangs from what seems like a branch of a large tree. If there's a branch, there must be a full tree around somewhere. I tap and feel the branch; it's the solid feeling of the fluffy purple trees outside of the cave. It's so weird to be here in the middle of a cave.

I'm scared, worn out, and not sure if I can climb anymore. My other option is to go back down the vine. But I trust Zussta when she said hold on, plus, I saw her fall into the ground – so, yeah, going back down isn't a good option. Besides, I know I'd never be able to climb the vine again.

I have to climb onto the branch. Whether I think I can or not, I have to.

I rest for a couple of breaths first.

I look around. There are some light holes higher up. How big is this tree? And how can it grow in a cave?

Never mind, that's not the problem to worry about.

I take a deep breath and grab hold of the branch. First one hand, then the other. It's scarier than the vine. I'm hanging in midair with my feet dangling.

Before I get too afraid, I throw my right foot and leg over the branch and manage to pull myself up until I'm lying belly flat on the branch.

I breathe.

I'm lost in a cave, in a tree, on a purple planet, and Zussta is gone.

But I'm still alive, so there is that.

I sit up, with one leg on each side of the branch, and look around. As the old guys said, calmly figure out a way to solve the problem.

My problem is I'm in a tree in a cave, and Zussta is gone.

Yeah, that's a big problem to try to solve

I need to get down and find Zussta. Since I'm on a branch, the tree must be growing out of the ground… I assume. But then again, we are on a strange planet. For all I know the tree could be floating in the sky, or maybe on a cloud. I set that thought aside and hope for the ground, but keep the floating tree idea as a possibility. I look forward and backward, debating which way is toward the tree and which way is further out on the branch.

If I go further out on the branch, it might bring me to a wall where I can climb down to the ground.

Or the branch could break.

If I climb to the tree, I could maybe scale down to the bottom.

Or the tree could be too big or floating.

Branch or tree? Branch or tree?

I wish Zussta was here to tell me what to do.

I decide to crawl towards the tree. If I can't scale down the tree, then I'll go back and crawl further out on the branch.

I'm happy with my good decision-making skills.

I look both ways to try to figure out which way to the tree. The branch gets a bit thicker in one direction, so I go that way.

The branch isn't big enough for me to walk on, and what if I lose my balance? No. I decide to use my legs, knees, and hands to half crawl, half scooch my way up the branch.

I can do this. I can do this.

I slowly make progress, moving carefully so as not to fall.

It feels like hours since Zussta and I entered the cave. I'm not so sure I want to be a treasure hunter anymore.

I shake my head and get my thinking straight.

I have to find Zussta.

That's all I need to worry about right now. Find Zussta.

I was right; the branch is getting wider. I get onto my knees and start crawling.

Crikey, how big is this branch? And how big is the tree?

"Zussta!" She has to be okay. She just has to be.

I make it to the tree trunk and can stand, holding onto the tree for balance.

I look up. And up. And up.

I see one large light hole way, way up in the ceiling of the cave.

I look down.

That was a mistake.

I get dizzy and grab a hold of the trunk. Oh boy, that's a long way down. But not as far away as the top. And at least there is ground.

Not a floating tree. That's good.

I feel around for a way to get to the bottom. Other vines grow on and around the trunk of the tree. I bet I can hold onto those and make my way down.

I have to.

I have to find Zussta.

I begin to descend carefully.

I use my hands to hold on tight to the vines and my feet to work into the tree truck as a foothold. I gently test each foothold first before I put my weight on it.

I slowly begin my descent. Holding tight and climbing down.

I look up to see how far I've moved, and then I look down. I'm relieved to see I'm about halfway to the ground.

I can do this!

With a new rush of confidence, I keep myself in check, still paying attention. I sometimes get too excited and move too fast. I can't do that here. Move slow; find Zussta.

I make it to the bottom and gently tap it with my foot before stepping all the way down. I don't trust the ground is actually the ground anymore. Okay, good, it's solid. I hop down and look around, trying to figure out where I am. It seems I'm in a tunnel off to the side of the main area where we were running. I guess we were going so fast that I didn't even see it.

I follow the direction of the branch and walk slowly down the side tunnel to get back to where we were. I peek my head out into the main tunnel, and a beam of light shoots past me.

What is that and why does it keep shooting at me?

I get down and begin crawling towards the invisible hole that swallowed Zussta. I'm on the wrong side of the hole. Shoot, I was hoping I would come out on the other side of the abyss.

"Zussta!" I call out again.

"Britt?" I hear a quiet voice from the hole.

Zussta is alive! "I'm here! Are you hurt? Can I help? Can you get out?" I lean into the hole, hoping I can see her.

"I come up," is all she says. That's okay, I don't mind her not answering any of my questions. I'm so happy she's alive!

I keep straining my eyes, watching for her. Then, out of the dark, I see her form climbing up the side of the wall. She is moving slowly, but that's probably because she is having to pull herself up. "You can do it," I call an encouragement to her.

It turns out she isn't using hand or footholds; she is pulling herself up by the suction cups on her fingers. OMG, she is strong. And she is coming up the side of the hole we were trying to reach.

I watch as she slowly climbs to the top and pulls herself out of the hole. She flops onto her back and lies still for a moment. "You're on the wrong side," she says.

I almost start to cry with relief.

"I not know how to get to your side. I just here. Are you okay? How deep is the hole? What did…?"

She cuts me off, "No questions right now please."

Yeah, okay. I get that.

I sit with my legs criss-cross-applesauce style and wait. I'm not great at quietly waiting, but I know it's important right now. I begin to hum to myself. I start to rock back and forth to the tune I make up. I must be humming out loud because I hear Zussta chuckle. "Okay, we figure out." She slowly pushes herself into a sitting position.

Yeah, let's figure out how to get out of here.

Chapter 45

Zussta stands up, so I stand up. We look at each other from across the big hole. "How did you get down? And why down on wrong side?"

"I climb up." I point up the vine. "Up to a tree, and then I climb down and walk here. I no mean to be on wrong side."

I know she's not mad at me. She's wondering how I got here. I can tell she is still tired, so I try to stay calm and not ask a lot of questions. Except, I can't help myself. "Now what?" I ask, looking at her across the huge hole.

Zussta sighs. "We find a way to get you here. Look for pictures."

Pictures. A clue. Okay, I can look for a clue. What kind of clue? I don't know, and I'm pretty sure she doesn't know either, but I look around anyways.

I walk slowly along the ledge of the hole. I don't want to fall in, and I don't have suction cups to get me out.

A clue.

A clue.

I feel along the weird wall, tapping my hands on the side and my feet on the ground. I keep tapping until my foot hits empty air. I quickly step back and look down. There's a small hole in the ground. Not a huge one, not even one big enough for my foot to fit into. Just a hole barely big enough for my hand to fit into.

"Zussta." I get her attention. "I found hole."

She stands up. "What in it?"

She's crazy if she thinks I'm sticking my hand in a dark hole in a cave on a weird planet. "I not know. I not see."

Zussta reaches into her frontpack and pulls out a torch. "Here," she calls as she tosses it to me. I scramble to catch the light. I would hate for it to fall and break. Then we would really be in trouble.

I fumble with the torch and finally turn it on. Why weren't we using this the entire time? I know she can see pretty well, but this would have been nice for me to have. I wonder what else she has in that pack.

I shine the torch into the hole, holding my breath even behind the clear mask. What if a snake jumps out at me? OMG, an alien snake.

Now I'm terrified.

I shine the light inside.

It's empty.

Whew.

Now that I know nothing is going to jump out, I look closer. A small knob or switch sticks out from the side, towards the bottom of the hole. "There a …" I don't know the word for switch. How do I possibly explain a switch or lever to her? "The hole is like my hand. It go like this." And I make the hand signal for flipping a switch or lever.

"Can you move it?"

Yeah, that's the big question. Should I flip the switch? Should I pull the lever?

I don't want to make that decision. I let Zussta decide.

She looks at me with her big eye, then moves to the side of the cave. "Okay, move it. Be ready run. Okay? Be ready go fast."

I take a deep breath and nod.

I can do this.

I can do this.

I stick my hand into the hole… and it gets stuck.

My hand doesn't fit.

"Hand no go in. Hand big." I explain to her.

We both give a big sigh.

Think. Stop and think.

What can I use to move the switch? Zussta is searching in her bag, so I start patting down my clothes. I totally forgot about the washer and string that I left in my pocket.

I pull it out, looking at it.

Could this work?

I look up at Zussta who is looking across the hole at me. "What is?" she asks.

"It make noise, remember?" I hold it up so she can see.

I start to spin it when Zussta yells, "No, Britt!"

I instantly stop. Why shouldn't I make the noise? I don't ask out loud. I totally trust and believe her. Okay, if I can't spin it, what can I do?

I look at the hole in the washer, then down at the lever.

Will it fit?

I look back at Zussta who nods at me. She gets it.

I hold the end of the string and slowly lower the washer into the hole. If I'm right, the washer will slide around the lever, and I can pull it up that way. It's like a carnival game, trying to get the washer over the lever.

It takes me three tries, but then it works. The washer is in place. I look at Zussta again, and she gives me a nod.

I pull up on the string.

I pull the lever up.

A low hum begins. A kind of hum that I can feel through the ground somehow. I drop the string and scramble to the side of the cave. The hole begins to shimmer even more and then becomes solid. As if the hole is gone, and there is only regular ground instead. Well, as *regular* as the ground on a purple planet can be.

That's it? I pull the lever, and the hole closes?

It almost seems too easy. But then again, there is no way a Zobian hand or even finger could have reached in that small space. So maybe it would have been impossible for anyone but me.

I crawl to the edge and tap the floor, and I see Zussta doing the same – except she isn't crawling because nothing scares her.

We both tap the ground a couple of times. Zussta starts walking toward me. "Britt, stay." Yep, I wasn't planning on moving just yet.

She walks all the way across the closed hole and to me. She squats to my level. "Are you okay?" she asks.

I jump into her arms, and she catches me. I'm too shaken to speak right away… but it doesn't last long. I start rambling in English. "Did you see that? We were running then I was swinging, and you fell in the ground. I climbed up the vine and to the tree. Then I come back to find Zussta. You climb, but still big hole. Then hole closed, and here we are."

That about sums it all up.

I hug her as strongly as I can, and she hugs me back.

"Britt good and brave," she whispers in my ear. I don't feel brave; just glad to be back with Zussta. She stands up, "Let's go."

I'm with you, Lady.

"Not all okay. Be careful," Zussta warns me. Shoot, we aren't out of here yet.

We begin walking forward through the cave again. At least this time we aren't running, and beams of light aren't shooting at us.

Zussta walks right down the center of the cave. I walk kind of next to her while being a little behind her. I'm not brave enough to just stride through an alien cave yet.

"Are we done?" I ask. I want us out of the cave and back at the ship.

"Almost done," she answers, glancing down at me but never looking far away from the cave walls. I move closer to her.

"Stop!" She hollers.

I freeze just as a beam of light zips in front of us. Zussta makes her way to the side of the cave. "Stay back," she warns as she inches closer to the cave wall.

I stay directly behind her.

Zussta examines the hole where the beam of light came out. She waves her hand before the hole, and sure enough, light shoots out.

I duck, but of course, nothing happens since it went in front of Zussta.

She looks at me with her back-of-the-head eye. "Stay low. See here. Stay below here," she says as she points to the hole where the beam comes from.

Got it; stay below the hole in the wall where a deadly beam of light shoots from. I nod.

But she is tall. "Zussta stay low?" I wonder how she will avoid the beam.

"Britt go under, Zussta go over."

Oh, she'll jump. Got it.

"We run fast, you go low and I go over. Britt go fast." She is directing me down the cave tunnel with her hand. "Ready?"

No, but I'm ready to be done. "Yes, Britt ready."

"Britt run fast, go low when I say." She stands up and studies the tunnel. "Not far. Run fast, then we are out."

Yeah, let's get out of here. First, we were followed by a bad guy, then we almost died in this tunnel, and we never found the pala. Yeah, I'm ready to go.

"Go!" Zussta yells.

And we both take off running.

"Down." I drop to a fast crawl as Zussta jumps when a beam zips by.

"Run." We run.

I see a light at the end. This is it!

We run out of the cave and slide to a stop.

We are done. We are out of the cave and in the purple jungle.

"The ship is close by. We go home." Zussta says as she smiles at me.

It's a good thing I'm a young whippersnapper. I can see how a lazy kid would not be able to survive with Zussta. But even I wouldn't mind a bit of a break.

"Can we rest?" I ask her. I don't know if we're in a hurry, but I know it's best to pace myself instead of getting worn out and unable to walk at all. I doubt she wants to carry me on her back.

We stop, and I sit down. Zussta hands me the water ball. I don't think I've ever been so thirsty in my entire life. I press the area behind my ear and drink as much water as I can in one breath. I press the area behind my ear again and breathe. Then I do it again, drinking more.

We sit quietly for a while, gathering our thoughts and energy. But before long, I decide I want to go home.

When I think of *home,* I'm not thinking of the group home on Earth, I'm thinking of Zussta's home.

"Ready?" She asks as she holds the rope to me.

I push myself up. "Yep, I'm ready."

Do I really have a choice?

We start at a fast pace through the trees. I'm still holding my end of the rope and trot to keep up with her.

I feel like a teacup poodle on a leash.

We make it back to the ship faster this time since we came out the other side of the cave and didn't have to go the long way around to trick Jama. His ship is still here. Did he follow us through the cave or did he go back out the first way? If he were smart, he went the long way around. I wonder if he is still on the other side waiting for us to come out of the cave that way.

Zussta opens the door and picks me up, placing me inside. I crawl over to my seat. It seems odd that there isn't a door on this side, like a car, but whatever. I'm starting to give up on trying to make sense of alien technology. I can't compare it to things are on Earth.

She does a full scan of the area, but doesn't see Jama. I would rather know where he is than be surprised if he jumps out.

What if he's inside our spaceship?

Don't freak out.

Don't freak out.

I look all around but, thankfully, don't see him.

Zussta walks all the way around the ship, checking it and the surrounding area. Maybe Jama put a tracking device on the ship, and he's hoping we will lead him to the next clue.

I bet he's one of those slimy aliens who would rather let us do the work and just sneak around behind us. Lazy and not smart, that's what I think of people (and aliens) like that.

Satisfied, she climbs into the ship. "Britt good see pictures on wall. Britt run fast and is smart. We make good team." She holds her arms up over her head in our yay way.

I can't help but beam at the compliment. "Yay!" I throw my hands up. "Good team."

She starts the spaceship. "We go home?"

Yeah, after all of that, I'm more than ready to go home.

Chapter 46

Home never felt so good. Yep, I consider this my home now. It's great to go somewhere new, but even better to come home. After sleeping for probably two days straight, Zussta and I fall back into our regular routine. I sleep when I want and she feeds me when I'm hungry.

I'm happily coloring a galaxy when Zussta interrupts me. "Britt. We go out?"

Sure, I'm always ready to go out. I quickly throw my paper and crayons into my room and race back to the bubble door. I'm ready before Zussta.

She laughs and pats my shoulder as she arrives at the door. We bubble up, and it's pitch-black outside.

I freeze in place.

"Oi, I can't see." I remind Zussta. Did she forget that I can't see at night? What if I trip and break a leg? Well, that probably won't happen, but it could.

"Okay, I got you." Zussta bends down and awkwardly picks me up and holds me facing outward with her arm around my waist. It's not the most comfortable position, but I don't complain.

Why are we going somewhere during the night with no moon to see by? Oh, imagine what the tree Lamenana looks like under a full moon.

She easily walks forward, and I make out the shape of the spaceship. Oh, we're going somewhere else, not just outside. Great…maybe. What happens on this planet at night?

No lights come on when she opens the spaceship's door. Odd, I figured all ships would have a light inside like cars. But then again, I guess Zussta doesn't need a light if she can see in the dark.

I slide over and settle into my seat. It's exciting to go somewhere new. We aren't restricted to the area around the house. We can go anywhere in the galaxy or to another galaxy. The possibilities are endless. Going out at night is a bit scary, but I can handle it.

"Where we go?" I ask.

"To fix my hair. Too far to walk, so we fly only a short way. We be there almost right away," she says as the ship rises out of the ground.

Huh. I never thought about flying around this planet when we can go anywhere in the universe. But maybe just because we *can* go anywhere doesn't mean we *have to*. I guess if a human just needed vegemite or something, they would run to the closest store, not the next town or country over.

I sometimes forget to keep things simple.

And I look at her hair. It isn't as bright as before, and beginning to droop. It must be time for her to get a haircut.

When she starts the ship, the soft glow of the instrument panel helps me see a bit better.

I look closely at her hair. It is a little longer than when I first arrived. And it's not as bright as it was.

I'm worried I'll be bored and I didn't bring my paper and crayons. I begin to fidget.

"You will be okay." She must know I'm anxious.

"But you busy, and do something." I try explaining to her. I don't need to get in trouble on my first outing on this planet.

"You will like this. Trust me."

Yeah, famous last words.

The ship rises to barely above tree-top level, and starts moving forward. We are definitely staying on this planet.

Maybe since we aren't going through any wormholes, she'll let me kneel and watch out the window. As soon as we are in the air, I get up and place my hands on the window.

We are zipping over the land, and my eyes are adjusting more. I can't figure out if I'm seeing buildings or trees, but whatever it is, I'm seeing something.

I wonder how fast we are going. Maybe it's like Mach 1 or some airplane talk like that. Whatever it is, it's fast. And I love it! I finally tear myself away from the window. "What you do to your hair?" I ask Zussta. She's flying easily, not having to pay too much attention since we aren't in outer space.

"The same, only better. Maybe we find you a *bakichi*." She says a word I don't understand. What? Something for me? Now I'm really curious.

"What is *bakichi*?" I pronounce the word she said.

"It's something for you to do. Something you like."

A toy? She's going to get me a toy? That's so wonderful!

What does a Zobian toy look like?

Now I really can't sit still.

I start quietly singing in English and Zobian and seat dancing a little bit. "I get a toy. I've never had a Zobian toy, but today I get one. Will it be big? Will it be small? What will it be, after all? Can I hold it or throw it? Will it make me fly or cover my eyes? What will it be, this toy for me?"

Zussta smiles at me. "We are almost there."

I scramble to my knees and look out the window. It's dark, but I see colored lights on the ground, but that's about it. Not like Christmas lights strung around, but lights built into the ground.

I was kind of hoping to see a huge city with tall buildings, aliens everywhere, and spaceships flying around.

Deflated, I turn and look at Zussta.

"It's all underground," is all she needs to say to me.

I didn't even think that they would have stores underground. It's like the marketplace where I saw Marco. That was underwater, so it makes sense.

I'm excited again. I'm wiggling back and forth as I watch out the window. Our ship slows down and then start going straight down. I peer at the ground and watch as a trap door opens. We aren't landing in a hole; instead, it looks like a landing pad.

Zussta makes a gentle touch down, and the landing pad lowers us into an underground garage. Not much different than a parking lot, just below the surface. We stop and she shuts down the ship.

"We leave ship here?" I'm wondering how many landing pads there are.

"We leave it here and they fly it to a spot." She is trying to explain it in simple terms as well. Oh, someone parks the ship for us. It's like rich people have someone park their cars for them.

She helps me out. "Stay close. Do not run or get lost. There are lots of Zobians here, so watch where I am and where you are."

I was thinking she doesn't have to tell me twice to stay close, but on second thought, yeah, she probably does. I easily wander off. But I solemnly nod like it won't be a problem.

We bubble down some more, and the doors open to a large cave-like area. Heaps of Zobians are mingling, talking their language, and not noticing me.

I stop and take it all in.

I've gotten used to Zussta being bigger than me, but being surrounded by tall aliens is a bit scary. I grab ahold of her leg, trying to look everywhere at once.

We are in a different style of marketplace than where Marco lives.

There is color and noise everywhere. I think I even hear music playing. Do Zobians even like music?

I hear talking, laughing, feet running, and some strange noises that I have no idea what it is or where it's coming from.

This is so awesome!

It's more like a carnival than any hair-cutting place I've been.

Even when Jordie brought me to have my hair trimmed, it was quiet and peaceful - but not this place. This is like a social gathering for the entire town.

The place is made up of separate stalls rather than shops. It's more of an open area with tables and dividers around the outside of the room, and each has its own theme, and vendor. The center is wide open. I bet you could fit four basketball courts in here.

Zobian kids are running around and hollering back and forth. Wow, kids will be kids no matter if they're alien or human.

Zussta gives me a slight nudge, and we begin to walk through the crowd.

A few of the aliens notice me and point and stare. I smile and wave; I know I'm unique. They must not know what waving means, so I talk.

"Hello. How are you? Hi there." I'm saying greetings every way I know how in their language (and some in English).

My talking surprises them.

I bet I look like a little dog that's happily barking at everyone. I laugh at this because they don't know I'm really a superstar treasure hunter.

Zussta keeps looking down and checking on me. "Britt okay?"

"Britt very good!" I give her two thumbs up.

There are no separate salons, just areas that have Zobians sitting in chairs. Some are having their hair done; some are having pictures painted on their bodies; and some are having beautiful jewels attached to their arms.

Of course, there are stalls to sell items as well.

Zussta guides me to a stall and begins to talk with the alien. The store worker looks at me without answering her. I bet it's because my hair looks great today.

"Hello. My name is Britt." I would offer to shake his hand, but that's not their custom.

"Is that a human?" he asks Zussta instead of talking to me.

"Yes, this is my human. Her name is Britt."

Uh, yeah. I just said that.

"I've never seen a real human. She is small." He still isn't talking to me.

I guess even on Earth we spoke with other humans and not to the pet right away.

Zussta continues to answer him, "she is young; that is why she is small."

He reaches out to touch me, and I step back. Nope, I don't want to be pet or tapped on the head, or whatever he was going to do.

Zussta realizes my concern and quickly steers the subject away from me. "I need my hair done." She and the stylist begin discussing her hair, and I quickly lose interest.

I turn and watch the Zobians as they walk by. Some of them notice me and others don't.

"Look!" I hear what I assume is a kid pulling at his mom's arm and pointing at me.

"That is a human," she says as she stops and lets the kid stare. He runs at me like he wants to hug or tackle me or.

I quickly duck behind Zussta's legs and avoid the loud child. He probably has sticky hands.

Gross.

He darts around her legs, trying to grab me, but I keep dodging him.

I know I'm a kid too, but I also know which ones to stay away from. No matter what galaxy I'm in, there is always that one spoiled, sticky-hand kid that causes trouble.

I start tapping on Zussta's leg, saying "No, no, no" over and over. She quickly picks me up, saving me from the terror of a kid.

The spoiled alien child gets mad and starts yelling. Of course, he does. His mom storms over and starts scolding Zussta. "He wants to touch your pet. He has never seen a human. You should let him touch it."

Oh, this lady doesn't know who she's messing with.

Zussta won't put up with her rudeness. "Britt does not want to be touched," she answers the lady, and keeps turning to keep me away from his grabbing hands.

The lady gets all huffy and finally pulls her kid away. Good riddance.

"Thank you," I tell Zussta. "Why do you not yell at her?" I mean, she could have torn into that lady.

Zussta squats as she sets me down, looking me in the eyes. "We fight only when we are in danger. That lady was no danger at all."

I'm not sure if that was a life lesson or just an explanation.

I guess both.

Zussta is in the stylist's chair getting her hair worked on. I'm being good and patient, waiting for them to finish. But there is just too much going on for me to stay still. The area next to us has square objects that bounce up and down from the floor without stopping. I wander over there – it's just one stall over.

The vendor guy sees me. I point to the block bouncing high over my head. "What is?" I ask.

"Well, hello, human. This here is a *zabhara*."

Okay, well that doesn't tell me what it is. He catches one and brings the block down to me. It is small enough that I can hold it in my two hands.

Is it like a super ball?

I slam throw it to the ground. The bouncy square must hit on a corner because it flies into the center of the crowd, hitting a Zobian man in his back. He probably should have seen it coming with his back-of-the-head eye, but he didn't.

So, the cube hits a male alien on his back.

He makes a noise and spins around, bumping into a lady next to him.

She drops her package and the contents spill out.

Two alien teenagers don't see the bag and trip on the lady's spilled items.

They begin to fall and reach out to grab anything to catch them.

One teenager grabs a kid and brings him down with them.

The other doesn't grab anything and falls face-first.

Everyone stops to stare.

It all happens so fast that me and the vendor guy stand there with our mouths open, watching it unfold.

Zussta must have heard the commotion and quickly finds me. She snatches me up, hustling me off to the side – kind of hiding us from the crowd that has gathered.

"What happened?" She asks once we are out of sight from everyone.

"I no mean to," I start with my explanation. I don't know the words to tell her what happened.

She sighs. "Britt, stay near me. No wander off." She looks sternly at me.

Yeah, okay. I get it.

Then she starts laughing.

I break down laughing too. We are laughing so hard that she has to set me down, and I'm doubled over. Just thinking about it all again is hilarious!

She gets herself under control. "We get you an easy toy. Then I get my hair fix and we go home."

I have the coolest owner ever!

She leads me to a stall with kids milling about. I stay close while she picks something out for me. With an object in her hand, we make our way back to the first stylist. He smiles at her, ignores me, and sits her in the chair.

I don't need to watch; I know what happens when someone gets their hair done. Instead, I examine the toy she got me.

I sit on the ground nearby so I don't get in trouble again. I'm pretty good at figuring things out. Plus, that's part of the fun. The toy is bigger than the *bouncing cube of trouble* but still small enough for me to hold. It's shaped like a large hot dog bun. I let it go, and it falls to the ground – ok, it doesn't float.

I pick it up and throw it down like the cube. Nothing, it doesn't bounce. It's probably a good thing given what happened when I did that with the cube.

I pick it up and try squishing it. It's soft, but not soft enough for me to completely squeeze it together.

I bang it on the ground several times, and it suddenly lights up.

Like, a gazillion different colors glowing from the inside of the toy are blinking and changing.

It's beautiful!

I laugh and hold it up to Zussta. She smiles but can't nod since the stylist is working on her hair.

It's only about ten minutes total before Zussta stands up. "We are done, Britt."

Already? My hair takes longer than that. But then again, I have a lot of hair.

I study her. Her hair is a vibrant blue, but this time with shades of purple streaked through the strands. And her mohawk is standing up straight again. She's right. She's done.

"It look good," I tell her. I think everyone, even aliens, likes a compliment saying they are pretty.

She holds my toy as we get back to the ship and fly home. She probably doesn't want me bouncing it around the ship.

We get home, and Zussta hands me my toy and makes her way back to the treasure map table.

I sit in the main space, banging my new toy on the ground, making it change colors and even wiggle.

Zussta calls to me. "Britt."

I quickly look up. I didn't think I was doing anything wrong.

"Come look." She is pointing to her table. I drop the toy and climb onto my box next to her.

"Do you remember writing on wall in cave? It said that we go to the clouds."

Of course, I remember, it was just the other day. I don't think she's really asking if I remember, just talking about the writing.

"We go to clouds. Are you ready?"

Today? We're going to the clouds today? "Yes!" I'm so excited I can't control my voice, "I ready!"

And with that, we are off on yet another adventure.

It feels like every time we leave the house, it's an adventure, whether at the hair place or on a treasure hunt.

And this girl from Earth likes adventure!

Chapter 47

I barely had time to relax when we are back in the ship. It's bright outside now. I think this is my first time staying up all night. I look for the sun, but I don't see it rising like it does on Earth. It's as if it suddenly gets dark and then suddenly is light – without warning.

Weird.

"Are you ready to go to clouds?" Zussta asks from her seat in the spaceship.

Hopefully, she won't almost die again. That was scary.

I'm not tired, so sure, let's go treasure hunting again! "Yes, to clouds!" I exclaim while pointing to the sky.

Zussta laughs with me, and we take off.

"We go to one cloud, or will we fly around and see something? What we look for? I see things good. I see mabo, and I can see pictures." I'm not bragging and don't say it with a snotty voice. I can see the wormholes and I truly want to help.

Zussta laughs, "Yes, you see very good. The pictures say where to look. We go there first."

"We fly and find pala?" I'm already looking out my window, trying to spot anything unusual.

Zussta is tapping on the computer screen when she answers, "No, we stop and walk and look."

Well, that confuses me.

"But you said we go to the clouds?"

Now she is confused too. "Yes. We go to the clouds and walk." She speaks a little slower and clearer like I don't understand.

I understand the words just fine; it's the meaning that confuses me.

"You walk on clouds?" I ask.

She turns and squints her one big eye at me. "You don't?"

I blink several times before I answer. "Um, no. On Earth, they soft, no walk."

"Well, then, what good are they?" she asks.

Oh, another time to learn about each other's planet. I never thought I would be telling an alien about Earth.

"They have *rain*," I say the word rain in English. "Water falls from the sky and help trees and plants be big. Clouds very important."

I know this because we were starting to learn about clouds in school. I'm trying to remember the different kinds of clouds besides being called soft, fluffy clouds and dark, stormy clouds. I forget the name of them. But I don't think she cares about their technical name.

Am I going to forget about what life on Earth was like? I don't want to do that; I always want to remember my home planet. I bet I'll remember lots. Maybe not all the different homes I was in. I never loved going to school, but now it seems weird that I'll never go again. I suppose I don't need to learn all the Earth things since I'm not there anymore. But how am I going to get smart about Zobian things? Maybe Zussta will home-school me.

I make a mental note to ask her about it when we get home.

"What clouds do here?" I ask.

She shrugs. "They are like the ground - but different."

Oh, well – that answers absolutely nothing.

I stare at her, waiting for her to further explain, but she doesn't.

I guess I'll figure it out when we get there.

We fly straight up and into the blackness of space. I look at the ship screen and see that it has the wormhole marked, but I already see it in the distance. I look around to find more wormholes or maybe new planets that I haven't seen yet.

It's still new and amazing.

Maybe one day she'll let me fly the ship. I wonder if you have to be a certain age like you do on Earth to drive a car.

But then again, pets don't drive cars, so I probably won't be allowed to fly the ship.

But I'll still try.

We are about to enter the wormhole. "Here we go. Are you ready?" She smiles as she asks.

"Totally." And I am. I'm totally ready for this adventure. I sit back.

The black and white zips by us as we swerve right then left.

I don't even feel sick. I'm an old hand at this.

We get to the end and shoot out, stopping instantly. I still think it's funny how my arms and legs keep going. I giggle, and Zussta laughs with me.

Almost right away I spot the purple planet of Sononi. I guess once I know what I'm looking for it's easy to spot. That, and we've been here before.

Zussta checks the computer screen, and we fly over Sononi a bit before she makes our descent. Maybe the writing on the walls said where in the clouds to look for the next clue. Otherwise, searching an entire planet of clouds could take us a lifetime.

We are at cloud level, and I notice she is steering around the clouds instead of through them. I guess when they are solid or semi-solid, you want to avoid hitting them.

Looking for a pala.

Looking for a pala.

I'm looking out the window for something unusual; whatever that may be.

And then I see him.

"Zussta! There Jama!"

Sure enough, he is following us. How did he know we are here?

He stays on my side of the ship and a little way behind us. He thinks he's being sneaky, but we are better at treasure hunting than he is.

"Hold on," is all she says before the ship makes a sharp turn and dives straight down.

I didn't even get time to hold onto anything. Thankfully the seat keeps me in place. I bet without it, I would have hit the windshield, the roof, and everything else inside the ship.

She turns again and aims the spaceship straight up, straight for Jama's ship.

I hold my breath.

His ship quickly darts out of the way. Yeah, he's running now.

Zussta flies directly behind him. Are we going to shoot him out of the sky? It would be nice to be rid of him, but I don't want to kill anyone or anything.

Thankfully, she doesn't shoot.

This is so exciting!

We are zooming through a purple sky, dodging purple clouds, chasing a bad guy… and then I see it.

There is a small box sitting on a cloud.

It confuses me so much that I can't say anything right away.

I stare at the grey box lodged halfway in the cloud like it's half buried.

I have my hands on the window and face planted against it, trying to see the box again.

How can there be a box sitting on a purple cloud? This entire situation is so odd.

"We get rid of Jama," Zussta says with some force in her voice.

What does she have in mind?

Chapter 48

I look out the front window and see Jama's spaceship take a hard right. I brace myself and am ready when Zussta swerves our ship to follow him. Spaceships move much easier than cars. Up, down, side-to-side, without any roads to drive off. It's funny how cars seem so limited now that I'm flying in a spaceship. It's weird what we get used to. I never knew how much more was beyond my world.

But what's 'out there' right now is Jama's ship, and we are chasing it down. I'm not sure what Zussta's going to do when we catch it. Can one ship catch another? Like with a net or fishing pole?

That paints a funny picture in my mind, and I laugh a little bit. Zussta must think I'm laughing at the excitement we're having because she looks at me and smiles big.

Yeah, she is one of those people (or aliens) who thrives on adventure.

I guess I'm one of those people too.

"What we do to Jama?" I ask, but I'm not sure I want to hear the answer. I take that back; I want to know the answer. Good or bad, I like to know what will happen rather than sit back and wait.

"Jama afraid. He follows others and try steal their treasure, but he doesn't like fight. He will be scared and leave. Then we leave too."

What? That's our plan? To go home? Sounds like a sucky plan to me. But I keep my thoughts to myself. Zussta hasn't been mad at me yet, and while I'm not afraid, I don't want her anger aimed my way.

I cross my arms and look out my window. I still think this is a sucky plan.

Zussta nudges me. "We not give up. We come back tomorrow when Jama not here. He not see pictures to look in the clouds, and I not want him to know."

That does make sense.

I like that she explains things instead of dismissing me like a pet. I remember some adults act like their pet doesn't exist unless they feel like petting it or showing it off. I'm glad that's not the case here.

One time, my bunkmate, Amy, was with a family for three days before she knew they had a cat. It stayed hidden, and the owners didn't even look for it. I'm glad Zussta doesn't ignore me.

We are still chasing Jama's spaceship when he suddenly shoots straight up into outer space. She was right; he's running home. He's a scaredy cat.

"There he go." She says to herself as much as to me.

"Just like you say." I nod and answer.

She looks sideways at me. "I know Jama. He is nothing to be afraid of. But maybe one day he go too far. I keep my eye on him."

"Yeah, your one big eye." I accidentally blurt out. I meant it as a joke, but I realize she may not think so. I look at her in horror.

Zussta bursts out laughing. "Yes, both big eyes. And now your little ones too."

I laugh with her. She can take a joke. Good to know – but I don't want to push it too far and offend her.

She looks out the window past me and yells, "Look out!"

I don't even have time to look when I feel a crash. We are in a crash.

The ship is pushed sideways, but thankfully the seat holds me in.

It's all happening so fast.

I look out the window and see that Jama's ship hit us. I turn and look at Zussta; her lips are pressed together tight. Her one eye squints straight ahead.

Oh boy, she is mad.

I can't believe Jama hit us. Like on purpose, hit us. I'm worried he is going to do it again.

I grab the edge of my seat and hold on. We don't fall out of the sky, so that's good. You usually pull over and stop when in a car accident, but not us. Nope, we turn and start going after the other ship.

This isn't fun anymore.

Once again, we are chasing after Jama; this time Zussta means business.

We zip through the sky, zigging right, left, up, and down.

Jama turns behind a cloud, and he is waiting for us when we get there. Zussta has to swerve to miss hitting him head-on. She turns hard, and we hit a cloud.

We hit a cloud?

I thought we would fly through one like on Earth, but not here.

Nope, we hit a cloud.

And hard.

So hard that our ship starts to wobble and slow down. Even I know a plane, or I imagine a spaceship, has to keep moving in order to keep flying.

We begin to fall from the sky.

Zussta holds the steering control so tight that I'm worried she might break it. I'm not sure which is scarier, falling from the sky or the steering control breaking… what if both happen? What if the steering control comes out of the front of the spaceship, and we fall out of the sky? I don't want to crash on the purple planet.

Close my eyes or keep them open?

I keep them open; I want to know what's coming. Plus, I'm too scared to close my eyes.

Where do I look, at Zussta or out the window? Is Jama still coming for us or running home?

I manage not to scream or panic. I know enough to keep my cool in a bad situation. I have to trust Zussta.

We crash onto a cloud.

The spaceship ends up sitting on the cloud, a little sideways and a little rough, but at least we aren't upside down. "Are you okay?" Zussta asks, instantly checking on me.

I think I'm okay.

I move my feet, move my hands, and turn my head to face her. "I okay," I confirm. Then I have a terrifying thought. "Are you okay?" I ask her.

What if Zussta is hurt? And we're stranded on this cloud on another planet? I try to wriggle out of the seat to get closer to her. She pats my arm, "I okay too."

Oh, thank goodness – for her and me.

She taps a button on the screen, and the seat releases us. She puts on my face shield before opening her door. I press around the edges to double-check, too, just in case.

She doesn't close the door, so I climb out after her. She assesses the damage like an adult human after a car accident. The side is scraped, and the front is dented. That's all I can see; I don't know what might be wrong with the engine.

I look around while she inspects the ship. Of course, the cloud is purple.

But I'm walking on a cloud.

It's not as bouncy as I imagined, but it's not as solid and hard like the Earth, either. I jump up and down and feel the cloud beneath me give a little, but it still holds. I stop jumping just in case. I don't want to fall through.

But it's not completely flat here. I walk towards a cloud wall, wondering if it all feels like the cloud or like a wall. The wall is further than I first thought. I guess I can't tell distance because everything is different shades of purple. It's kind of like mirrors on cars – you know how it says objects are closer than they appear – that's this planet, except objects are further away than they appear.

I turn around and see how far I am from the ship. Oh my, I did wander off; it's far away. But I can still see the ship and Zussta working underneath it.

I look around a bit more. Is that a plant?

Is there life growing on this cloud?

I go to check it out.

It is a plant. It has a light purple stem and a dark purple flower with white tips. White is the only other color I've seen since I've been here.

Wait, is white a color or the absence of color? My art teacher, Mrs. Yang, taught us all about the colors and how to mix them together to get other colors. I know white makes other colors lighter, but I remember her saying something that, technically, white is a color, but not really. Now I'll never be able to ask her to clarify that.

I can't help it; I need to touch the flower.

My fingers are about to graze the petals on the flower when it pops down into the cloud and disappears.

What the...?

There's another one over there. I walk softly towards it, trying to sneak up on the flower. I hold my breath and slowly reach down.

Pop. It disappears into the cloud.

I keep following, trying to catch them.

There's a group of three, so I try running as fast as I can to grab one before they know I'm there. I'm at a full run dive for the flowers.

Pop. Pop. Pop. They all disappear.

What are these, and where do they go?

I try digging into the cloud, but it's not dirt, and I can't dig into it. I'm completely baffled.

I look up to ask Zussta, but I don't see her.

I don't see anything but purple – and another flower.

I must have wandered further than I realized.

Oh no.

Oh no.

Oh no.

I'm lost on a strange planet.

I don't see Zussta or the ship. Right about now, I'd even be happy to see Jama.

I look around for anything familiar, like the wall I saw near the ship. But there are several cloud walls all around. And there are flowers in all different directions. I don't know if any of those are the same flower or if they pop up all willy-nilly.

Oh no.

Oh no.

Oh no.

Don't panic.

I panic. I start hollering for Zussta.

"Zussta! Zussta!" I walk in a circle calling her name.

What do I do? Should I walk the way I think I came or stay put? On the one hand, I might find her, a town, or another alien. But on the other hand, if I stay in one place, she may come and find me. But how does she know which direction to start looking for me? What if I walk in the wrong direction and get further and further from her?

I know; I'll walk in a circle and then start making my circles bigger. But I need a starting point, something to stay in the center of the circle so I don't start circling away.

I look for a rock, or a different colored flower… anything.

It's like being lost in fog.

I find a rock, but it looks like all the other rocks around. So, I gather three rocks and pile them together.

"Zussta!" I keep yelling.

She found me when it suddenly turned dark; maybe she'll find me now.

"Zussta!"

I still panic.

I have to stop and get myself under control. I need my ninja street skills. The old guys always told me to stop and look at a problem instead of making decisions without thinking it through. I sit down, close my eyes, and take a series of deep breaths. I think of being calm; I think of my heart rate slowing to a normal pace. I think of my deep breaths. I think about not crying. I think of a calm picture.

I think of the majestic tree, Lamenana.

I picture myself under the tree, looking up at the colors. I take deep breaths.

Okay, I'm calm now.

I open my eyes and have developed a plan. I decide to walk in one direction for fifty big steps. If I don't see Zussta, I'll walk back fifty big steps. Then I'll turn around a quarter of the way and walk fifty big steps in that direction.

I've never done this before, and I'm a bit impressed at what a good idea I have. I wonder if the tree gave me the idea.

Thank you, Lamenana.

Here we go. One, two, three. I keep stepping and counting. I want to look around, but I'm afraid I'll lose count.

Forty-nine, fifty. I stop and look around.

Nothing but purple in all directions.

"Zussta!"

I wait for a reply but don't hear anything.

I turn around and take fifty steps back to my starting point. I then turn sideways to my left and start again.

I count my steps to fifty and look around. Again, nothing.

That's okay. I still have two other directions to go.

I get back to where I hope is the starting point, turn to the left again, and start the paces. This time I count out loud and watch all directions around me. Imagine if I walked right by something. That's almost funny. Almost.

Nothing in direction one, two, or three. This is it. I only have one direction left to go.

I start the steps. One, two, three, four…

I get to fifty and still don't see anything.

What do I do now that my plan didn't work?

I panic, that's what I do.

"Zussta!"

I stay in place hollering. I don't even bother to go back to the starting point. What's the use? Lost is lost. I fall to the ground. I'm lost, scared, and have no idea what to do next.

Is this how a dog or cat feels when they run away? I used to wonder, when a dog would sneak out of the house, was he running the neighborhood and having a grand time? Or is he scared and lost? Maybe like me, he was having fun until he didn't know where he was.

If I were lost in the outback, at least I would know to look for shelter and water. But here, I have no idea what shelter looks like, and I'm sure there isn't a nice stream for water.

I lie on my back, looking to the purple sky for answers.

Chapter 49

I think of what someone on television would do if they were stranded in a strange place. They always seem to write the word HELP in case a plane flies over.

I sit up. That's not a bad idea.

Maybe Zussta will fly over.

Except I don't know how to spell the word 'help' in Zobian. I don't know how to spell anything in Zobian.

I look around and see another wall close by. Walking to it, I notice some small rocks scattered in the clouds. Is this hail or just hard cloud pieces? Either way, I don't care. I cup the bottom of my shirt to make a basket and start collecting rocks.

When I have about all I can gather, I drop them in a pile.

Now what?

And all the rocks are purple, like the ground. Will Zussta even see it if she flies over? I have to hope that, yes, she will see it. Maybe they are different shades to her and don't all look the same.

I have to hope for that.

I can't write help…. So, what do I write?

I keep gathering rocks while debating what to write with them. I could do a happy face. That would stand out.

Even in bad times, I manage to make myself smile.

I climb on top of the wall to look around.

And then I see it.

The box.

The box I saw from the spaceship.

Is this another clue?

I drop my rocks and run to it.

I have visions of gold and jewels inside it. Like a treasure chest. I'll be rich, or Zussta and I will be rich.

I'm not scared anymore.

It's half buried in the cloud. But at least the top half is sticking out.

I grab ahold of it and pull hard. It takes some work, but I finally pull it out of the cloud.

I search for a lock; I can use one of the rocks to break the lock and open the treasure chest of all the riches in the galaxy.

There is no lock, and the top simply opens.

How can someone not lock up treasure?

I hold my breath and look inside.

There is one rock inside. It's big enough that I have to hold it in both hands.

That's it, just one plain-looking rock?

Well, that's disappointing.

Until it floats out of the treasure chest.

Whoah! The rock floats out of the chest and stops at eye level.

Just floating.

I drop the chest and grab the rock.

Then I start to float!

I scream and drop the rock, and fall back to the cloud.

Good thing it's soft.

The rock floats back down and hovers in front of me again.

I try again. I grab the rock and start to float.

I let go of the rock, fall, and it floats back to me.

Oh, now this is cool!

I run ten steps in one direction, and the rock follows me. Or maybe it's following the treasure chest.

I run ten steps in the other direction, and it follows me again.

I set down the chest and grab a hold of the rock. And just like last time, I begin to float. I let go and fall back to the cloud before I get too high up. I wonder if there is a way to control the rock and float in the direction or height I want.

I pick up the treasure chest and catch the floating rock. Thankfully we don't float away. Okay, the treasure chest keeps it in place. Got it.

Now I really want Zussta here so I can show her what I found.

I set the chest on the ground and gather some more rocks. This time I make sure not to wander too far away.

Once I get enough rocks, I sit down and rest. I'm glad Zussta keeps me active with the obstacle course. Otherwise, all of this work would have worn me smack out.

What design to make… what design to make?

I think back to when I would chat with the old guys. They always said to keep things simple and straightforward.

What's more straightforward than an arrow?

I get to work making an arrow out of rocks, and then I'll sit at the tip of the arrow. There. A sign that tells Zussta exactly where I am.

Plus, it's easy to draw an arrow.

I start laying out the rocks in a straight line. When I figure it's long enough, I start drawing the top of the arrow with the angle going out. I count out fifteen rocks on one side and then start counting rocks for the other side.

I only have fourteen more rocks. I guess it's not a big deal that my arrow isn't perfect. You can still tell it's an arrow.

I pick up the treasure chest and smile as I plop it down to be the point of the arrow.

Perfect.

I sit down at the point of the arrow to wait.

And I wait.

Yeah, I'm not so good at waiting.

I lay on my back and stretch out. In the past, I used to look at the sky and stare at the clouds, trying to find shapes in them, like a rabbit or a horse. But now I'm lying on a cloud, and the clouds around me don't float and change.

What would a dog do in this situation? Probably run off. This could be why humans make good pets, we are problem solvers. And my ninja street skills help.

I pretend I'm lying under the tree, Lamenana. I close my eyes and picture the light coming through all the colors.

And then I hear it.

A quiet hum.

Is that a spaceship?

I jump up, scanning the sky.

The hum is getting louder.

I hope it's Zussta and not Jama. I would hate to have Jama find me and kidnap me. I hate to think what it would be like to be captured by an alien.

Ha! Here I am, a captured pet on a strange purple planet, and I'm scared of being captured by another alien!

I would laugh more if I wasn't so scared.

Please be Zussta.

Please be Zussta.

I see a grey ship. Good, it's not Jama. I start jumping up and down and waving my arms. At least my white shirt and yellow pants should stand out on the purple cloud.

I'm hollering and waving my arms like a crazy person. "Here. I'm here!"

The ship slows and begins to come straight down like a helicopter.

Like Zussta's ship.

I want to run and hide until I see for sure who steps out of the ship. But I'm here, right out in the wide open, with nowhere to hide.

My mouth is dry as I try to swallow. I pretend to be brave.

I stand up tall and wait.

I hate waiting.

Before the door is fully open, Zussta rushes out and grabs me.

It's Zussta!

She is on top of me so fast I barely register it's her.

It's Zussta! She is hugging me and talking so fast that I have no idea what she's saying, and I don't mind.

Zussta found me!

She is twisting me all around, checking me over to make sure I'm okay. She's still talking faster than I can understand. She finally stops and gets face-to-face with me. Her big eye is right in my face. "Britt, are you okay?"

I was worried her first words would be scolding me for wandering off, so I'm happy she is more concerned than mad at me.

"Zussta found me." I smile big and accidentally slip into English. "Look, I made a picture out of rocks. I hoped you would look for me, so I made this. I didn't mean to get lost. There was a flower, and when I tried to touch it, it went away into the cloud. Then I saw another flower, and it did the same thing. Then I saw another flower and another flower, and soon, I couldn't see you. I tried to find you, but everything looks the same here."

I realize I'm speaking the wrong language and continue in Zobian. "I make a picture, and you see me."

Zussta looks at my arrow. "I not see picture," she says. "But I see light. Something different, like a light that turn off and on. Then I see you."

My face scrunches up. What blinking light? If I had a blinking light, I would have definitely used it. I look at Zussta, and we both look at the arrow.

Well, I'm studying the arrow, and she spots the treasure chest.

"What is this?" She almost whispers as she picks it up.

"Oh!" I jump up, all excited to tell her what I found. "I find! I see from the ship before we fall. But then I find rocks, and then I find this. I hope for more, but it only a rock. But look, it go up." I open the chest, and the plain rock floats out, staying in front of my face.

Zussta sucks in her breath. Her one eye is open wide, her mouth hanging open too.

I freeze. What did I do?

"Where you find it?" She quietly says in awe. She's still staring at the rock floating in front of me.

"In the box. It open easy. I thought be open hard, but no. When I open the box, the rock right there. Not even special, just there in the box. On Earth, special rocks colorful and pretty, but not…"

"Britt," Zussta interrupts me. "You did good."

Yeah, I'm pretty proud of myself, too.

"Woo hoo!" Zussta lets out a loud whoop.

"Waaah!" I scream.

I'm totally looking at the rock when Zussta lets out a loud whoop. It scares me so bad that I yell too – and I think my heart stops, and my stomach drops. I spin and see Zussta with the biggest smile I've ever seen on her face.

"You find the pala, Britt. You find the pala!" She picks me up under my arms, holds me high over her head, and spins me around and around. "You find the pala!" She laughs.

Wait. That plain-looking rock is the pala?

"I find the pala!" I start laughing too.

She finally sets me down. "Now, we go before Jama comes back."

I've forgotten about Jama for a moment. "Where is he? What happened to him?" I search the sky for a white ship.

"He is gone," she assures me. "He see us crash, he stay a little. But he go away very fast when he see we okay and I was mad. He is not good, but he didn't want to kill us. And he *really* not want me mad at him after the crash."

I totally understand that.

Zussta takes my hand, "Let's go home."

Yes, let's go home.

Chapter 50

It's probably been about an Earth week since we found the pala. Zussta gave me some homework that I'm busy with. What pet has homework besides me? Ugh, isn't it just my luck that I get an owner who makes their pet learn stuff?

Well, maybe that's not so unusual. I saw a video once that the dog would push a button on the ground that said what he wanted, like '*treat*' or '*out*.' But I don't need buttons, I'm getting much better at speaking the Zobian language.

Today I'm studying solar systems and galaxies. It's amazing to think there are so many solar systems inside even more galaxies. And I'm learning the ones closest to us. I guess this is their version of geography.

"Hey, Britt." Zussta gets my attention. "Want to go see the other human today? Maybe your bag is ready. Then we can sell the pala."

"Yes! Yes, to it all!" Oh, there were so many great things in that one question. I get to see Marco, I get a bag, we are going somewhere to sell the pala. I jump up and run to my room. I quickly change clothes, try to tame my hair, and choose a nice headband to match my pants. I almost leave my dirty clothes on the floor, but remember that Zussta likes me to keep my room clean.

I sprint back into my room; I make sure the blanket is rolled away into my floating bed. I put my crayons and paper on the dresser, throw my dirty clothes in the bathroom, and close the door.

There, all clean.

I run back to the main room. "I'm ready," I announce.

Zussta is still at the table. "We not go yet. Wait." She says without looking up.

Well, that's disappointing.

I climb up on the box next to her to see why she is so busy. I get distracted when I see the treasure chest on the table. "Is that the pala?"

She put it away as soon as we got home last week. I haven't even had a chance to study it.

"Yes." She distractedly answers.

"Can I hold?" I try asking quick easy questions, hoping she'll hand it to me without thinking it's a bad idea.

"Sure." She hands it to me without looking up from the table.

Score!

Holding it close, I hop off the box and slowly open the top of the treasure chest. The pala floats out and hoovers in front of me.

I zig to the left, and it follows me.

I zig to the right, and it follows me.

I run across the room, and it stays with me. Like right with me, not just following.

I climb on the couch, and it's still in front of me.

I grab it and begin to float.

I rise about a meter before I get scared and let go. Thankfully I was above the couch and had a soft landing.

I grab it again and rise further before I let go, falling to the couch.

This is so much fun! I can see why the pala is so popular.

I grab it again and float to the ceiling before letting go. "Woo hoo!" I whoop as I fall back to the couch.

Well, that got Zussta's attention. "Britt! What are you doing?"

"Watch." I show her how I float up and fall back onto the couch. "It's fun! Do you want to try it? Can the pala lift you, too, or are you too big? How big can the pala hold?"

I'm glad that I don't get in trouble. "The pala can hold much bigger than me, thank you very much." She smiles as she says this.

"If we are outside, how high does the pala go?"

"Too high."

Oh, well that kind of scares me. On the clouds, if I didn't let go it could have taken me into outer space. Then what would I have done?

I wonder if I can control how I float. Like, can I float forward and backward, or only up? I grab it again and begin to rise. I float in a standing position, then I try leaning forward a little more… wham, I'm floating stomach down, and my back hits the ceiling.

OK, so I didn't go forward. But it gives me another idea.

I let go and fall to the couch. I straighten my hair and clothes, take a deep breath, and grab the pala again.

As soon as I start to float, I try doing a summersault. I wobble, and my hands fly outwards, letting go of the pala.

I crash land on the couch again.

I try again.

And again.

Finally, after about the fifth time, I do it. I totally do a full front flip while floating!

"Zussta watch!" I holler.

"I have been watching. You are very good."

I look, and she is sitting on her chair, but turned away from the table and looking at me. She has been watching me without telling me to stop. And she is smiling.

"You learn that fast."

Yeah, I'm pretty proud of myself too.

"Okay, please put that away now, and we will leave. We will go to Oonala first."

I almost forgot that we are going to see Marco.

I quickly put the pala back into its chest and run back to Zussta, handing her the treasure chest. Then I run to the door. "I'm ready. Do you have my face mask?"

I'll be happy to have my own bag where I can have my own face shield, maybe another headband, and maybe that water ball. My ninja street skills taught me to be ready to be on my own.

"Yes, I have everything." She says as we bubble up.

I squint as we stop outside. The trees and plants are shining bright today. I take a deep breath, admiring the beauty of it all.

Okay, that's enough. I'm ready to go.

I rock back and forth, trying to be patient as the spaceship rises from the ground. It's still dented from where Jama hit us. "Will you fix that?" I ask as I point to the damage.

"If we get a good amount for the pala, maybe I'll get a new ship."

A new spaceship? The pala is worth that much? Yay!

Maybe her treasure-hunting business is so good that she was able to buy me. Jordie said that humans are rare pets, so we must be expensive.

Yeah, I'm worth it.

We climb into the ship, and I take my normal position looking out the window. It's weird watching the ground fall away, but I love looking at the colors as we go up and up.

And just like that, we are in outer space. Zussta turns the ship, flying higher. I see the wormhole she is aiming for. "Mabo," I say to remind her that I know the word.

"Yes, this mabo will take us to Oonala."

"Can I learn all the mabos and where they go?" I ask while still looking out the window. When she doesn't answer right away, I turn to see Zussta staring at me.

What? What did I say? Am I not supposed to learn that?

"Why do you want to learn mabos? You do not fly a ship." She squints her big eye, looking at me like I'm crazy.

I mean, she has a point, but still. "If I learn about planets and solar systems, maybe I can learn how to go to each place. I see the mabos when you can't. It might be good one day."

See, I'm always thinking ahead. Well, okay, not always, but I think this is a good argument.

"We'll see." Is all she says.

I guess that means '*no*' in every adult language.

I sit down in my chair as we get closer to the wormhole. I'm ready as we zoom through it. The black and white flashing by. Maybe our new spaceship will have a sunroof so I can see out the top when I'm sitting down. I'll make that request.

We zoom right, left, up, and down. I'm laughing the whole way. I see the end of the wormhole and try to brace myself. We come out and immediately stop, my arms and legs flying forward. This ride is still great.

I learned that Oonala is only one solar system away from Janti; that's why we only need one wormhole.

See, I like knowing these things.

I start singing and rocking back and forth. "*I get to see Marco, he's another human. 'Cuz I make friends easy, even on other planets. Human Marco made a bag for me, la tee da, la tee dee. Maybe we will see the dragon, maybe we won't. Maybe I will learn to swim, maybe I won't. But either way, the pala lets me float.*"

I realize that I'm singing in Zobian. Oh, I'm getting much better at this whole language thing! Zussta is trying not to laugh at my singing, but I know it's a happy laugh. She isn't making fun of me. It's nice to not have to worry so much about what other humans think. It's freeing.

We land on Oonala and Zussta puts on my face shield. I know we could wait until we are out because Marco breathes above ground, but that's okay; I don't mind having it on early. It's not uncomfortable at all.

"Ready?" She asks.

"Ready," I confirm.

We get out of the ship and head to the water. I hope Marco is at the store. "What if Marco is not there?" I didn't think of that earlier.

"Then we will ask for the bag." Is her simple answer.

Well yeah, but I want to see Marco more than I want a bag. I'm not sure how to say that, but we are already in the water up to my knees, so I really don't have time to explain it anyways.

I start to doggie paddle as Zussta is still walking deeper. How does she know where to park and where to swim? I guess it's something you just learn, like knowing what store you want to go to.

"Ready to go down?" She is looking at me. She is lucky she doesn't need a face shield.

I nod and she grabs my hand, pulling me down. We swim to the dome, and she easily finds the outer door. It's open, so we swim in, and she presses the button to close it. I keep floating, waiting for the water to drain. When it's done, she presses the next button to open the inner door.

We step into the market and off to the side so she can remove my mask. I try to straighten my clothes and hair and look at her. How does her hair stay in the same sideways Mohawk in water?

I look at all the aliens walking by as she puts my face shield in her frontpack.

They are so tall and blue and have those flipper feet and four arms.

Two aliens stop and point at me.

I wave.

They open their mouths wide, which I know is smiling. So, I decide to do a spin for them. I twirl around and land back facing them. I hold my arms out. "Ta da."

Their mouths open even wider.

They love me.

They come closer and talk to Zussta in their language. Somehow Zussta knows their language. Well, I suppose she would if she shops here. I'm sure they are talking about me. I hear Zussta tell them my name, and who knows what else they are saying.

I'm bored already. It's like standing here while adults talk.

I look up through the dome and watch the oddest-looking fish swim by. Long fish, yellow fish, all kinds of fish; but no dragon.

Zussta nudges me. Oh, I think she was talking to me. "What?" I ask.

"I was telling them you are learning our language very well." She explains as she motions to the two aliens.

Does she want me to talk like a performing pet? I'm not mad. She wants me to talk and be like an actor; a showman. I can do that.

"Hello fine blue aliens. How are you? My name is Britt." I also give them a little curtsey.

They smile big and clap their two hands on the right side together and their two hands on the left side together.

I take a bow. "Thank you, thank you. I'll be here all week."

With that, they close their mouths and tilt their head, looking at Zussta. "I'm not sure," she shrugs. "She sometimes says things I don't understand."

They don't stay long, and soon, we are walking to the store. I keep close to Zussta, I bet getting stepped on by their big flipper feet would hurt.

Most of the aliens who see me stop and smile and point. I start doing my parade wave. Smile and wave, smile and wave.

I'm a hoot.

Zussta nudges me, laughing. I stop and laugh with her.

I recognize the store coming up and hold my breath. Is he here?

We get closer to the shop.

I see Marco.

Chapter 51

"Marco!" I can't stop myself from hollering.

His head snaps up, looking around a bit surprised and scared. I get it, he probably doesn't hear another human calling his name very often.

I break into a run and slide to a stop directly in front of him. "Hi there! It's me, Britt!" Yep, I have totally surprised him.

A huge smile covers his face, "Britt!"

"Zussta," I point at her as she is finally catching up to me, "let me come with her today. We came to check if the bag you made for me is ready. But I really wanted to see you, too. I mean, I love being with Zussta, but it's great to see a human. I was worried I forgot how to speak English, but I haven't. So that's good. How are you?"

"It's great to see you, too. Yep, I have the bag all ready for you. Wait here, don't leave." He says. I make a motion to plant my feet and not move. He turns and runs into the store, saying something to the shopkeeper as he passes by her.

Does he work at this store? He's been here both times, and he knows the alien working here. Wow, he's a pet that makes a product and works. Dogs have their job of protecting the homes, but I've never heard of one working at a store.

But then again, I'm a treasure-hunting pet – so I guess neither of us is a normal pet.

Marco comes back holding a backpack that is the perfect size for me. "I finished it and have been watching for your owner. I wasn't sure if you would be able to come with her."

He hands me the bag and I start inspecting it. It has a flap that folds all the way around. I open it and peer inside. Yep, this will hold my face shield, an extra headband, and the water ball. And I still have room for more.

"It's perfect," I tell him

I notice he stands a little taller when I say that. He's proud of his bag, as he should be. The fact that he makes a bag that keeps water out is pretty amazing.

I start to put it on like a regular backpack when he stops me. "You wear it on the front, like this." He helps me put it on, with the bag hanging on the front.

"Why on the front? This feels weird." I squirm.

"Trust me. If it's on the back, the drag makes it hard to swim. Wearing it on your front makes it easier."

I shrug. "If you say so." I continue to adjust how it hangs on me.

I turn to Zussta and speak in Zobian. "Look, he made the bag. And it goes here. It is great." I show her the bag hanging on my front.

"Yes, it is very great." She agrees. "Stay here, I need to go inside."

I bet she has to pay for it.

My first alien bag made by a human.

"So, your first owner taught you how to make these, and he died? Now, where do you live?" The whole thought of what he must have gone through scares me.

"Yeah, Jutte made bags for a long time and sold them to several stores, and then another alien killed him. But now I live with Bakao. He is married to the lady who runs this store, so I get to make the bags and sell them here. I'm not always here."

Wow. What a life he has.

"Are you still friends with the dragon?" I ask looking up and around, hoping to see it swim by.

"He shows up sometimes, not all the time. How about you? Do you like your owner?"

"I love Zussta. She is fierce but so nice to me." I don't know if she wants me to tell him that we are treasure hunters. I look for Zussta, but she is still talking to the alien lady. I guess I can tell Marco some little stories of what we did. "Guess what? We went to a planet that was all purple. Like, everything was purple - the trees, the ground, everything. Then we flew to the clouds. We, for real, landed on the clouds and walked around on them."

He gives a sharp intake of breath. "You walked on clouds? Too cool."

"I know, right?"

There, now he sees that I have a cool owner and life, too.

"Maybe Zussta will let me come see you sometimes. Should we ask?" We run to the two alien ladies talking, Marco and I both interrupting them.

"Zussta, can we come here now and then? I be friends with Marco?" I ask in Zobian while Marco is probably saying the same thing to the other lady.

The two aliens look at each other and talk in Marco's language. He is watching both of them, listening to their conversation. He probably understands the language better than I understand Zobian since he's been here longer.

"What are they saying?" I whisper and pull on his sleeve.

"Shhh, hold on." He waves me off and whispers back.

I scoot closer to try to listen, but it doesn't matter; I still can't understand them. Marco breaks into a smile, so I know they agree.

Zussta looks down at me. "Yes, we can see them sometimes."

Yes!

And Marco looks as happy as I do.

"We are now officially friends." I beam at him.

"Yep, your owner will bring you by here sometimes, and we can hang out."

I beam up at Zussta. "Thank you." And I sincerely mean it. She bends down and hugs me.

"I'm glad you are happy. But we cannot stay today. We must go now."

Oh, that's right, we are going to sell the pala.

I turn to Marco. "She says we have to go, but we will be back another day. Thank you so much for the bag. I love it, and it will work perfectly."

"Sure, anytime. I'm glad I could make it for you. So, I guess I'll see you again." Then he gets all fidgety, like debating if he should hug me or shake my hand. Instead, he punches me in the shoulder.

Boys are so weird.

"Okay, bye." We both say at the same time. Zussta and I leave the store. She walks normally, and I happily jump and hop and dodge alien flipper feet. I don't know how they can all walk around looking straight ahead instead of up at the top of the dome. I could spend all day watching the fish swim by.

We get to the exit, and she bends down and puts my face shield on. "Ready?"

"Yep, I'm ready. Maybe we can swim slow and See fish? Not too slow, but a little slow?" I ask.

"Okay, a little slow." She agrees.

We pass through the first door, and she presses the button to make the water come in. By habit, I hold my breath while the room fills up. But then I test it again, and the face shield still works.

She presses the other button and takes my hand helping me swim out into the ocean. True to her word, she swims slowly, dragging me along as I look all around.

It's a whole other world down here.

Another alien world. I'm still not used to all the new worlds I'm seeing.

The dragon doesn't make an appearance, but maybe that's a good thing since we aren't with Marco. He might not recognize us.

We get back to land and to the spaceship. I peel off my face shield and wring out my hair. Maybe a towel will fit into my bag. And once again, Zussta's hair is dry and in place. I don't get it.

I settle myself in my seat while Zussta closes the door and presses buttons, starting the spaceship. I look down as we take off, trying to see the dome under the water.

"Now we sell the pala?" I ask.

"Yes, it is a little far away. You can relax."

Yeah, like I can relax while flying in a spaceship. Nope. I stay on my knees, watching everything. We are in space, and she starts with another lesson.

She tells me the names of the planets in Marco's galaxy, and I say them back to her. I really am trying to learn, but I doubt I'll remember all the names of all the planets in all the galaxies. But since we will come back here for visits, I try to learn these planets.

I'm saying planet names and pointing out wormholes.

All in all, this is not a bad way to travel.

I study Zussta. Looking at her big eye on the front and back of her head and her sideways blue Mohawk. I shake my head. How did I get here?

And now we are going to sell our treasure.

It turns out that I am able to relax and sit down. Zussta stops with the lesson plan and starts chatting. She's not saying much, but I think it's her way of helping me learn the language more.

She is always teaching me something.

"This is our last wormhole. Then we will be near Balaratas. That is where we sell the pala." She informs me.

I brace myself for entering the wormhole.

Zoom!

Left, right, right, right. Oh, it's a good thing I still don't get motion sickness.

We pop out in a totally different solar system. I scramble to my knees and look out the window.

Every planet is yellow.

I blink and look again.

Yep, every single planet is yellow.

"You will like this. There are many treasures to see." She says without even looking my way.

Oh, I didn't even think that I might see heaps of cool things.

I can't even imagine what aliens think are treasures.

I rock side to side with anticipation.

I get to see cool things. I get to see cool things.

La la la la la la la.

Chapter 52

We make our way to one of the yellow planets. Instead of landing on the ground, she flies to what reminds me of a dock floating in the sky. There are several ships lined up, and she pulls into a slot and stops.

"Let's put your face shield on," she says as she leans to me. She puts it on my face, and I press all around it just to make sure.

She steps out on the dock-thing, holding the treasure chest, and waits for me. I scoot out and jump down. The dock isn't solid! So, when I land it bends and kind of pushes me back up. I suppose since it's floating it might not be stable, but I still wasn't expecting that.

I jump up and down two times to test it, and both times I am pushed up higher than when I started.

Oh, this is like a trampoline!

I jump higher, and then higher, and then…

"Britt!" Zussta hollers and grabs me. Which scares the heck out of me.

My heart is pounding, and I can't speak at first. I catch my breath, "What? What's wrong?" I'm looking all around in case something is about to grab me.

Zussta also takes a deep breath. "Please stop jumping. You could fall."

Oh, I didn't even think that I might not land back on the dock. I get down on my hands and knees and peek over the edge. I can barely make out the ground. It must be like a hundred kilometers below us.

Gulp.

I scoot back to the center of the dock and hold onto Zussta's leg. "I won't jump." I solemnly tell her.

Staying in the middle of the dock, we start walking to the end where there is a building. Except it's floating, like the dock.

We are on a yellow planet where buildings float, but I don't.

This is so weird and cool.

We are about halfway to the building when Zussta freezes and grumbles under her breath. I stop and look where she is looking.

Jama, the bad alien from the cave just got out of his spaceship.

Oh no, I wonder if Zussta is going to fight him.

I debate if I should hold onto her leg tighter or let go.

Jama sees us and actually hesitates. Yep, he knows he did us wrong when he hit us and then left us alone on the clouds. Granted, it's how we found the pala, but he doesn't know that.

What is he doing here? Did he follow us?

He squints as he sees Zussta holding the treasure chest.

He starts walking towards us, but Zussta stands her ground and doesn't move. I know she's not afraid of him, but I'm not sure what's about to happen.

"What do you want, Jama?" She begins talking first.

"What do you have there?" He sneers at Zussta, but he doesn't look scary. He looks like he is trying to be scary but failing.

Zussta answers, still not moving and not allowing him to walk past us. "Nothing for you. Why are you here? Are you following me?"

Hah, that's what I thought too.

If an alien can look guilty, he is doing it. "No!" He protests and whines.

Even I know he's lying.

Zussta takes a threatening step towards him. "Back off, Jama," she angrily says.

"I'm just going inside; I'm not following you." He tries explaining. "You can't stop me from going inside."

Actually, I bet Zussta could stop him.

Zussta steps aside, "then go ahead."

I get it. She doesn't want him behind us. She's smart. But I think he is a little afraid of having us behind him.

He hesitates, standing there deciding what to do.

He looks at the treasure chest again. I see Zussta has her suction cups out, holding on tight. There is no way he can grab it from her.

Before he can speak, run, try to snatch the chest, or anything else, she looks down at me. "Let's go."

Ha! She stood her ground and then dismissed him.

Zussta rocks.

I'm still holding onto her leg because even if he can't get at the treasure chest, he might try to grab me. I walk a little faster and a bit in front of Zussta's leg.

As we get closer to the building, I look under it. Is it sitting on something or just floating? Nope, nothing underneath; we are about to walk into a floating building.

This day just keeps getting better.

As soon as we step inside the door, the strangest alien I've ever seen welcomes us. I've now seen many different species, but this one freaks me out.

He is probably five meters tall and dark maroon in color. He has four legs, which somehow don't get tangled and trip him when he walks, and has three arms. But what scares me the most is his head is huge. Like, way too big for his body huge. His neck is so long that I don't know how it's holding that head up. He doesn't have hair, ears, or a nose… but he has three rows of sharp teeth in his huge mouth.

I totally scoot behind Zussta. I'll take my chances with Jama rather than this guy.

Zussta, of course, isn't afraid.

"Hello, Ka." Zussta pleasantly greets this creature.

"Hello, Zussta. It is good to see you today. How may I be of assistance?" He glances at me. Not in a scary way, but a nice hello without saying it.

He's polite and not surprised to see a human.

My head is spinning.

Zussta answers her. "Firstly, I want Jama removed from this building. He has tried to steal from me, and I don't want him here while you and I do business."

Ka bows his head and walks to Jama.

I have to see what happens. Zussta stays facing forward, but I turn around, staring.

Ka leans down and speaks quietly to Jama. He starts to fight and raise his voice. That's when Ka actually roars and shows his teeth.

I yelp and jump back.

Jama jumps too. I guess he didn't realize who he was dealing with.

Ka talks to Jama quietly again and starts moving all four arms towards him. Jama holds his arms up in surrender and quickly leaves the building.

I repeatedly tap Zussta's leg. "He's gone. He yelled at Jama and showed his teeth, and now Jama's gone. That was so cool. You missed it."

Zussta gives me a small smile. "I saw it."

Oh yeah, her back-of-the-head eye saw everything.

Ka comes back to us. "Now then, how can I help you today?" He is very polite and formal again.

"I have a palabonosabrana." Is all Zussta says.

If Ka is surprised, he doesn't show it. "Certainly. This way please." He turns and leads us towards the back of the building. I begin to follow but start looking around.

The place is filled with floating shelves, and each one has a strange-looking treasure on it. Oh, this must be all the cool items Zussta told me about.

There must be at least a hundred shelves. Some are floating high in the air, but others are lower to the ground. And each has something cool-looking on it.

I bet each is a treasure of some kind.

There are large objects and tiny ones – each on its own shelf. Some are colorful, while others are plain-looking.

I want to touch them all.

I wander to a shelf that is my height but has a tall, white, thin strand standing on top. I have no idea what it is, but it's on display, so it must be something important.

I touch it.

The strand bends, twists, and shapes itself into a human finger and touches the tip of my finger.

I freeze, and it freezes.

I drop my hand, and it goes back to a tall, straight strand.

I move my finger towards it again, and it shapes into a finger again.

I hold my entire hand up to it, and it shapes into a hand.

I stick my face close to it, and it shapes itself to my face.

And as soon as I step back, it returns to its original shape.

I laugh and look at another low floating shelf.

There is nothing there. I start to back up when I notice there is a glob hanging on the bottom of the shelf. Did someone stick gum under the shelf?

I look closer. The first thing I notice is the smell, this blog smells wonderful. How can a blob smell so good? I can't figure out exactly what the smell is, but it makes me feel warm and cozy. Like having a soft blanket wrapped around me and cookies baking in the oven.

I lay on my back under the shelf and look up at the blog.

It blinks.

"Waaah!" I scream and scoot away and get up and run.

I scurry in the direction that I last saw Zussta and Ka going. "Zussta!" I holler.

A side door immediately opens, and Zussta runs out.

"It had an eye. Or it was an eye." I have no idea how to explain what blinked at me.

"It's okay now. Come in here." Zussta guides me into the room. It's an empty room with just the three of us and a table with the treasure on top. I take a deep breath and calm down.

After she sees I'm okay, Zussta turns back to Ka. "I cannot tell you where we found the palabonosabrana. But it is here now and beautiful."

Do they think the plain rock is beautiful? I shrug and keep listening.

"You are correct," Ka answers, "this is a beautiful treasure, but smaller than others. We may not be able to give you as much for it."

Oh, they are deciding on a price.

"It doesn't have to be big to work. This palabonosabrana is perfect."

Ka bows his head a bit. "Yes, it is perfect. Here is my price." Some writing appears on the wall next to us. Is the entire wall a screen or just that spot?

Zussta must like the price because she doesn't argue. "This is fine."

The price disappears, and Ka reaches an arm out, touching the wall in a different spot. "Funds are now in your account."

Zussta smiles, "Thank you, Ka. Once again it was a pleasure doing business with you."

"And you as well." He politely answers.

Zussta taps my shoulder, "Are you ready to go?"

It took less than 30 minutes to sell the pala. It almost seems too easy for all the hard work we went through to get it. But the price must be pretty good.

I guess so. I wouldn't mind staying and checking out what treasures are on the shelves, but I guess that will have to wait for another time.

As we are walking out, I pass by an object on a shelf that I recognize. I move closer.

Is that what I think it is?

There, sitting on a shelf in a treasure store in another galaxy…

Is a pencil.

"Zussta," I get her attention, "is that from Earth?" I point to the pencil

She turns to Ka and asks him the question. She then turns back to me, bending down to my level. "Yes, that is from your planet, Earth. Do you know what it is? Ka said it is very important."

A pencil is important? Ha, who told her that? But I know enough not to laugh at Ka.

"It's a very common tool to write with. Everyone has one, even us kids. It's not special to us at all."

Zussta leans in close. "Let's not tell Ka."

Yeah, good idea.

But wait.

If a pencil is here, that means that an alien was on Earth.

Maybe Jordie sold Ka the pencil.

Okay, even I doubt that.

"Let's go." Zussta leads me out the door. I look back at the pencil and then follow Zussta.

I notice Jama's ship is gone. I guess he is someone we just have to always watch out for.

I lightly bounce on the dock all the way back to the spaceship.

"Let's go home," Zussta says once we are settled in our seats.

Just going to a building is a surprise. I bet this is what my life will be like from now on… treasure hunting and surprises.

I like that thought.

Chapter 53

I bet it's been about a month since we sold the pala. I sleep when I want and keep learning about planets and wormholes. I'm lying on the ground coloring a picture of the planet Sononi, where we found the pala.

I think we are getting on a good schedule because right about the time my stomach rumbles and reminds me I'm hungry, Zussta is already getting my bowl ready. She hears my stomach and blinks at me with her back-of-her-head eye.

I'm too busy thinking about what I want to eat to be embarrassed. Do pets even get embarrassed? I remember when Mikey told us about how he went and stayed with a family called the Franklins, and they had a dog that would pass gas – a lot. Mikey and the husband would plug their noses and groan at the dog. "Oh man, Frankie, that was horrible." Yeah, they named their dog Frankie. Frankie Franklin. The dog would get embarrassed and hide behind the wife. She would pretend not to smell him, but Mikey said he could see her holding her breath. But she was too polite to make a big deal like Mikey and the husband did.

So yeah, I guess pets get embarrassed, but I'm not when my stomach growls.

I scoot into my chair and close my eyes. What do I want today? I've already had brekky, so I decide this is lunch. I want a BLT. I imagine a bacon, lettuce, and tomato sammie – with extra bacon. She hands me my bowl, and I dig in. The bacon is salty, the lettuce is fresh, and the tomato is juicy. I start to do a happy dance in my chair.

I finish and hand my bowl back to her, stretch, and realize I'm tired.

Here's the great thing, I can sleep whenever I want. I used to think cats were so lucky to sleep all day, and now here I am, able to crawl into bed without anyone thinking badly of it.

"Zussta." I get her attention. "I'm tired and going to sleep for a while."

She gets up and walks into my room with me. "Let's get you comfortable," she says as she helps me into my floating bed. It's nice having someone tuck me in.

When I wake up, I stumble to the main room, looking for Zussta. She's at her table working, but I'm not ready for a lesson yet. Instead, I flop into my beanbag chair.

Zussta makes me cube puzzles. Once I learn how to open each box, she makes a new one for me. I see a new one beside my chair and get to work.

It's nice to ease into the day without tons of other kids running around.

I like my life on Janti with Zussta.

"Britt," I hear and look up to see Zussta standing over me. Wow, I didn't even hear her walk up. I'm still surprised at how fast and quietly she moves with that stocky body. "Do you want to go outside?"

"Yeah. Let me get dressed." I jump and run into my room. I throw on new clothes and try to tame my hair. It doesn't settle down, so I pull it back in a headband. Good enough for now.

I run back to the main room and stand by the door, waiting to go outside.

One day I'll learn how to call the bubble down to me… that will be my day of freedom!

Imagine if dogs could let themselves in and out as they please. Would they run away? I wouldn't.

Anyways, I wait.

I sit down.

I lie down.

I stand up.

I'm bored and go sit back in my chair.

Again, I now feel bad about any time I made a pet wait for me to be ready to do something.

"I'm sorry, Britt, that took longer than I expected. Are you ready now?"

I can't help it; I'm excited and ready. I jump up and run to the door again. We bubble up to the surface, and I look to see which way we are going. Are we heading to the obstacle course, the tree Lamenana, or just going for a walk? I'm good with us doing any of these.

"Do you want to go to the tree?" She asks. I wonder what would happen if I told her 'No.' But truthfully, yeah, I want to do that.

Before she can say anything, I tap her and take off running. I hear her yell and laugh behind me, and I have a good head start. I'm laughing too hard, and she quickly catches up with me. We run side by side all the way to Lamenana.

We are still laughing as we crawl under the colorful limbs. Amazed at the beauty, I lie on my back next to Zussta. I bet this is what it feels like to be a globe surrounded by stained glass windows.

I squint and examine each leaf separately. The black outline and see-through colors still dazzle me. Then I open my eyes and bask in the glory of Lamenana.

Without looking at me, Zussta begins talking. "Are you happy here?"

Wow, that's a loaded question. Adults ask that, and I know they secretly hope I holler 'Yes,' and tell them there is no other place I'd rather be. But with Zussta, I know she cares and wants to know how I really feel.

So, I tell her the truth.

"I am happy here. I know I'm a human, but sometimes I think I'm more than just your pet, I'm your family. I miss Earth, but I always knew I would move away from the group home. And I love that you let me find the pala with you. And you ask how I'm doing. It's nice to have someone ask that. Not every day, but sometimes it's nice. And I like the obstacle course and being here under the tree. Did you know I named the tree? It's so pretty and makes me feel good. And I like the food. But I do miss real human food, but what you give me is good. Do you know that I'll grow and need more clothes and shoes? I wasn't sure if Jordie told you that. I'll be an adult one day, but until then, I'll stay a kid. I like my age right now. Some kids want to grow up too fast, but not me. Are you happy with me?"

I'm surprised she let me talk that long. But she was looking at me and actually listening, not just pretending to listen.

"I'm very happy with you. I didn't know what to expect when I contacted Jordie to get a human pet. I hoped for a human to keep me company and maybe go with me on treasure hunts. But you're more than that. You are my family."

She doesn't say as many words as me, but what she does say is important.

We both get quiet and look at the tree. After a while, I begin to get restless. I'm not so good at staying still for very long. Zussta has figured this out about me.

"Are you ready to go home?"

I'm ready. But this time, we quietly walk next to each other.

We bubble down, and Zussta instantly heads to her table.

I climb on my box next to her, careful not to bump, touch, or break anything. "What are you looking at?" I ask. There are different planets on the screen, not Oonala and not Sononi. Maybe she's looking at a different galaxy.

Zussta turns to me, looking at me full-on with her one big eye. "Do you remember the vibo monster that hid the pala? He is missing. If we can find him and make sure he is safely returned to the lake, he may gift us with more pala."

She smiles.

Her big eye glints as she looks at me.

"Do you want to go on another treasure hunt?"

"Yes!" I jump up, all excited.

I have the coolest life ever!

The End

Acknowledgment

There are so many people I want to thank for helping me publish this book.

 I owe so much to my husband, who fed my dreams of becoming an author and helped make it happen.

 I send huge hugs to my parents and sisters for encouraging and believing in me.

Thank you to my friends for not only being supportive but putting up with me constantly (and I mean constantly) talking about my books.

 To Kathryn: Thank you for your encouragement every step of the way, even during the bad first drafts.

I'm eternally grateful to my writer's group for listening to my wild ideas and then making them better. You all encouraged, helped, and saw this book come to life.

Thanks to my beta readers: Andrea, Ivy, Nancy, DJ Mays, Sydney, Leslie, and Michael who all took the time to read through the rough drafts.

And thank you to you, the reader, for choosing this book. I hope you enjoyed it.

Books written by Tiffany Jo Howell
The Finder's Tales: Marco
The Finder's Tales: Britt

Since her early days, Tiffany Jo Howell has been telling stories of helping her friends get in trouble and instigating mischief. Maybe she never grew up because children still gravitate to her wherever she goes. Perhaps this is why writing in an easy voice for the younger ones comes naturally to her.

Tiffany originally hails from Minnesota but now lives with her husband and most perfect, Sweet Pea, along Florida's Gulf Coast. One of her favorite writing spots is at the local sports bar with music playing and sweet tea flowing.